"Read my

Kendra said. "This is the last time I'm going to say it. I do not pop pills and I do not make up stories, and I resent your treating me as if I do."

She broke off with a gasp as he closed in on her, placing one hand on each side of her shoulders on the back of the couch. His eyes were deep, dark and terrifyingly unreadable.

"If you've been telling me the truth, then why am I making you so nervous?"

"You aren't," she told him, but now her defiant stare faltered.

Alex knew she was lying to him. He followed the downward drift of her lashes. His hand swept across to touch their softness, and his anger evaporated.

Slowly he lowered his head.

Dear Reader:

No doubt you have already realized that there's a big—and exciting—change going on in Intimate Moments this month. We now have a new cover design, one that allows more room for art and has a truly contemporary look, making it more reflective of the line's personality.

And we could hardly have chosen a better month to introduce our new look. Jennifer Greene makes her second appearance in the line with *Devil's Night*, an exciting and suspenseful tale that still has plenty of room for romance. Old favorites are here, too. Barbara Faith's *Capricorn Moon* and Jeanne Stephens's *At Risk* show off these two authors at the top of their talent. Finally, we bring you a newcomer we expect to be around for a long time. Once you read Kaitlyn Gorton's *Cloud Castles*, you'll know why we feel so confident.

In coming months, look for favorites like Marilyn Pappano, Nora Roberts, Kathleen Korbel and Paula Detmer Riggs, as well as all the other authors who have made Silhouette Intimate Moments such an exciting—and romantic—line.

Leslie J. Wainger
Senior Editor

Cloud Castles

KAITLYN GORTON

Silhouette Intimate Moments

Published by Silhouette Books New York

America's Publisher of Contemporary Romance

SILHOUETTE BOOKS
300 East 42nd St., New York, N.Y. 10017

ISBN: 0-373-07307-0

First Silhouette Books printing October 1989

Printed in the U.S.A.

KAITLYN GORTON

is a former librarian and college lecturer who now lives in Maine. She has published both adult and young-adult fiction, as well as a biography of Nelly Bly and a study of sixteenth-century women. In addition to history, her interests include wildlife, camping, photography and bagpipes.

To Carolyn Marino
With thanks for all those encouraging words

Chapter 1

Rain spattered against the windshield in immense, dripping blobs. Equally large drops danced into her headlights as Kendra Jennings squinted, straining to see if there were hazards on the road ahead.

"I must have been out of my mind," she muttered under her breath.

She'd been driving since midmorning, when she'd left Burlington, Vermont. Everything she cared about was in the five-year-old Eagle with her, moving at a cautious thirty miles per hour along a desolate rural road in western Maine.

Even rotating her stiff shoulders failed to ease the building tension. She didn't dare release the steering wheel to rub her neck. Neither could she risk brushing back the one limp strand of cinnamon-colored hair that had worked its way down her high forehead. She tried blowing at it, but it settled back in the same spot, just at the edge of her peripheral vision.

Kendra fought the sensation that she was in a tun-
nel, the rain slanting toward her, yet sucking her in. It
drummed loudly on the roof of the car and drowned
out the mournful lament of a country singer. Kendra
had chosen the radio station by default. It was the only
one that seemed to come in here in the mountains.

Her hands began to ache next. When she'd stopped
for supper, her palms had already been red from gripping the hard wheel too tightly. She'd hoped a break
would relax her. Instead, she'd felt worse since leaving the small, homey diner. The beginning of a headache throbbed behind her temples.

Would it be better to continue, or find a place to
turn around? She could head back to the nearest vil-
lage. That quaint little white clapboard bed-and-
breakfast place she'd spotted on her way through was
starting to look better and better. The problem was
finding a place to turn.

Kendra tried to concentrate on her driving, to fight
the unexpected light-headedness stealing over her. It
dulled the aches in her tired muscles, but it was
numbing her reflexes as well. She couldn't let herself
fall asleep at the wheel. If there wasn't a spot big
enough to turn around in, she'd have to press on. She
just hoped the house wouldn't turn out to be totally
unsuitable. She didn't really want to face the long
drive back to town, not even for clean sheets and a soft
bed.

Surely Cousin Olive's place couldn't be much farther. Kendra felt as if she'd been driving forever, and
had lost all sense of distance. The winding, roller-
coaster roads and the need to drive slowly in the rain
were confusing her, and with each passing minute she
felt sleepier. She couldn't account for the sudden las-

situde. Hadn't she forced down two cups of bitter coffee with her meal just so she would stay alert?

"Remind me of this trip the next time I decide to do something impulsive," she told the radio announcer.

A wry smile played across Kendra's lips. She appreciated the irony of her situation and was glad she could still laugh at herself. A sense of humor might keep her going when she finally saw her new home.

Anything might be waiting at the end of this journey. All Kendra knew was that she'd inherited a house in rural Maine and the five acres surrounding it from a previously unknown cousin, Olive Andrews. When the lawyers had first contacted her, in early January, she'd been convinced they had the wrong person.

Now it was the first Monday in May, and she was driving through an early evening downpour toward that inheritance. She planned to live there for at least six months no matter what shape the house was in. A week ago she wouldn't have believed it, but a week ago she hadn't dared dream there was life beyond her stagnant, unrewarding job as a junior-high schoolteacher.

This is going to work out, she told herself firmly, wishing she could recapture the excitement she'd experienced earlier in the day. That morning at the bank she'd felt more like nineteen than twenty-nine. She'd been off to a brave new life, shedding the old and dull like so much dead skin.

Quiet elation crept back, filling her with contentment. Yes, she'd been impulsive, but not foolish. Hugging her delicious secret to herself, she drove on. Not even her mother knew what had prompted her, less than twenty-four hours ago, to telephone Henry Damon and resign.

Forgetting Henry was one of her new goals. Their relationship had been over for months, and now the job was part of the past as well. The only thing she couldn't understand was why it had taken her so long to realize neither was right for her. She'd taught for more than eight years. For two of them, she and the principal of her small, private Vermont prep school had been lovers. They'd talked of marriage. Then, almost too late, Kendra had discovered that under Henry's handsome, intelligent, cultured exterior was an insensitive, self-centered, small-minded bigot.

Yawning, Kendra peered through the rain, looking for the last crossroads before her turn. The waitress at the diner had given her clear, concise directions, and a comment: "You wouldn't catch me living all alone out there." At the time, Kendra had laughed and said she was looking forward to the solitude. Now she wondered. Just how isolated was Cousin Olive's place? Kendra hadn't seen a house for at least two miles.

Ahead and to the right she saw the headlights of another car. Surely that was the intersection she'd been told to watch for. The turn she wanted would be a mile farther on. Yawning once more, Kendra automatically took her foot off the gas to slow the car and checked to make sure her seat belt was securely fastened. The rain continued to fall in torrents and the road felt slick under her tires.

Through damp, gray fields and dark, skeletal trees, Kendra's headlights picked out the other car. The vague shape seemed to lurk there, difficult to see clearly, waiting at the crossroads for her to pass.

Rule one of defensive driving: Never trust the other guy. Even as the thought flitted through her mind, the other vehicle lurched forward into the road. Kendra's booted feet pumped the brake pedal but nothing happened. It was too wet. The car skidded, headed directly for a large maple tree and did not respond to her frantic efforts to steer away.

Kendra didn't have time to cry out. She threw her arms up to shield her face and closed her eyes as tree limbs crashed against the windshield and the sound of scraping metal and wood echoed around her. She felt her car slam into the tree, then shudder and spin away. After what seemed an eternity it came to a sudden stop as the back end collided with a second solid object. Kendra's upper body bounced forward only to be jerked back with bruising force by the seat belt.

Very slowly, she opened her eyes and lowered her arms enough to peek through her fingers. Unhurt, but shaking uncontrollably, she saw that her car was, miraculously, still right-side up. It was pointing back the way she had come. She sat still, trying to take in what had happened. The engine coughed and died. The radio issued only crackles and hisses, but the windshield wipers were still working, scraping with eerie precision over a long crack in the glass. With one trembling hand, Kendra reached out to turn them off.

It seemed to her that she was moving in slow motion. Concussion? She didn't remember hitting her head, but with each passing second she felt more and more light-headed and confused. She didn't have the strength to get out of the car. Through the rain she had a misty view of the other vehicle. Had she hit it? She didn't think so, but the only light came from its headlights and it was turned sideways in the middle of the road.

A door opened and the dome light illuminated its passengers. Teenaged boys, her numbed mind told her. Kendra had to fight back hysterical laughter. It was a bad dream. Her former students were coming after her.

She closed her eyes again. Just for a moment, she promised herself, but she couldn't seem to make them open again.

When Kendra came to, she was lying on a hard, narrow bed. She was cold. Her clothes had been removed and replaced by a short cotton gown and a lightweight blanket.

Slowly, she opened her eyes and surveyed the room. Hospital, she thought, and wondered why that disappointed her. Daylight streamed in through a window curtained with tiers of dotted swiss. Otherwise the bed, table, chair and doors were exactly what she'd have expected to find in any medical facility.

Kendra's mind was still fuzzy, as if she'd slept too long, but her memories quickly began to return. In fits and starts, the way she'd recalled the one college fraternity party at which she'd had too much to drink, the accident came back to her. Bits were very clear. Other parts were impossibly blurry. Almost all the images puzzled her. She couldn't shake the feeling that something very peculiar had happened to her.

"Good, you're awake."

Startled, Kendra sat up too quickly and had to grip the sides of the bed until her head stopped spinning. The woman in hospital whites watched her from the doorway. She made no attempt to offer aid or comfort.

When she judged Kendra's dizziness had passed, she moved with silent authority into the small room. She was in her fifties, Kendra guessed, and in her youth had been beautiful.

"Where am I?" Kendra asked.

"You're in my clinic in Quaiapen, Maine. I'm Dr. Colleen Gray."

She checked Kendra's pulse and listened to her heart. After a pause during which she examined Kendra's pupils, she added, "You're in good shape, considering."

"I hate to ask, but how long have I been here?"

"Overnight. It's Tuesday morning, Ms. Jennings."

"How do you know my name?"

"You had identification in your pocketbook." Dr. Gray seemed surprised by the question.

Kendra touched her forehead with her fingertips, a puzzled look stealing over her face.

"Are you still dizzy?"

Experimentally, Kendra rotated her head. "No. My neck is a little stiff, but it was before the crash. I'd been driving all day. I just feel...odd. Sort of...hung over." The laugh that accompanied her words faded into a sputter of indignation as she saw the doctor's face turn to stone. "That's how I feel, not what I am!"

The protest was useless. Dr. Gray's opinion was clear in a voice gone taut with ill-concealed disapproval. "Deputy Moreau's been waiting to talk to you. He has a few questions about your accident."

"So do I. Did I hit my head?"

"No. Your body received very little damage. You were apparently quite relaxed by the time your car hit that tree."

"Relaxed? I—"

"Ms. Jennings." The doctor cut her off with a raised hand and the stern, lecturing tone Kendra herself used when assigning a week's detention to a rebellious thirteen-year-old. "Let me offer you a word of free advice. Go easy on the pills. They say God looks after fools and drunkards, but next time you might not be so lucky. Next time you might hit another car instead of a tree."

Before Kendra could defend herself the doctor had gone. Her quiet footsteps made no sound in the corridor. After a moment, Kendra heard the murmur of voices in the distance.

Struggling out of the bed, she made her way to the bathroom where she dashed cold water on her face. She'd never felt so disoriented.

Revived, but still wondering what on earth was going on, Kendra carefully examined her face in the mirror. Did her pupils seem smaller than usual? It was hard to tell. She had faint shadows under her eyes, but they had been there for weeks, the result of overwork and stress. Her hair was a tangled mess.

Kendra ignored the snarls and struggled out of her short hospital gown, wincing at the contortions required to untie the two bows that held it together in the back. Then she twisted in front of the small, high mirror until she was able to examine her body.

There was a huge bruise on her left breast where the seat belt had caught her. That and a bruised knee, which had likely struck the steering wheel, were the only damage she could find.

She was not vain about her looks, but she was relieved to find she was still in one piece. She liked her body the way it was. Her breasts were high and firm, and her waist trim. If her backside and stomach were not quite as small as they had been when she was eighteen, they were still in very good shape for someone who was nearly thirty, and her legs were as slim, shapely and supple as ever.

Satisfied, Kendra slipped back into the hospital gown. She'd just retied the second bow when a memory overwhelmed her. She stood perfectly still as the details came back to her.

She'd thought she was floating, then realized she was being carried. Her arms had been draped limply around the stranger's neck, her head cradled against his broad chest. Slowly, she'd opened her eyes, but her vision had been blurry. She'd tried to focus on what was nearest—a strong, clean-shaven jaw and a mouth. Lips, full and delightfully sensuous, had swum before her.

In the distance she'd heard the wail of a siren. She'd wanted to lift her eyes, to see what features were above those fascinating lips, but she hadn't had the strength. She had wondered if she was badly hurt and if she was going to die.

Kendra shook her head. That was all there was.

She came out of the bathroom in a rush, forgetting that she might not find the room empty. When she caught sight of the man, and the gleaming silver badge on his chest, she drew in a startled breath. Heat rushed into her face as she remembered the short, thin cotton gown she wore.

Waves of confusion returned. Kendra's mind registered details, but couldn't seem to assimilate them. He must be the deputy Dr. Gray had spoken of. She saw the dark brown, long-sleeved uniform shirt and its contrasting tan tie. Low on his hips rode a thick

leather belt, loaded down with the tools of his trade—
a portable radio, a flashlight, a can of Mace, a night-
stick and a service revolver.

All that was normal, expected. What disconcerted
her was her profound awareness of the muscular male
body underneath the uniform.

The enigmatic look she surprised in his eyes was
gone before she could identify it, replaced by an
expression that was carefully blank. She stared at the
hard, angular planes of his face, taking in molasses-
brown eyes flecked with gold and hair the color of
mahogany. His nose had been broken at least once,
but it added to the appeal of a strong chin and broad
forehead.

"I'm Deputy Alex Moreau." His voice was a gruff
baritone rumble.

Kendra felt her pulse flutter as she continued to stare
at him. The room had grown alarmingly smaller since
he had come into it, and when he took a step closer she
instinctively moved back.

"I'd like to ask you a few questions."

"Of course," she murmured. She had a few for
him, too, if only she could make her heart stop ham-
mering.

It was absurd to be so flustered. She felt almost
afraid of him, and there was no cause. He was simply
doing his job. If he was any good at it, he already
knew that the accident had not been her fault.

"Dr. Gray says you've been released." His voice
sounded impersonal, even cold. "You came out of the
accident without a scratch, but your car is another
story. I doubt you'll ever drive it again."

"I'll have to rent one. My purse... was my money—"

"We checked your valuables when you were admitted. You were carrying a great deal of cash. Ever hear of traveler's checks? They aren't a bad idea."

Looking up, she caught him watching her with narrowed eyes. Why did he seem so suspicious? Trying to keep her voice light, she thanked him for his advice. She did not tell him she'd deliberately rejected traveler's checks because they could be traced. She'd chosen to avoid leaving a paper trail.

"Where were you headed?" The question was issued as he sank into the room's one chair and flipped open a spiral notebook. Taking a pen from his breast pocket, he waited, apparently relaxed, the upper half of his body inclined slightly forward.

Mindful of the gown gaping open behind her, Kendra sidled toward the bed and caught the edge of the light blanket. Wrapping it securely around her, she risked a perch on the end farthest from him, carefully smoothing the pale green blanket ends over her knees.

She couldn't understand why he made her so nervous. He was a powerfully built man, and his presence dominated the small room, but he hadn't touched her, or accused her of anything. Why did she feel so threatened? Kendra tried to attribute her uneasiness to frayed nerves, a natural aftereffect of her car crash, but didn't quite convince herself.

Remarkably, her voice sounded self-possessed. All those years of teaching came to her rescue. "I was on my way to a house I recently inherited from my cousin, Olive Andrews. I got directions from the waitress at the Quaiapen Diner."

Alex Moreau avoided looking at her as he fired rapid questions in her direction. In short order he'd learned she was single, unemployed, knew no one in

Quaiapen and did not want to phone her mother in Florida. He continued to elicit information and scribble notes until Kendra mentioned the other car. Then the pen stopped, and his unsettling eyes lifted. So did one skeptical brow. "There was no other car at the scene."

"It came right at me," she insisted. "When I tried to stop I skidded. The road was too wet. Maybe the other driver panicked and drove away."

"Can you describe this car?"

"Big. Dark. Black, I think." She spread her hands in a gesture of futility, momentarily forgetting her state of undress. The blanket slipped, opening to show an inch-wide strip from shoulder to thigh. "I was too busy getting away from it to worry about the make and model."

"You're saying someone tried to ram you?"

She heard the disbelief in his voice and saw a flicker of regret in the brown eyes as they slid up her long, bare legs. They rested, briefly, on the swell of her bosom, stopped at her lips as she nervously dampened them with the tip of her tongue, and then swung away as she jerked the blanket closed and hugged it more tightly around her.

"I know it sounds absurd, but that's the way it happened. I don't know. Maybe the car skidded in my direction accidentally, but it was stopped when I approached the crossroads. I am a very good driver. I don't run off the road for no reason at all."

"The only skid marks at the scene were made by your tires, and I think there was a reason, Ms. Jennings." He took a small, ornately decorated pillbox from his pocket, rubbing one blunt thumb over the raised filigree on its top before he placed it on the edge of the bed nearest him. "This was found in your purse when we looked through it for some ID. You want to tell me how many of these you took?"

Puzzled, she reached for the box. It still felt warm from his hand, reminding her that for all his professional reserve, Alex Moreau had an aura of tightly leashed virility about him. Kendra fought back a shiver as she closed her fingers over the box.

It was heavier than she'd expected. Though she was no expert, she suspected the box was an antique and probably quite valuable.

Because Moreau seemed to expect it, Kendra fiddled with the lid, trying to figure out how it opened. Just as she was about to give up and ask for help, she located the catch.

Three small white pills and a single capsule lay nestled on the silk lining. Kendra stared at them for a long moment. Both drugs looked familiar. Kendra had confiscated plenty of uppers at school, and the tranquilizers were the same brand her mother had taken for several weeks after Kendra's father died. They'd calmed her nerves but she'd been warned not to stay on the prescription drug very long because it was one on which it was easy to become dependent.

Very carefully, Kendra closed the box and returned it to his end of the bed. The doctor had implied she was taking pills. Now Alex Moreau thought this was her pillbox. To tell the truth, she felt as if she had been drugged, though she hadn't ingested anything stronger than coffee.

What was going on in this little town? Uneasily, she remembered a third-rate women-in-prison movie she'd seen on late-night television. The heroine had been driving innocently through a small Southern town when the local sheriff decided he wanted her. That's absurd, she told herself. Fiction.

Then she remembered a story that had not been the creation of a writer's mind. She'd heard it second-hand from a fellow teacher, but she'd believed it. A young woman, driving home alone from a party, had been stopped by a state policeman. He'd made a deal with her. He'd forget about a breath test and a speeding charge if she'd have sex with him in the back of his cruiser.

When Kendra spoke again her voice wasn't quite as steady. "I don't know where you got this, but it isn't mine."

"Then how do you explain that I found it in your purse?"

The images in her mind were blurry at first, but as she wrinkled her forehead and closed her eyes they came clear. She'd been slumped against the car seat, right after the accident. There were noises at her left side. Someone had been trying the door, but it wouldn't open. Of course not, she remembered thinking. It's locked. A tap on the glass had sounded next, but she hadn't responded. She'd wanted them to go away so she could sleep.

A rustling on the seat beside her, off to her right, had brought Kendra back from semiconsciousness. Dimly, she'd been aware that someone had crawled in through the hatchback. He'd been fumbling with her purse. She'd decided he was robbing her, but had lacked the strength to care, much less do anything to prevent it. She'd barely been able to force her eyelids open far enough to catch a glimpse of the thief.

"He had blond hair," she said aloud. "Young. They were all young. I thought they were a nightmare."

"Now you're saying someone was at the scene after the accident and left you?"

"Yes." Why did he sound so angry? It was the truth. "They got out of the car. The black car. Three boys. Teenagers. And then one of them had his hands in my purse. I wasn't really with it the whole time. I think he climbed over the back seat to get at it. The rain had stopped. I remember thinking how eerie the sudden quiet was."

"So you're claiming that some kid planted these pills on you?" The small container was dwarfed by his hand.

"I know it sounds fantastic." Kendra's fingers clenched on the edge of the blanket. "I'm not saying I saw him put anything inside. I just saw him open it. I thought he was going to steal the money."

"If there had been a boy, I'm sure he would have. I counted over $8,000."

"Eight thousand two hundred forty-five before I left this morning. I mean, yesterday morning. I bought gas, though. Twice."

"Why?" There was a rough edge in his voice, a tacit challenge in his eyes that made her want to defy him.

"The car won't run without it."

Kendra regretted her smart remark as soon as it was out, but she had no intention of explaining why cash had seemed such a good idea at the time. Or that she'd simply enjoyed the feel of all those hundred-dollar bills. It was none of his business, anyway. It was her money. She could carry it any way she pleased. She'd meant to open a checking account in Quaiapen as soon as she got settled.

"Make things easy on yourself, Ms. Jennings. Tell the truth. It will come out anyway when we get the results of your blood test."

"Go ahead. Take a blood sample. That will prove I'm telling the truth."

"We already did."

"When I was out? How dare—"

"It's standard procedure in a car crash when the driver is unconscious. Look, denying you have a problem with drugs isn't going to do you any good. There's help for people like you. All you have to do is admit it." The gruffness in his voice faded until he sounded almost sympathetic. "Prescription drugs can be dangerous, as volatile as PCP or crack if you misuse them."

Kendra wasn't listening. Another memory had started to resurface. She recalled fumbling with one limp hand for the window crank. She'd only managed to lower it an inch before her energy evaporated. Slumped against the seat, she'd watched through half-closed eyes as the blond boy walked back to his car.

His voice had carried well in the still, damp air. He'd said, "It's all set. She never knew what hit her."

Kendra struggled to make sense of his words, but it was hopeless. Maybe she had been dreaming.

"Another boy was a redhead," she said slowly. "He said, 'Let's get out of here before the cops show up.'"

A puzzled frown furrowed her forehead and she caught a strand of hair in one finger, curling and uncurling it as she tried to sort fact from fiction. How many teens had there been? Something had made her think of gangs. They'd had identical jackets, but not black leather.

"They wore ski jackets."

A spark of emotion flared in his eyes and was quickly gone. "So does half the population of the state. You'll have to do better than that."

Still another vision invaded her mind. This time the same figures, shadowy and threatening, were moving toward her through the fog. She was powerless to get away. Just as they converged on her wrecked car, they disappeared.

Blinking rapidly, Kendra stared down at her clenched hands. Clearly that had been imagination. Had everything been produced by a fevered mind?

Risking a glance at Deputy Moreau, she saw that he radiated skepticism from every pore. He didn't believe there had been another car, and he certainly wasn't buying the idea of a towheaded teenager who carried antique pillboxes full of drugs. She had trouble with that part herself.

"Are you sure I don't have a concussion? There has to be some explanation."

She didn't like suspecting someone had deliberately caused her accident any more than he did. That would mean she'd been set up. Some unknown enemy had meant her harm. Kendra wasn't ready to accept that possibility, even though she knew she wasn't lying about those pills. She'd never seen the small, deadly box before.

"Dr. Gray said there was no sign of concussion."

"Where is she? I want to talk to her."

"Gone home. She was up all night with you. This is a small town, Ms. Jennings, and a small clinic."

Quaiapen *was* small. One main street held the entire business district. She'd passed Dr. Gray's bright green one-story clinic and spotted Wakefield McKee's real estate office on the opposite corner when she'd pulled into the parking lot of the Quaiapen Diner.

McKee. She could ask him for help, she supposed. He could tell her where to rent a car. She had to see him anyway, to tell him to take the house off the market. She'd meant to do it on her way, but it had already been too late in the day when she reached Quaiapen. A Closed sign had been hanging in the realtor's window.

Kendra remembered deciding to have a good meal, since she doubted there would be food in a house that had been standing empty for four months. Afterward she'd planned to drive straight there. She had a key. The lawyer who'd handled her cousin's estate had sent that, before McKee came into the picture.

Her waitress had been plump, white-haired and motherly. The name tag on her faded pink uniform had identified her as Millie, and she'd been happy to provide explicit directions to the house along with the special—New England boiled dinner.

"So you're the heir." Her friendly brown eyes had carefully recorded Kendra's appearance, noting the oversized sweatshirt she'd chosen for comfort, the lack of makeup, the long, straight hair and the snug designer jeans. "Wakefield didn't think you'd bother to come and look at it until summer."

Wakefield McKee hadn't managed to sell the place, either, but Kendra had seen no reason to give Millie grist for a small-town gossip mill by complaining. "I've decided to live in the house for a while," she told the other woman. "If I like it I may even stay on."

Millie had given her an incredulous look. "You wouldn't catch me living all alone out there."

"What's wrong with the place?"

"Not a thing, honey, if you're into communing with nature."

Kendra would have pressed her further, but other customers had come in and Millie was the only waitress.

Relaxed by the quiet atmosphere, Kendra had spent much longer than she'd planned over the meal. Watching people and speculating about them was one of her favorite pastimes. A man and his wife hardly spoke, but put away huge platters of roast beef. Had they quarreled, or were Monday nights at the diner a long-standing tradition, no longer enjoyed but still indulged in? A man in a business suit ate alone and spoke sharply to Millie when she tried to be friendly. Another man reminded Kendra of a lumberjack with his plaid flannel shirt and high boots.

By the time Kendra had finished the second cup of coffee Millie insisted she needed "for the road," the sky was dark as night and it had begun to rain. Back in the car she'd felt a pang of unease when the last light disappeared in her rearview mirror but had shrugged it aside, anxious to press on.

"Ms. Jennings?" Alex Moreau's voice brought her back to the present.

"I must have hit my head. Nothing else makes any sense."

"You were still securely fastened in your seat belt when I got to the scene. There wasn't anything there you could have struck. Check for yourself. You have no bumps, no bruises."

"Maybe not, but neither did I have any pills in my purse!"

He frowned, looking back at his notes. "Do you know what time it was when you hit that tree?"

"It couldn't have been much after six. I left the restaurant around 5:30."

"I pulled you out of the car at 6:10, Ms. Jennings. That leaves very little time for all you claim happened to have taken place."

"You pulled me out?"

The remembered sensation was one of pure pleasure. Someone had run warm, firm hands over her neck and spine and ribs, soothing the aches. He'd been checking for broken bones. Still groggy, she'd thought she was imagining the light, arousing touch, but had concluded dreams didn't have smells. The scent of spicy after-shave had filled her nostrils. "You smell wonderful," she'd murmured.

Abruptly the hands had withdrawn. Kendra had felt her seat belt release and her own body slump forward. She had been too weak to control it. As those same strong hands caught her shoulders, she'd drifted off again, collapsing against him with a little sigh of contentment.

Now Kendra watched him through lowered lashes. He was only a few inches taller than she was, and no more than a few years older. As he bent over his notes, his tailored uniform accented well-muscled arms and broad shoulders.

"I could read you your rights and take you in for operating under the influence." He did not look at her and for a moment his meaning did not sink in.

"I wasn't!"

"So you say." He was still avoiding her eyes, toying with his pen. "I'm not going to do that, Ms. Jennings, but only because the charge is difficult to prove. You're a very convincing liar. And chances are good the level of drugs in your system isn't enough to get a conviction. I'll lose less time and waste less of the taxpayers' money if I just see to it that you get where you're going with no more fuss."

Abruptly he closed his notebook and stood up. At last, almost reluctantly, unreadable brown eyes turned on her. Kendra slipped off the edge of the bed and moved closer.

What had been disguised by the overpowering hospital scents of ammonia and medicine now drifted toward her. Very faintly, weakened by a night of waiting for her to regain consciousness, came the familiar aroma of spicy after-shave.

Millions of men wore that brand. Her father had, though without the same effect. As Alex Moreau moved past her toward the corridor, Kendra knew it had never been quite so potent on any other man.

"Get dressed," he snapped from the doorway. "I'll drive you to this house of yours."

An almost military bearing made him look stiff, unyielding and sternly professional, but Kendra ignored the facade and stared at his lips and chin. She felt the strong pull of attraction.

"I must be out of my mind," she muttered as Alex Moreau tugged the door closed behind him. If he had any feeling toward her at all, it was contempt.

Chapter 2

In the hall outside her room, Alex bit back a string of frustrated curses as he shrugged his arms into his uniform jacket. What right did she have to be so alluring? Wrapped in a blanket, hair in disarray, face bare of makeup, she should have looked pathetic. Instead she radiated fragile loveliness that made him want to take her in his arms and kiss her troubles away.

Worse, why did she have to sound so convincing? She had to be lying. Black cars. Teenage hoods who left cash behind. Next she'd be trying to sell him a bridge in Brooklyn.

The money bothered him. She hadn't been just nervous when he asked her about the cash; she'd been evasive. The instincts that had kept him in law enforcement for more than ten years convinced him there was a piece of the puzzle still missing.

Alex ran agitated fingers through his already tousled hair and sank back against the smooth hospital wall. The corridor had been painted a soft, reassuring blue. Doc Gray said that color had a calming effect on waiting families. Nothing had helped him.

They'd found those damn pills right off, but even knowing the kind of woman she was hadn't erased the memory of how right she'd felt in his arms when he'd lifted her out of that car. For one insane moment he'd wanted to kiss her right there on the rain-soaked pavement. Then she'd passed out, and the ambulance had pulled in, tires squealing, to carry her away.

Cursing his own weakness, Alex had spent the rest of the night trying to convince his rebellious body that he couldn't be attracted to any woman who misused drugs. He'd stayed on patrol until he went off duty, but instead of going home for some much-needed sleep he'd found himself back here at the clinic, waiting for her to wake up. He'd done enough checking while she slept to know she had a Vermont driver's license, car registration and teaching certificate. The computer insisted she was clean as far as arrests and traffic violations were concerned.

And then he'd seen her again, coming out of the bathroom in that sorry excuse for a gown. He'd needed every ounce of self-possession to tear his eyes away from her long, shapely, silky legs. A sudden vivid picture of those legs wrapped around his waist had left him speechless.

Alex blinked. Stick to business, he told himself sternly.

Technically the case was closed. It was at his discretion as investigating officer whether or not to press charges. An hour of paperwork and she'd be just another statistic. He could forget about her. By the same token, he could ask her out, even sleep with her, and it would no longer be unethical. The thought was tempting, but imbued with another kind of danger. He'd been burned once by yielding to an overwhelming desire for a beautiful woman. He did not intend to let history repeat itself.

In self-defense, Alex slipped mirrored sunglasses into place as soon as she came into the hall. Only then did he allow himself to look at her. His gaze lingered on the perfect oval of her face. He was bemused by the shimmering cap of her bright hair. Even tangled, it was lovely.

She wore the same sweatshirt and jeans she'd had on when he brought her in. The pale blue top was large, long and loose, and would have disguised the lack of a bra if he hadn't had firsthand knowledge that there wasn't one. Under his steady gaze she looked away.

In spite of his determination to stay objective, he let his eyes rove lower, over the snug jeans that hugged her firm hips and thighs.

His survey stopped at her feet, where he was finally able to force his thoughts into safer waters. Kendra's fashion boots had narrow, two-inch heels, and if they were waterproof he'd eat the regulation Stetson he refused to wear. She was good-looking, probably available and up to no good. She didn't belong in this rural county, and she wouldn't fit in at Olive Andrews's house. In spite of the desire that surged through him every time he looked at her, or maybe because of it, Alex abruptly changed his mind. He'd file the accident report, but he wouldn't forget about the loose ends. He'd send her blood sample to the lab and do a little checking into her background. By the time he was done, he'd know everything there was to know about the lovely Ms. Jennings.

Forcing a casual smile to his face, he pushed away from the wall. "Ready?"

"I need my purse." Her fingers plucked at the bottom edge of her sweatshirt.

She was nervous. Good. If he could keep her off balance she might let something slip. He dipped his head in the direction she should go and fell in behind her to enjoy the view. Her walk was graceful, giving her hips a gentle, sensuous sway. No, he was not through investigating Kendra Jennings. Not by a long shot.

Unaware of Alex's quickening interest, Kendra waited as he removed a key from beneath the blotter on the reception desk and unlocked its file drawer to retrieve her purse. With no office hours until afternoon, no one either questioned or hindered her departure. She had been the clinic's only patient.

"Don't I have to pay the doctor?"

"She'll send you a bill, don't worry."

"Awfully trusting."

"I can find you, Kendra Jennings." He smiled when she dropped her gaze. She hadn't been quick enough to hide a flash of fear. "Don't forget this." The pillbox lay in the palm of his hand, extended toward her.

Like a small child, she clasped both hands behind her and refused to take it. "Keep it. I've told you it isn't mine." Then her chin tilted up defiantly. "Maybe you can put an ad in the local paper and find the real owner."

She searched his face, frustrated that he could hide his thoughts behind the mirrored sunglasses. She sensed he was trying to intimidate her, and it made her angry.

Alex found Kendra's emotions laughably easy to read. "The cruiser is this way." He motioned her ahead of him toward the door. The silence was not broken again until they reached the outskirts of Quaiapan.

There were police and citizens band radios between them on the seat and a rack that held a clipboard, various report forms and a box of tissues. Kendra kept her eyes straight ahead as they drove down the tree-lined street, past brightly painted homes and old-fashioned storefronts.

The apple trees were just starting to blossom, and lawns, in spite of frequent patches of brown and the stray streak of rusty white snow, were putting on spring colors.

"I must be keeping you from your family," she said softly. "I'm sorry I've been so much trouble."

"No."

"No trouble?"

"No family. Make no mistake, Ms. Jennings. You are a troubling woman."

He sensed her watching him as he drove and could have kicked himself for saying so much. His voice was harsher than he intended when he pulled into Benji's Auto Salvage and stopped the car. "You did a thorough job on it."

Puzzled, she looked in the direction of his abrupt gesture. Her face drained of color, leaving it dead white. For a moment, Alex thought she might faint, but she got control of herself and reached for the door handle.

Her car, or rather what was left of it, had been towed in during the night. There was no hope it would ever run again. The front end had been pushed in so

that the hood was almost folded in half. The headlights were gone, the bumper was bent, the sides
bowed, and even the tires stuck out at odd angles.

Taking a deep breath to steady herself, Kendra
stepped out of the cruiser. Slowly, she crossed the lot
and lifted the hatchback. The latch was broken.

"You were lucky," Alex said as he came up behind
her and reached for the first suitcase. "The car might
have rolled over, or you might have neglected seat belts
and been thrown out, or you might have been going
faster." She might easily have been killed.

"Or my car might have burst into flames?"

"Not likely. Every time in movies. Very rarely in
real life."

"Thank you so much for sharing that with me." She
grabbed the two small cases and reached inside again
for a portable computer.

"You should picture this car next time you start
popping pills, Ms. Jennings."

The color rose in her cheeks as she turned to face
him. He felt the impact of her fury as plainly as if she
had struck him. "I have never taken a tranquilizer in
my entire life." Hands clenched at her sides, she was
fighting back tears.

Reaching past her, he extracted the last suitcase.
"Anything else?"

Miraculously, she regained her composure. "My
coat was in the back seat. And an umbrella."

In silence, he retrieved them. She was good, he'd
give her that. Maybe she'd done some acting. For a
moment he'd almost believed her.

"Did my cousin have a car?"

Alex gave her a sharp look. "Don't you know?" At her glare, he shrugged. "There's an old Jeep at her place."

"I don't suppose it has automatic transmission?"

His short bark of laughter was answer enough.

"Got a ten-year-old Nova we're working on that'll be ready tomorrow," Benji told her. He was small and wiry, his hands and overalls stained with grease. Bright, birdlike eyes glittered. "I'll take that Eagle in trade for scrap and let you have it for $500."

"What if I wait? Could I have it today?" There was a note of desperation in her voice. Frayed nerves were close to the surface.

"Tomorrow. Best I can do. We've got the engine out of her."

"How am I supposed to get back to town for it?"

"Expect young Alex there will give you a lift." Benji shot a gap-toothed smile in his direction and looked puzzled when it wasn't returned.

That was the trouble with living in a place all your life, Alex thought. The locals knew you weren't as tough as you tried to look. His attention shifted to Kendra Jennings, noting the slumped shoulders, the nervous fiddling with her hair. She looked utterly defeated, as if this news that she was still dependent upon his goodwill, unimportant as it was after all she'd been through, was more than she could bear.

Alex resisted the urge to put his arms around her shoulders. He simply loaded her luggage into the cruiser and waited until she'd paid Benji, in cash, for the car. The sight of that wad of bills hardened his resolve to find out what she was up to and reminded him he could not trust her, no matter how sad or sweet she looked.

Twenty-five silent minutes followed. He drove slowly, watching for her reaction when they passed the accident site. She didn't seem to notice, although the corner was made distinctive by two dead elms that still defiantly lifted leafless limbs toward the sky, and a maple much the worse for having stopped Kendra's car.

Finally, after a left-hand turn, he spoke. "Another mile."

They were on a dirt road not much wider than the car. All around was pine forest, beautiful in the pale sunlight, but eerie as well. The closer they got, the more nervous she became.

"I haven't seen a house or a telephone pole since we turned off the paved road."

"That's right," he said, and swung into her dooryard.

The house stood alone in a clearing, a simple wooden dwelling with a red brick chimney and a railed front porch. Late-morning fog still rose off the lake beyond and extended delicate fingers toward the patrol car, giving the scene a dreamlike quality. Lost in the moment, Kendra simply stared.

Years of training had Alex looking over his shoulder, examining the surrounding wilderness carefully as he parked the car. The place was familiar to him, but never before had he been more aware of its isolation.

Olive Andrews had fit the milieu. He'd never worried about her alone out here, though events proved he should have. Kendra Jennings was out of place, with her high-heeled little boots and her soft skin. Why on earth had she come? And how was she going to cope? Scowling, he thought he had that answer. She probably had a good supply of those damn pills, maybe something stronger, to wile away the days.

"It's very secluded," she said faintly.

"The middle of nowhere." Agreeably cheerful, he took the glasses off and grinned at her. That made her even more nervous.

Kendra slid away from him, reaching behind her for the door handle. "Thank you for bringing me out. If there's a taxi in Quaiapen you can send that out for me tomorrow."

"No taxi."

She can't be as innocent as she looks, Alex thought. There were too many inconsistencies. What was a teacher doing out of work at this time of year? Why was she carrying all that cash? The money nagged at him. Nobody carried cash these days. He didn't seriously believe she'd robbed a bank on her way to Quaiapen, but the sixth sense that had served him so well in his years in law enforcement insisted that he keep digging until he got to the truth.

Abruptly, he got out of the car. At once he saw the tire prints. Someone had been in here since the rain the night before. Kids, parking? Maybe, but this was a long way out to come when there were lovers' lanes much closer to town.

In the ordinary course of his patrol, he might have swung in to check this empty house during the night. He'd been tied up with Kendra's accident. Then there'd been a domestic dispute on the other end of his patrol area. He'd never gotten back this way.

On the far side of the car he heard the whisper of fabric as she got out and stood looking at the house. "No taxi, no phone, no power. How did Cousin Olive live out here?"

"Very comfortably. I take it you never visited her."

"I didn't even know she existed until four months ago. She never met me. She just left me everything she had."

"Why?"

"I wish I knew." Kendra squared her shoulders and reached back inside the car for her shoulder bag and the computer she'd insisted on placing on the floor under her feet for the trip from the junkyard. "Thank goodness this thing runs on batteries."

"You a writer?" He kept his voice casual.

Her laughter sounded forced. "I told you. I'm unemployed."

"You must have done something before. Some job."

"Once I was a teacher." Her sharp look pierced him. "Why are you asking so many questions?"

"Habit."

"Is it habit that has you scanning the forest as if you expected to find terrorists hidden in the trees?"

"You're very observant, Ms. Jennings. Do you know how to use a gun?"

Eyes widening, she took a step backward, almost losing her balance as her heel landed in a mud puddle. "I hate guns. Why on earth would I—"

"In case you haven't noticed, you're on your own out here."

"My cousin lived out here, all alone, for many years."

"She died out here, too. It was a week before we found her body." And Olive, he added silently, never looked as vulnerable as Kendra did now.

"Why are you trying to frighten me?" The color had drained from her delicately chiseled features. He felt a twinge of guilt. He hadn't meant to terrify her.

"You okay?"

"No, I'm not okay." Anger rippled just under the surface as she fought to control her temper. Once again her emotions were transparent. Her eyes revealed every thought.

Alex blinked, suddenly realizing that such openness didn't square with the idea she was lying. It was an act. It had to be. But he believed the fury he heard in her voice.

"If it isn't too much trouble, could you explain what happened to my cousin?"

"She apparently took a fall. She hit her head on a rock, then died of exposure. We had a couple of good snowstorms right around then and by the time her road was plowed..." His voice trailed off and he shrugged.

"Don't you patrol?"

She'd hit a nerve, and his jaw tightened. The words came out clipped and cold. "Do you have any idea how big this county is? It extends clear up to the Canadian border, and the northern patrol officer, that's me, has the biggest half. I could drive for an entire shift and never leave the main roads that connect the thirteen small towns I serve."

Why was he defending himself to her? The anger turned inward as she swung away from him and moved swiftly toward the house. He'd done his job. Old Mrs. Andrews had been alive and healthy the last time he'd been by. She'd fed him homemade doughnuts and patted his head, and told him to be a good boy and not fuss about her.

Alex Moreau took one more look around before he released the trunk catch. Inhaling deeply of clean, damp air, he caught the scent of moist loam and wet pine needles. The earthy smells settled him. He'd grown up in Quaiapen. His parents owned a camp less than a mile away. They hadn't used it since they retired and moved to Arizona, but Alex knew and loved the country around him. He'd known and liked Olive Andrews, too, and he'd never once heard her mention Kendra Jennings.

Dark eyes narrowing with renewed suspicion, he studied her as he circled to the trunk and removed her luggage. What was she doing here? She was as out of place as a rose blooming in January.

Kendra was wondering the same thing. The house shone like a gem in its misty, dreamlike setting. The outside had been painted white with dark green shutters, and the yard, in spite of the recent neglect, showed evidence of having been planted, arranged and lovingly cared for. Rosebushes, still covered against the winter frosts, stood on either side of a wide set of steps leading to a porch that ran all along the front of the building.

Cousin Olive's place had a rose-covered cottage sort of appeal. Kendra wanted to like it. If only it weren't so isolated. Once Alex Moreau left, she'd be completely cut off from the outside world.

Burlington was hardly New York or San Francisco, but it was a city. Her experiences with country living were limited, and she'd never tried camping out. She had the feeling she was about to.

Nervously Kendra inserted her key in the dead-bolt lock. What would it be like inside? And what was she to do for heat and light? She supposed she could manage a wood stove, if the wood was already split and she had plenty of kindling, but she hoped she wouldn't have to rely on oil or kerosene in order to see. Any kind of liquid fuel terrified her. A fire, out here, would never be noticed until it was too late.

"Wait a minute!"

Kendra froze in the doorway as his shout knifed through her. At least she hadn't jumped out of her skin this time, but her tone was annoyed as she swung around to face him. He really had to stop trying to scare her. "Now what?"

"I'm going in first." He brushed past her, so close that his coat sleeve touched her breasts.

The unexpected contact jolted her, sending sensual shock waves up and down her spine. Kendra sucked in her breath, trying to still the frantic beating of her heart. It was insane to be so aware of him, so affected by a touch he hadn't even noticed.

He was intent on searching her house. Did he really think something amiss, or was this just an excuse to go through the place? Her stomach muscles tightened in anger. He was doing a thorough job of the first floor. She waited until he came back to the entry hall to comment.

"If you're expecting a stash of tranquilizers you're out of luck."

He answered her sarcasm with his own as he started up the flight of stairs directly in front of the door. "The place has been standing empty for months. As you've already pointed out, my patrols are inadequate. Would you rather be left here alone to find a vagrant or a burglar?"

Muttering to herself, Kendra hoisted the largest suitcase and went inside. She seesawed between irritation and attraction when it came to Alex Moreau and she disliked both reactions. It was safer to stay angry at his high-handed ways, but even then his presence provoked a subtle sexual pull.

Frowning, she looked around. She was standing in a small hall, with wide, arched doors on either side. Before she could begin to explore, he was back. "Everything's fine. Sometimes people break into these places, and the summer camps along the lakes, but there's no sign anyone's been here."

"Why do they break in?"

"Looking for liquor, antiques, firearms, stereo equipment. Anything they can sell. You'd be amazed the stuff summer people leave behind." As he talked, he retrieved the rest of her suitcases and motioned her ahead of him up the stairs to the bedrooms.

"You've been here before." She didn't make it a question. Something about the sure way he turned at the top of the stairs spoke of long familiarity.

"I was through the whole place after we found her. And I've been in and out of her kitchen since I was a kid. She was a nice woman."

"Tell me about her. I don't even know how old she was, or whether she'd been married."

One thick brow lifted, skeptical. Did he question her claim to ignorance, or to Olive's house? She supposed she couldn't blame him. The inheritance was inexplicable.

Kendra glanced around as he deposited her bags. Her throat tightened as she realized they were in a bedroom. Her cousin's bed was the high, soft, old-fashioned kind, with an elaborately carved headboard and footboard. The image of Alex Moreau on that bed, decidedly out of uniform, flickered across Kendra's mind before she could stop it.

As heat and color flooded her cheeks, she lowered her eyes, hoping he couldn't read her as well as most people seemed to be able to. She'd never been able to hide her emotions, any more than she'd been able to learn to keep her thoughts to herself. She tended to blurt out whatever reaction first crossed her mind, and realize too late that she'd said the wrong thing.

His voice seemed lower, more sensual, in this setting. "Olive was widowed many years ago. There's probably a picture around somewhere."

Risking a glance in his direction, she was relieved to find he wasn't watching her. Instead his eyes roamed the cozy, comfortable room. Hers followed. A matching dresser and highboy and blanket chest took up most of the space. Olive's bedroom was one half of the upper floor, under the eaves. The oversized furniture made the room seem small. Alex Moreau's presence made it shrink all the more.

"Nothing has been touched since her death." A sudden change came over his voice, a gentleness, but it only served to underscore his rugged virility.

He must have been fond of Olive. Did he blame himself that she hadn't been found in time? Kendra wondered.

No one had troubled to protect the furniture with dust covers or pack the small knickknacks that seemed to be everywhere. Olive's framed Currier and Ives prints broke the pattern of fading flowered wallpaper, and the mail she'd collected that last day still lay on her dresser, unopened.

Curious, Kendra glanced down at the mailing label on a rolled newspaper. Olive had rented a post office box in Quaiapen. She'd had to drive all that way just to get her letters.

"Don't you want to see the rest of your...inheritance?" His voice was soft, too soft. Kendra left her purse behind and scurried ahead of him toward the stairs, barely taking time to glance into the other room and see that it had been used exclusively for storage. Contrasting with the neat, orderly appearance of the bedroom, trunks and boxes lay strewn everywhere.

At the foot of the stairs she turned left, then stopped, charmed, at the sight that met her eyes. The living room was dominated by a fieldstone fireplace. One picture window overlooked Square Lake. A second, drapes drawn, would show the porch and the dooryard beyond.

An overstuffed sofa and two cheerfully mismatched chairs, all covered in bright flowered percale, had been grouped facing the hearth. The huge oval of a multihued braided rug covered the hardwood floor in front of them. Around the room an eclectic collection of knickknack shelves, occasional tables and plant stands hugged the dark paneling that covered the walls. Two old-fashioned cedar hope chests served as window seats.

"The dining room is on the other side of the hall."

For a moment Kendra forgot about Alex as she explored the delights of an overflowing china cabinet that matched the rosewood dining table and chairs. Here Olive had kept a collection of bisque figurines. They were hardly valuable antiques, but they had appeal and varied from dainty shepherdesses to piano babies to self-important white cats. It was some time before Kendra tore herself away from them and passed through the room's second door into a brightly decorated kitchen.

Alex was just firing up the huge black cast-iron wood stove. "Did you think about supplies?"

Dismay echoed through her words. "Apparently I didn't think about a lot of things." She smiled warily back at him and perched on one of the wooden stools surrounding a section of counter fitted out as a breakfast bar.

The urge to let exhaustion overwhelm her was strong. Kendra hadn't yet had time to absorb the confusing events connected to her car crash, and here she was facing wilderness survival. The civilized dining room had momentarily made her forget. Olive might have lived here year-round but her house was really a camp. It was miles from the nearest power line.

Taking a deep breath, Kendra examined her surroundings more closely, hoping against hope for some easy way to cope. Painted bright yellow and decorated with framed prints of Kliban cats, the kitchen was a pleasant, cheerful room. Had it boasted an electric oven, Kendra would have thought it perfect. She closed her eyes, took several deep breaths and looked again.

This time her eyes roamed to the end of the countertop and stopped. An electric fry pan? Scanning the room the third time she found an electric toaster tucked away on an open shelf. Disbelief was followed by expectation as she spotted an electric outlet and a light switch.

Alex was watching her, amusement relaxing his features and for the first time rendering him approachable. There was a sinuous charm about the way he moved in this room, at home in the rustic surroundings.

"Tell me there's a way around roughing it and you get your pick of anything in the house."

She regretted the words as soon as they were out, but only the brief glitter of laughter in his eyes indicated he'd caught the unintentional double meaning. He kept his distance.

"Olive has an electric generator. And a CB radio. I'll show you how they work before I leave."

He was as good as his word, and followed up by starting a fire in the fireplace against the chill that had crept into the house during the long months it had stood empty. Then he used her cousin's electric coffee maker to brew enough for both of them. As the room warmed, he shed his uniform jacket and gun belt, hanging them on the coatrack in the hallway.

Kendra took a mug of steaming coffee from the tray he held, and smiled. "You are a lifesaver." He seemed less forbidding now, less suspicious of her.

"That's my job." Savoring a slow, warming mouthful of the coffee, he let it trickle slowly down his throat but he never took his eyes off her. This was not turning out the way he'd planned. Instead of trapping her in her own lies, he found himself liking her. And now, her stockinged feet curled under her on the sofa, she looked as young and vulnerable as a teenager.

What was he doing, staying here? He'd delivered her to her destination, settled her in. There was no need to do more. In fact, he had leads to follow up this afternoon, and it was already well past noon. He had sleep to catch up on, too. So why wasn't he leaving? Why did he suddenly want to move in and take care of her?

Kendra's thoughts echoed his. She didn't want him to go, not yet. She felt safe with him around. Maybe it had to do with his profession. Policemen protected. Her heart skipped a beat when he loosened his tie, and she blurted out her thoughts before she could stop herself. "Don't you have to get back on patrol?"

"I've been off duty since two this morning. Right now I'm on long weekend."

"In the middle of the week?"

"This week, yes. Cops don't work standard hours."

She took another sip of coffee to avoid meeting his eyes. Why was he here if it was no longer part of his job?

"You must be anxious to get to bed. I mean, to go home. I'm sorry to have taken up so much of your time. Do you live far from here?"

Babbling, she realized. If she kept sounding so jittery he was going to think she had something to hide. That she did was not reassuring. It was only a little secret, but she'd sworn not to share it with anyone.

He took another pull on the coffee before he answered her. "About halfway between here and Quaiapen. Alone."

He set his mug on a coaster shaped like a turtle and rose.

In confusion, Kendra blurted out, "Before you leave, I just wanted to repeat that there *was* another car, a black car that, I think, tried to ram me. Those boys—"

Alex's derisive snort stopped her in midsentence. He still didn't believe her. Eyes flashing, she spoke in short, clipped tones. "Read my lips, Deputy. This is the last time I'm going to say it. I do not pop pills and

I do not make up stories and I resent your treating me as if I do.''

She broke off with a gasp as he closed in on her, placing one hand on each side of her shoulders on the back of the couch. His eyes were deep, dark and terrifying unreadable.

''If you've been telling me the truth, then why am I making you so nervous?'' His voice had gone soft and coaxing and infinitely more dangerous.

''You aren't. Not a bit,'' she told him, but now her defiant stare faltered.

Alex knew she was lying to him. He followed the downward drift of her lashes. His hand swept across to touch their softness, and his anger evaporated.

Why should lies bother him, as long as he knew going in that they were lies? He had no illusions about women anymore. His ex-wife had cured him of such foolishness. She'd given him a crash course in lying and cheating. He wouldn't be sucked into that kind of trap again.

Slowly, he lowered his head. She didn't try to move away. Like a deer caught by a jacklight, she seemed frozen, unable to escape her fate.

Kendra felt muscles clench all up and down her stomach and abdomen. Alex Moreau's dark eyes were suddenly as readable as her own. They flamed with desire for her as he bent closer. The hard pressure of his lips claimed her mouth while his hands gripped her shoulders. In one smooth motion she was pulled upright and crushed against his broad chest.

Her hands, moving instinctively to protect herself, were trapped between them. She knew she should push against him until he released her, but her fists opened instead to caress the slightly rough texture of his shirt and feel the hard muscles beneath.

Strong, ruthless fingers traveled downward, molding her body to his as she clung helplessly to his waist. Breasts flattened, she could feel the imprint of his badge and hear his heart pounding next to her own. Her skin was tingling, and she was almost painfully aware of the pleasure his touch brought. She knew she should squirm away, stop this madness before it went further, but she couldn't resist the temptation to taste and feel just a little more of him.

As if he knew her need, his hands tightened on her hips, pulling her closer. He wanted her, and wanted her to know it. With tender urgency he deepened the kiss, plundering her mouth with a darting, marauding tongue. He tasted of coffee with cream and sugar, and of something more deeply sensual and dangerous.

Abruptly, he released her. What had begun as an effort to show at least one of her lies for what it was had quickly turned into something more basic, more shattering. Alex was as shaken as Kendra, though better able to hide his emotions. When she reached for him, pure undiluted desire surged through him, but somehow he managed to turn his back on her and stalk toward the door.

She didn't move, except to brace her back against the wall of the fireplace. Emptiness, almost unbearable, enveloped her. Her own weakness appalled her. She'd never responded this way to a man before and it was a frightening experience.

His voice was harsh and ragged, and seemed too powerful for the size of the room. "I'll be back tomorrow morning to drive you into town for your car."

She nodded.

"You've got canned goods in the kitchen, but you'll need supplies."

What was this man playing at? She knew he had wanted her, and he was experienced enough to know how weak she'd become under the onslaught of his kisses. She'd been his for the taking. She'd have regretted it later, but why should he care about her feelings?

Kendra forced herself to look at him and found him glowering back. "Plan on buying a gun. Olive didn't own one."

"I don't have a permit." She felt idiotic as soon as the words were out. He was the law. He could probably issue her one.

"Not needed." His lips quirked into a wry smile as he buckled his gun belt around his lean hips. "In this state you're not only allowed to have as many guns as you want, you're allowed to shoot an intruder. Make sure he's actually inside your house. And just before you kill him, tell him you're going to shoot. If you miss the first time and he's in the dooryard by the time you nail him, drag him back inside before you call me."

Shocked out of her lethargy, she pushed away from the fireplace and took a step toward him. "That's sick."

He shrugged. "A little black humor. Goes with the job. It's also true. I'll be here by ten in the morning."

"I won't buy a gun."

Very slowly, he turned to face her. "You feel safe here, alone?" His grin was a brief flash of white as he lowered his voice. "If you stay," he said softly, ''you're the sort of woman who's going to need protection.''

He was gone, coat slung around his broad shoulders like a cape, before Kendra could cross the room. The cruiser engine roared to life just as she reached the lock and turned the key to secure the dead bolt.

Still shaking, she returned to the sofa and sat huddled by the warmth of the fire. She needed protection all right. She needed protection from herself.

Chapter 3

All the way back down the dirt road to the highway Alex argued with himself. Twice he almost stopped the car and backed up. The persistent ache in his loins was telling him he'd been a fool to stop, but his head insisted he'd have been more foolish to stay.

She was bad news. If she sincerely believed she hadn't taken any drugs, she was only deceiving herself. He'd be crazy to let anyone that mixed-up into his life. Hell, next thing he knew, she'd be filing charges against him for sexual assault. It wasn't unheard of.

And yet, there was something about Kendra Jennings that made him want to trust her, made him want to believe she really felt something for him. Most of the time he'd known her she'd been prickly as a cactus, but those few moments when they were in each other's arms there had been a softness, a yielding.

Was she without guile, open and honest?

He couldn't claim she'd been coming on to him, either. Just now he'd forced her to kiss him, and she'd reacted to the stress of the situation. There should have been gentle words between them after a kiss like that, but no. He'd had to go and scare her to death by talking about guns.

Some said no one but another cop could tolerate a cop's perverse sense of humor. Jody certainly wouldn't have been able to accept him or his outlook on life, not that she'd stuck around long enough to try. Maybe that was why he'd felt driven to subject Kendra to the worst of his pessimism. Some subconscious instinct for self-preservation was working with the odd circumstances under which they'd met to drive her away before she got too close. Alex had the uneasy feeling that his instincts had kicked in too late.

Why else had he promised to come back? He could have sent someone. He wasn't really concerned about her safety, though he still wondered who had been in her dooryard last night. She had a good lock on the door, and he'd shown her how to call for help on the citizens band radio.

Alex reached the main road and made a decision. Instead of turning toward Quaiapen and his apartment, he drove north, toward the Canadian border.

The Moreaus had owned their camp on Square Lake for three generations. Alex's parents had modernized it, putting in plumbing and indoor-outdoor carpets, but it still looked as it had fifty years before—small, rustic and peaceful.

The camp road in was more deeply rutted than the driveway leading to Olive Andrews's place, and the small bridge over Bubble Brook would need repairs soon, but Alex was distracted from such housekeeping details by signs of recent traffic.

Cautiously, he parked the patrol car out of sight beyond the bend in the road and walked the rest of the way, hand resting lightly on his holster. There was no sign of another car now, but smoke rose from the chimney. Someone was inside.

The cabin consisted of one open room with sleeping lofts above. With silent, catlike tread, Alex approached the back porch overlooking the lake, until he could see in through the picture window. No attempt had been made to close the curtains. From the back, Alex easily recognized the pale, scraggly hair, narrow shoulders and long, skinny legs. Those were extended to rest booted feet on the kitchen table. The chair was tipped back and its occupant was calmly smoking a cigarette and swilling beer.

Alex swore softly under his breath and, no longer making any effort to be quiet, threw open the door. "What do you think you're doing!"

The feet crashed to the floor and the chair fell over backward. Alex wrenched the bottle of Canadian beer out of his son's hand and tossed it through the still-open back door.

Sparks of anger flashed in eyes the exact color of Alex's own as the boy made a show of defiance. He was as tall as Alex but more slightly built.

"I asked you a question, Denny." Alex could barely control the urge to grab his fifteen-year-old son by the shoulders and shake him until his teeth rattled.

"Aw, Dad. I just needed to get away for a while."

"You're supposed to be in school."

"I hate school." The familiar whine Alex had learned to hate came into the boy's voice.

Extraordinary willpower was all that kept Alex from hauling his son in for truancy. He'd long since given up trying to undo the harm the boy's mother had done. The whine was hers. So was the defiance of authority, any authority. Alex's father had predicted Denny would be in jail by the time he hit thirty.

With one hand, Alex threaded a path through the thickness of his hair, more unnerved than he liked to admit by Denny's unexpected presence. It was bad enough if he was telling the truth, and just skipping school, but the tread marks in the driveway looked to Alex's trained eye like a match for those in Kendra's dooryard.

"How long have you been here?"

Sulkily Denny answered him. "Since yesterday. Me and the guys went up to Lac-Mégantic for the weekend. They dropped me here."

Alex didn't have to ask who "the guys" were. Denny ran with two older boys, George Marks and Gil Paradis. Both had a well-deserved reputation for wildness. They'd obviously bought beer in Canada. Maybe Gil and George had only stopped at Kendra's place to hoist a few more before driving on to Quaiapen.

Youthful high jinks, Alex tried to tell himself, remembering how he'd been no more than eighteen when he and two friends had started making regular runs across the border to bring back Canadian whiskey. They hadn't drunk it. They'd sold it, at a profit. That one summer-long venture into crime had gone unpunished, but Alex wished now it had not happened. He'd been one of the lucky ones. He'd figured out without being arrested first that easy money wasn't worth the risk.

"Does your mother know where you are?"

Denny gave a nonchalant shrug. Even Alex recognized it as the twin of his own habitual gesture. "George was going to tell her."

"Was George going straight there after he left you?"

Denny righted the chair and sat in it again. He put out the half-smoked cigarette before his father could snatch it away and shot an incredulous look in Alex's direction. "Where is there to stop?"

"Somebody pulled in at Olive's place."

A shadow crossed Denny's face. Olive had been good to him, too. "Maybe it was her cousin."

Alex's eyes narrowed. "What do you know about her?"

Denny started to grin. "Her, huh? You meet her, Dad?"

"I asked you a question."

"Okay, okay. Don't get all official on me. I just heard somewhere that Olive left the place to a cousin. You knew it was a she cousin, so I figured you must have met her."

"Come on, I'll take you back. You've missed enough school for one year."

Alex's thoughts strayed back to Kendra as he drove his errant son toward town. He still had time to make a few phone calls. Although he didn't know anyone in the Burlington Police Department personally, he'd been to the Maine Criminal Justice Academy with an officer who'd since gone to work in Rutland, Vermont. That officer might well have friends in Burlington.

Another of Alex's professional acquaintances, the good-looking but married juvenile caseworker in the probation and parole department, had a former college roommate who now taught high-school English somewhere in Vermont. She'd mentioned it one day at lunch.

Someone could get him a copy of Olive's will, too, Alex decided. Maybe the estate was the source of Kendra's cash. He hoped it was, but one way or another when he was through calling in favors, there would be no more secrets.

By the time Alex had made the phone calls to start the investigation and tumbled into bed for some long-overdue sleep, Kendra was feeling more comfortable with her house. She'd explored it thoroughly, even the dirt-floored basement, and discovered battery-powered lanterns and plenty of candles as backup for the generator.

As Alex had said, nothing had been touched. Olive's personal belongings were just as she'd left them. Kendra found empty suitcases in the spare room and packed the contents of the bedroom drawers and closet into them, feeling like an usurper as she made room for her own things. In a bottom drawer she found Olive's purse.

Inside was her driver's license, which gave her age as ninety-two. Kendra stared down at the deeply lined, strong-willed face for a long time, wishing she'd met Olive Andrews. She knew her in ways no one else had because of all her cousin had left behind, but Kendra wondered if she would have liked her.

The wallet yielded few other clues to its owner's personality. There was a collection of small bills, both Canadian and American, and a checkbook, but she'd carried no credit cards, no photographs and no medication. Nestled in a zipper pocket was proof she'd played the lottery faithfully. Tri-State Megabucks had been paid for her lucky number for the entire year. Realizing she'd inherited the lottery tickets too, Kendra burst into laughter.

As the afternoon light began to fade, Kendra ventured back outside. She wanted to look over the shed where Olive's Jeep was parked and survey the lake. Now that the day was no longer overcast she had a clear view of the opposite shore. Everywhere she looked she saw trees, mountains, water and sky.

If there were other houses, or camps, they were hidden. She was not, however, completely alone. Far out on the lake was the black dot of a loon's dark feathered head, and its distinctive cry echoed in the stillness. Then, in the shallows, less than a hundred yards along the shore, Kendra spotted a gigantic moose, watching her and grazing.

Kendra beat a hasty retreat into the house. Moose were notoriously stupid, and unlikely to attack unless they were protecting their young, but she didn't care to get any closer to something that outweighed her by several hundred pounds.

When she had finished unpacking, Kendra set up her portable computer on the dining room table. The manila file folder labeled Cloud Castles lay next to it.

"This is it," she said aloud. This was what she'd decided she needed—peace and quiet, no student papers to grade and plenty of time. Now all she had to do was sit down and work.

Alex had come closer to the truth than he'd realized when he'd asked her if she was a writer. She wasn't yet. By her own definition she would not be a writer until she'd had something published. For now she was an aspiring writer.

Experimentally, she sat. The chair was too hard. After a moment she moved everything to the brighter and more cheerful kitchen. The computer could sit on the counter. She could sit on a stool...and she'd have terminal backache in a week.

Her headache was returning with a vengeance. Restless, Kendra moved to the window and stared out into the gathering darkness. She was too unsettled to begin now. Tomorrow she'd start over. Then she remembered that Alex Moreau was returning in the morning. Tomorrow afternoon, she promised herself, and left the folder and the computer to return to the living room.

It was strange not having a television. Every sound in the woods outside, every creak in the house, seemed magnified. She was glad, suddenly, that she'd never read many horror stories. Her imagination was working overtime as it was.

Had there really been a black car? She thought so, but obviously Alex Moreau did not. Maybe there had been, and those kids had been scared that they'd caused her to go off the road, and they'd run off. That made sense. Or had she imagined it all, even the boy rifling through her purse?

She had a sensation of eyes watching her and hastily closed the heavy, insulated drapes. Immediately she felt foolish, but she did not open them again. There were too many shadows among the trees leading down to the lake.

"Idiot," she said aloud, and felt better at once.

"Okay," she said, again aloud. "What about the pills?" This was the time to think everything through and be done with it.

Dispassionately, Kendra searched her memory for clues and concluded that there was no proof she'd taken anything. She had been overtired and then, after the accident, suffered from shock. It was possible. People did peculiar things when a situation was extremely stressful.

Of course that's it, the rational part of her mind insisted. The only alternative was that the waitress had drugged her coffee, and Kendra could not by any stretch of the imagination envision mild-mannered, motherly Millie as the mad poisoner of Quaiapen.

"Okay. Shock. Overwork. Overactive imagination. But where did the pillbox come from?"

That was the one question she knew she might never be able to answer conclusively, but she had begun to construct a theory. Her shoulder bag was large, with a loose flap to cover several sections within. Two had zippers. The other was open. What if another woman had mistaken Kendra's bag for her own and dropped the pillbox inside?

Kendra hadn't emptied everything out for weeks. She could easily have overlooked such a small addition. Now that she was thinking about it with a clear mind, she realized that she could even guess when the mistake had happened.

That anniversary party at Monica and Bill's, she decided. They'd all left their bags and coats in the guest bedroom. Kendra didn't remember anyone else having a purse like her own, but it was a common style and color and there had been a number of people at the party she hadn't known. Some had been drunk enough to make such a mistake.

That makes sense, she told herself. The pills were prescription drugs one of Monica's friends had been taking. Kendra had gotten them by mistake. Back in Vermont there was a woman who was still searching for her lost heirloom. It was pure chance that the pillbox had only come to light after the car accident, and coincidence that Kendra's physical reaction to the trauma had resembled the results of an overdose.

Ignoring the nagging little voice that insisted her explanation had more holes than a slice of Swiss cheese, Kendra willed herself to forget the entire episode. She'd think only of the future from now on. She was here. Her new life was beginning. She was even, though with some nervousness, looking forward to seeing Alex Moreau again.

The next morning Kendra again contemplated her computer and again put off beginning. She told herself she didn't want to get involved and still be working when Alex turned up. Procrastination justified, she returned to the second floor instead and tried on three different outfits before settling on beige wool slacks and a pink silk blouse to wear into town.

Why on earth was she fussing? This was scarcely the way she intended to dress during her stay in Maine. Who was she trying to impress? But she didn't change back into jeans, and she didn't scrub off the makeup she'd applied so carefully.

Defiantly, she sprayed her neck and wrists with the expensive French perfume her mother had given her for Christmas, and wound her hair loosely into a twist.

When she'd anchored it with pins at the nape of her neck she glanced at her watch. It was still only nine.

She felt like a silly schoolgirl preparing for a first date. Here she was, dressed and ready way too early, just as she'd always been in college. Time would hang heavily if she did nothing but wait and grow nervous. Back then she'd played endless hands of solitaire. Now she went into her cousin's spare room. Rejecting her earlier logic, she decided that she would just as soon still be busy when Alex arrived.

Kendra had glanced only briefly into the trunks and boxes the night before. Now she bent to examine them more thoroughly, especially the one that contained family papers. She hoped that, somewhere, she would find a clue to tell her why this house had been left to her.

The pursuit proved unexpectedly fascinating. Olive had apparently been an amateur genealogist and had carefully recorded every detail of the direct line of her own ancestry. The connection to Kendra, however, was shown less clearly. That branch of the family was referred to only by a series of cryptic notations. A single line ran from Oliver Buttenbeck, Kendra's great-great-grandfather, to her own name. Reference numbers rather than names filled the gaps denoting generations between.

Olive's connection was to Kendra's father's side of the family. When the inheritance had first surfaced, Kendra had asked her mother for more information, but Mrs. Jennings had been puzzled, too. She was certain Kendra's father had never mentioned relatives in Maine.

An hour later Kendra was still poring over her cousin's enigmatic scribbles when she heard a vehicle approaching. Watching from the safety of the bedroom, Kendra saw Alex Moreau pull into the dooryard in a white pickup truck.

He hardly seemed the same man now that he'd exchanged his starched brown uniform for a white cable-knit sweater and faded jeans that hugged his body like a second skin. The threatening air of his masculinity remained. If he seemed less intimidating than before, he was equally impossible to ignore.

Suddenly it was important that she meet him outside, rather than in the confines of her small entry hall. She dropped the charts she'd been studying, barely aware that they skittered across the polished surface of her dresser and slid to the floor. She was down the stairs, seizing her shoulder bag and a cream-colored cardigan from the coatrack and dashing through the door before he'd reached the porch steps.

"Anxious to see me?" He stopped her with the light touch of a hand to her arm. Kendra's heart skipped a beat, but she let her breath out slowly and got a tight rein on her emotions before she answered.

"Anxious to get into town and pick up my car."

"All in good time. It's a beautiful spring day. I'm taking you to breakfast." Alex had a plan. He was determined to learn more about this woman.

"I've already eaten." Canned corned beef, a tin of apricots and stale coffee. There had been cereal in the cupboards, but mice had been at it.

"An early lunch, then." He moved the large, firm hand from her forearm to the small of her back and propelled her toward his truck.

Kendra stiffened, willing herself not to feel so much pleasure at the casual contact. Her whole body was starting to tingle, responding to the warmth of his splayed fingers and the low, melodic timbre of his speech.

The network of nerve endings just beneath her skin might be dancing with excitement, but her thoughts were troubled. What was he up to? She wanted to trust him. Some very primitive instinct told her that she could. Common sense dictated she avoid him like the plague.

"Relax. How can you not be cheerful on a day like this? Just look at those clouds." His eyes were twinkling and his full, fascinating lips crinkled at the corners, then opened in a genuine smile as he gazed upward.

Kendra followed the look to a sky impossibly blue and dotted with light, puffy cumulus clouds. As a child she'd loved nothing better than to lie on her back on the grass on a hot summer's day and let clouds like those spark her imagination. A soft, wistful sigh escaped her before she could stop it.

"I especially like the one off to the left," Alex said. "It looks like a race car."

"What kind?"

"One of those experimental models."

She laughed in spite of herself. For the first time, she felt a rapport with Alex Moreau that had nothing to do with the chemistry between them. Maybe, just maybe, he was the sort of man she could share a dream with after all. But not yet. This time she'd be sure before she bared her soul.

"First stop, bank?" Alex asked as he threw the truck into reverse and began to maneuver it out of her dooryard.

"Yes. I had no intention of hiding the money in my mattress."

Their eyes locked and the laughter faded. His were somber and slightly bloodshot. Hers were suddenly wary.

"Why the cash, Kendra? You're too smart not to know carrying a roll of bills like that is foolish."

"Impulse. Before I left home I closed both my savings and checking accounts. It just seemed easier to take cash. I was coming straight here."

She wanted to be open with him, at least up to a point.

"After I go to the bank, I need to talk to Mr. McKee."

She caught his quick frown only because she glanced at the rearview mirror at the right moment.

"The house is listed with McKee Realty. I just need to run into his office for a moment to take it off the market."

Alex was very still, but his mind was busy. Why was she lying again? There had been no For Sale signs at Olive's place. It had never been listed in the local paper, either.

Glowering, Alex didn't speak again until they reached the bank. As he circled in back of the truck, he checked the lock on the cap. Some habits he never broke. He always checked locks, and he never trusted Wakefield McKee. By the time he reached Kendra's door she already had it open and was jumping lightly to the ground. He forced a smile to his lips.

"I'll meet you at the diner in an hour. I've got a few phone calls to make."

"You needn't bother with me. I can walk to Benji's from here."

"Benji overcharged you. We're both going, and he's going to give you a little rebate. I'll meet you in an hour."

Fists thrust in his pockets, he set off down the street and didn't look back. If she picked up the car on her own, he knew where to find her. Meanwhile he had some investigating to do.

While Alex reread Olive Andrews's will and the accompanying documents, the sheriff's office patched him through to the Burlington number his contacts had unearthed. A few minutes later he was listening to an irritable male voice tell him Kendra Jennings no longer worked there. She'd quit her job with no notice at all and disappeared.

When Alex broke the connection he felt vaguely dissatisfied. Damon's words said one thing, his tone of voice another. Kendra had done more than leave a boss short an employee.

Without ever having met Henry Damon, Alex disliked him. Unfortunately that didn't mean he was any less suspicious of Kendra. She was hiding something, and he was as determined as ever to find out what.

He tried to piece together what he knew and failed to come up with a clear picture. She hadn't gotten thousands of dollars by embezzling the milk money, but she hadn't gotten it as an inheritance, either. There had been no cash left in Olive's estate after probate costs. Maybe Kendra was telling the truth about the money. Maybe it was her savings. If so, what did she plan to live on when that ran out?

Still speculating, Alex stormed into the diner, his swift, economical strides carrying him from one end to the other in seconds. "Errands done?" His voice was sharper than he'd intended.

Kendra sat at the far end of the counter. She had been chatting like an old friend with Millie. The waitress's snowy head tilted, and her hands went to her hips, but she said nothing. Kendra looked up and smiled, ignoring his surly look.

"Millie tells me I could have done my business with Mr. McKee the night I ate here. He was having his meal at the other end of the counter and I never even knew it."

"You didn't recognize him this morning?"

"I didn't see him this morning. His secretary promised to give him my message. I don't suppose I need to do any more. I'm no longer interested in selling my house."

Alex almost laughed. Secretary? He doubted Jody would care for that title, though it was more respectable than the word he himself would apply to her. He watched Kendra closely. If Millie had said nothing about his ex-wife Kendra hadn't made the connection. He was glad. In a town this size, she'd find out soon enough.

"I had time to window-shop at the secondhand bookstore, too," Kendra said.

They talked about books, and Tara Loomis, the slightly eccentric lady who ran Quaiapen Antiquarian Treasures, but the mention of McKee triggered Alex's sense of caution. What if Kendra was just another Jody? He'd be a fool to get involved with her. When they'd finished lunch and dealt with Benji, Alex told himself, that was it. He was going to stay away from her. Every time he saw her he came away confused. He didn't need that. He didn't need her.

Kendra watched him drive off and resolutely turned her attention to buying groceries. Then she returned to Tara's bookstore. Olive had not been a reader, and Kendra could not survive without books.

"Had lunch with the Moreau boy, I hear," Tara greeted her. "'Bout time he stopped pining for what's lost."

Tara Loomis was somewhere close to six feet tall. Her age could have been anywhere between forty and sixty. Her bony figure was hidden by a flowing purple caftan and the color of her hair by a matching turban that completely hid every strand. Lines were deeply etched in her cream-colored skin, but her eyes were as clear and earnest as a young child's.

"That's the second time someone's implied Alex is barely out of school," Kendra told her with a laugh. "Just how old is he?"

"Thirty-five," Tara answered with the certainty of a lifelong resident of a small, insular community. "Family's long-lived. His granddad died at ninety-eight."

"So he's a local...boy?" Kendra paused at a bin full of mystery paperbacks, her eyes lighting up as she spied a long-out-of-print treasure. When Tara looked away, she surreptitiously sniffed the pages, relieved to find no trace of mold or mildew.

"Oh, yes. Went away right after the divorce, but that was just to do his military service. Came right home again when he got out of the Navy."

So he'd been unhappily married. Pretending interest in the shelf in front of her, Kendra selected two more paperbacks without even looking at them. Perhaps that explained his peculiar attitude. Once burned, twice shy, as her mother liked to say. Deliberately, Kendra set about pumping Tara for more information, trying to sound casual as she asked the first question.

"Was his wife a local girl?"

Tara's derisive snort dispelled any doubt about who'd been responsible for the breakup of Alex Moreau's marriage. Ten minutes later, Kendra had an armload of books and a head overflowing with local gossip.

Alex's parents had only recently retired and moved to Arizona. Like Kendra, Alex was an only child, born when his parents were in their thirties. More important, he not only had an ex-wife, he had a fifteen-year-old son. And the ex-wife, Jody, was the woman Kendra had spoken to in Wakefield McKee's office.

Jody Moreau, Kendra ruefully admitted, was one of the most beautiful women she'd ever met. She made Kendra feel like a shapeless, styleless drudge. Her honey-blond hair was a startling contrast to sea-green eyes, and she dressed with expensive good taste that subtly accentuated voluptuous curves.

She was also, according to Tara, Wakefield McKee's mistress.

Chapter 4

Scraping sounds so faint she thought she was dreaming them disturbed Kendra's sleep. Slowly, she opened her eyes and let them adjust to the darkness in the bedroom. She held her breath, listening. The house was old. It creaked. Why was her heart pounding so loudly she couldn't hear?

Another sound brought her bolt upright in bed, pulse rate soaring. She clutched the thermal blanket and cotton sheet to her chest and fought back an urge to scream. She hadn't imagined it, and she knew instinctively that it was not natural. The house was not settling. It had been invaded.

A sense of foreboding crept through her tense muscles, making movement impossible. Someone was in the house with her. Taking a shallow breath, she willed her legs to obey her. She had to get up, to investigate. For the first time she wished she'd taken Alex up on his advice to purchase a gun.

Slowly, careful to make no sound herself, Kendra slid out from under the covers. She felt vulnerable in nothing but her nightgown, even though it was the floor-length, flannel kind, but she didn't dare fumble around for her fluffy robe. With icy fingers she felt instead for the flashlight she'd placed on the night-stand. Her hand was shaking so badly she almost lost her grip and sent the light sailing to the floor. She caught it just in time, then froze as the sound came again.

He was downstairs. In the living room.

Outside, thick clouds parted to reveal a three-quarter moon. Its light brought the furniture shapes of Kendra's bedroom into focus. She prayed it would stay bright long enough to see what was below. That she had to go down was unavoidable. She had no way to call for help from upstairs. She couldn't just stay in her room, waiting for an attack. At least this way she had the element of surprise in her favor.

Fear made her breath thready and her heartbeat ir-regular, but she forced herself to take one step after another until she was on the landing. It might be an animal, she told herself. It might be outside the house, scratching at the window. She wanted to believe that, but the faint glow of another flashlight spilling over into the hall below made such wishful thinking im-possible.

Her teeth worried her lower lip as she began to de-scend the stairs. Her throat had gone dry. Swallowing repeatedly, she hoped she had breath and voice enough for what she had to do.

Just at the bottom of the stairs, she stopped, peer-ing toward the living room. The light was gone. The room was lit only by wisps of moonlight, cut in silver ribbons by their path through clouds and trees and half-drawn curtains.

At first the looming black shadow seemed so much a part of the room that Kendra couldn't pick it out. Then it moved, becoming visible for only an instant before it blended with the massive bulk of the fireplace.

Moonlight and darkness combined to give an aura of unreality to the scene, but Kendra was sure. There was someone in her living room. Fright surged through her. She wanted to turn and run, to bury her head under the covers and pretend this wasn't happening.

Instead she flicked the switch on her flashlight, sending its powerful beam straight at the intruder. "I have a gun!" Kendra shouted, praying he wouldn't turn his light on her and realize she was bluffing. "If you aren't out of my house in thirty seconds I'll start shooting!"

The figure was dressed all in black, with a ski mask hiding his face. For one instant, pinned in her light, he froze. Then, so fast she couldn't believe she was seeing it, he lunged out of the beam and was gone. From Kendra's vantage point, it appeared as though he had disappeared right through the wall.

The flashlight wobbled erratically as a wave of sheer terror engulfed her. Part of her mind told her what she'd just seen was impossible. That didn't stop her knees from buckling.

She sat on the bottom step and took deep, calming breaths. He was gone. Whether he'd been ghost or man, at least he was gone. Shaking her head, she wondered if she had dreamed it all. She'd never known herself to sleepwalk, but anything seemed preferable to believing he'd vanished.

Pinch yourself, she thought. Find out if you're awake now. She was. Slowly her racing pulse returned to normal.

It was three o'clock in the morning as Kendra went from room to room lighting every lamp. She checked the locks on her doors, and every window. Nothing seemed disturbed. Finally, reluctantly, she turned to the fireplace. Feeling foolish, she began to look for a hidden catch. A secret door was preferable to a visiting spirit, but if there was one, Kendra couldn't find it.

She scowled at the citizens band radio set up on a small table in one corner of the room. Alex had shown her how to operate it and told her what channel to use for emergencies. She could call for help. She could even ask them to send Alex, though she knew he was off duty. She didn't dare. If he'd thought she was imagining things before, he'd be certain this time.

"There was no prowler," she said aloud. "I had a bad dream."

But she did not go back to bed. Instead she made a pot of coffee and reached for one of the paperbacks she'd brought home from the bookstore. It was one of the two she'd grabbed when her thoughts were elsewhere. A glance at the cover was enough to make her shudder. A girl in a flowing nightgown and windtossed hair was looking over her shoulder at an eerie stone house as she fled into the night.

Furious with herself, Kendra threw the small book across the room. The gothic romance struck the paneled wall and fell, its spine cracked, scattering pages to the floor. In fiction, Kendra thought irritably, a lucky pitch could hit the hidden button and release the secret door. Reality was less cooperative.

The hours until dawn passed with excruciating slowness, but at length bright sunlight had chased away the shadows and Kendra had reached a decision. After forcing down a hearty breakfast she went upstairs to dress. She stripped off her nightgown and strode toward the closet.

Nothing stirred below stairs. No sounds came through the open window from outside, except for bird song and branches rustling in the breeze. She was safe, and she meant to stay that way.

Still, Kendra found herself dressing in a hurry, slipping into the first things she came to in the closet. Then she flew down the stairs, pausing only long enough to grab her purse. She knew exactly where she was going. Halfway to Quaiapen, out on the highway, was a large sporting goods store.

Alex stood in the shadow of the back hallway and watched as Mickey DesJardins unlocked the store and let her in. Kendra's car had been parked in front of Suburban Sporting Goods for the last hour.

"I'd like to buy a gun," she blurted, as Mickey, with a practiced movement, flipped the Closed sign over to read Open. "How do I do that?"

Alert to the nervous little movements of her hands and the breathiness in her voice, Alex's gaze narrowed. Something had happened. She'd been dead set against his suggestion the other day. His scrutiny noted the jarring contrast of the shirt and slacks she'd chosen.

Something had sent her scurrying **out** of the house first thing in the morning to buy a **gun**. He didn't like it. In spite of his intention to avoid Kendra Jennings, he knew he had to follow his instincts. She was scared. She needed help. And she needed advice on this impulsive purchase.

Mickey hadn't questioned her request, but as he brought out a selection of revolvers, Kendra knew he was watching her closely. Kendra's hand shook. Would he refuse to sell her a gun if she didn't know how to use it? She glanced up just in time to see Mickey send a silent plea for help to someone behind her.

She knew it was Alex even before she heard his low, mellow voice. "Sell the lady a Chief's Special, Mickey. I'll teach her how to use it."

Biting back a brisk refusal, Kendra turned to find him less than a foot away from her. Quiet as a cat, she thought, frowning. She hadn't even heard the door open and close. He was wearing a hooded gray sweatshirt, baggy sweatpants and worn jogging shoes but managed to look neither tired or sweaty. He was probably one of those annoyingly perfect people who never worked up a sweat. Worse, he was grinning at her, as if to say, I told you so.

"That'll be $250 plus the tax," Mickey announced.

For a moment Kendra considered changing her mind. She hadn't planned to spend that much. She didn't want to spend time with Alex, either. But nothing had changed. She needed protection. "I also need bullets," she said aloud as she reached for her checkbook.

Alex took the Smith and Wesson .38 revolver and a box of ammunition from Mickey and waited while she paid for her purchase. She didn't look at him, or at the gun, but she followed him silently through the back door as soon as Mickey handed her the sales slip. She just wanted to get this over with and go away.

They came out on a firing range and at once Alex was all business. He scooped up what looked like a stereo headset and began her lesson. "You've got five shots, one round in each chamber."

He demonstrated the proper way to load a gun, then removed the bullets and made her try. Although she was not comfortable with it, the small gun easily fit her hand. She followed directions, fighting the tension that made her fingers stiff. She was terrified that if she dropped the gun it would go off. Eventually, all the bullets were in place and the cylinder had once again clicked into place.

"Now what?"

"Now you hold it in what's called a natural grip."

"There's nothing natural about this."

He shrugged. "When you aren't actually shooting, always hold the gun pointed up, toward the sky, for safety."

"Safety sounds good."

"You need to support your right hand with your left for stability," Alex said. His voice was unemotional, but in order to adjust her grip he stepped up close behind her and shadowed her arms and hands with his.

Gently he moved her extended arms upward, and she had her first good look at the target. It was in the shape of a man.

"Mickey's shooting range is used by the local law enforcement agencies to qualify in marksmanship," he said gently. "This isn't a game. If you fire this gun, you're going to be aiming at another human being. You'd better get used to that idea. And never point a gun, loaded or unloaded, at anyone unless you are prepared to fire it.''

At his deadly serious words she could only nod agreement. He'd obviously seen his share of accidental shootings, from hunting mishaps to kids playing with their fathers' guns.

They stood silently for a long moment, looking toward the target. Then a gentle nudge sent shock waves throughout Kendra's system. His leg, from behind, rubbed against the inside of her calves to correct her stance. That had always been a sensitive area, but never more so than now. For all the protection the thin material covering her legs provided, she might as well have been naked.

Fighting to steady her heartbeat and her hands, Kendra reminded herself that Alex had a beautiful ex-wife and an inherent mistrust of strangers. He was doing her a favor. He probably didn't realize that the slightest physical contact with him turned her on.

''Breathe normally,'' he said, close to her ear.

Kendra inhaled deeply and closed her eyes. She wanted to sink back against him, feel the protection of a hard chest and strong arms gripping her. Instead she took a small step away.

His arms dropped. Hers held steady, aiming at the target.

''Good. If you can, keep both eyes open when you aim. I'm going to slip a set of sound attenuators over your head in a second, to protect your hearing.''

Her mouth was so dry she could only nod. He tucked her hair behind her ears, then placed the headset over them and took a step back. With excruciating slowness, Kendra followed his directions for aiming and firing and finally squeezed the trigger.

She'd been prepared for the muffled sound of the shot, but not for the kick. Wrists, arms and shoulders all caught the force of it, jerking back. Alex steadied her and leaned close to shout encouragement.

Under his direction, Kendra fired ten rounds before he slid the headset off and moved up close behind her to gently massage the back of her neck. He stared past her cheek toward the target. "Not bad. You're consistently off to the right and high."

Kendra smiled. "I was aiming for his shoulder."

"You were what?" His voice was a whiplash. "If you're going to stop an attacker, you'd damn well better aim for the center mass. It's you or him, Kendra. If you can't deal with that, you'd be better off with no gun at all."

Temper flaring, she swung around to face him. "Fine. Take it!" She knew better than to point the gun at him to surrender it, but only too late realized the foolishness of switching her own grip to the two-inch-long barrel. Pain seared through her hand as flesh came in contact with heated metal.

He caught the gun to keep it from falling. His other hand captured hers and turned it over to inspect the burn.

The soft web of skin between her thumb and index finger was pink and tingling but not seriously damaged. "It's okay. My own stupidity."

He didn't release her hand. "Not badly burned, no, but you'd better run some cold water over it. Come on."

In spite of her protests, Kendra found herself mounting the back stairs behind Mickey's store. On the second floor, Alex ushered her through a door and into a small bath just inside. She barely had time to register the claw-foot tub and the kitty litter box in the corner before he'd pushed up her quilted flannel sleeve and plunged her burned hand under the faucet.

"Stay put," he ordered. In a minute he was back, turning the water off, drying her hand with a gentle touch and handing her an ice pack.

"You don't need to fuss, Alex."

"You might as well have the full treatment. Shoulders sore?"

"A little," she admitted, but she moved away before he could touch her again. His massage, no matter how innocently meant, would have a dangerous effect on her senses.

Kendra stopped, surprised, as she came out of the bath. She was not, as she had thought, in the store's rest room. She was standing in the middle of a compact kitchen, staring through the archway to an adjoining living room. Alex moved past her to a waiting coffeepot and filled two mugs. His easy familiarity with his surroundings told her what she should have realized earlier. This was his apartment.

Silently, she accepted the coffee and blew on it. "You're a good teacher," she said sincerely. "I appreciate how much patience it takes to explain something to a student who didn't have a clue to begin with."

He tried to wave away the compliment, but she wouldn't let him.

"I mean it. You'd be good in a classroom."

"Teach? You must be joking."

"No. It takes natural talent as well as knowledge of the subject. You have both."

He watched her over the rim of his mug. "Which were you lacking?" At her startled stare he elaborated. "You quit your job as a teacher a month before the end of the year. Why?"

Her shock that he'd been checking into her background changed quickly to dismay. Her voice trembling with affronted dignity, she glared at him. "I've got a better question. Why do you automatically assume people are lying to you?"

"Comes with the job. Humor me, Kendra. Tell me why you suddenly decided to give up on your career."

"Let's call it burnout," she said evasively. "You must have to deal with that in your line of work, too." Smiling too brightly, she added, "If you want a change, go into a classroom. You'd be a sure hit with the seventh graders."

"Why's that?"

"The girls would fall in love with you and the boys would try to imitate you. Men have a definite advantage in teaching kids that age." His eyebrow lifted, demanding elaboration. "A teacher dealing with boys entering puberty should be either large and male or old and female. If you're young and female, you haven't been around long enough to have a reputation for being tough, so it's an uphill battle."

"Discipline problems?"

"Partly."

"I'd think the boys would all fall in love with a pretty young teacher. That should make them putty in her hands."

"Hah! Boys that age are past puppy love. They're into lust."

Staring into the coffee, Kendra wondered if she'd revealed too much of the wariness she'd come to feel about some teens. She hoped he'd let the subject drop.

When she dared glance at him, she was relieved to find that he seemed lost in thought.

She took advantage of the opportunity to study the rest of his apartment. They'd moved into the living room, and she could see one more door that no doubt led to the bedroom. Everywhere she turned there were books. They filled floor-to-ceiling bookshelves on every wall to overflowing. They were piled in corners on the floor. They were scattered across the coffee table. Some had distinctive library coverings, but most did not. They covered topics as diverse as underwater archaeology and the poems of Robert Frost.

Of other personal items there were few. A wooden plaque from the Criminal Justice Academy hung between the windows at the front of the apartment, the only wall space not filled with shelves. He had a small television set, with a layer of dust on it to indicate how little it was used. And next to that was what Kendra at first thought was a stuffed animal. As her glance returned to it the eyes opened and it stared back.

"Good grief! It's alive."

Laughing at her expression, Alex scooped the huge orange and white long-haired cat into his arms and presented it. "Kendra, meet T.W."

"T.W.?"

His grin widened as he turned the cat around. It had nothing left of its once bushy tail but a short stub. "Tailless Wonder, the world's laziest cat. He lost it when he was still a kitten. Run over by a car."

"Poor baby," Kendra sympathized, taking the animal from Alex's arms. Their hands touched, and their eyes met over T.W.'s furry bulk.

"Careful. He's heavy. Close to twenty pounds. Maine coon cat. Mostly."

T.W. purred loudly, allowing himself to be fussed over and petted. Catching her elbow, Alex gently urged her toward the sofa. "Don't you think you ought to tell me what changed your mind about the gun?"

"It was nothing." Kendra stroked T.W. and tried to ignore the sensations Alex's nearness provoked. "Silly."

But he wasn't going to let her off that easily. "Tell me anyway."

Hesitantly, she gave in. "I had a nightmare, that's all." Briefly, she sketched the details, trying to make light of the experience. "When I saw my ghost disappear into thin air I knew I was dreaming, but it made me think things through. I decided I'd feel safer after all if I had some protection in the house. I don't think I could make myself aim to kill anyone, Alex. Not even—"

He put his fingers to her lips to stop the words. "Okay. It's okay."

T.W. howled an indignant protest at being trapped between them. He freed himself from Kendra's grasp, squirming and kicking off against her ribs. His claws snagged her shirt, pulling two buttons free from their buttonholes as he left.

"Did you train him to do that?"

Her joking words ended on a gasp as Alex's right hand closed over her fingers, preventing her from re-closing the gap. His free arm came around her shoulders and drew her closer, tilting her head back and lowering his mouth ever closer to hers. His fist clenched in her hair, holding her still. For a long moment, he studied her flushed face, as if unable to help himself.

"Kendra?" His voice seemed to come from a long way off, though she could feel the warm, sweet gust of his breath on her neck. "You don't really believe you dreamed it, do you?"

For a moment she didn't know what he was talking about. Then she remembered. The prowler, or ghost, or whatever. "I don't know."

"Did you take anything before you went to bed?"

A bucket of cold water could not have put out her inner fires more quickly. Kendra struck his hand away from her shoulder.

"I can help you, Kendra, if you'll let me. Who knows? It might do both of us a lot of good."

"What are you talking about?" Her fists clenched as she hugged herself, suddenly chilled.

"I think you know."

"What exactly are you suggesting?"

The little shrug she'd come to expect preceded his explanation. His eyes never left her face, and his fingers traced gentle patterns along her cheek and jaw until she jerked her head away. "You're a big girl, Kendra. You know there's chemistry between us. Hell, I can't remember when I've wanted a woman more. It'll be good for both of us. We'll get all kinds of things out of our systems."

"You arrogant oas—"

His lips cut off the protest, but Kendra was too angry. She pushed at him with all her strength and flung herself from the sofa the moment he released her.

"If I want a bodyguard I'll pay in cash!"

"How much?"

"Damn you!" The buttons refused to go back into their holes. "You know I can't deny that I'm attracted to you, but I don't need rehabilitation and I'm not some toy you can play with and discard. I can't be casual about . . . about—"

"The word is sex."

Kendra felt color rush into her cheeks and hated herself for the betrayal of her own body. Why was she trying to explain? Why didn't she just turn and run? Finally the shirt was safely closed, but she was blurting again. "I'm not as experienced as you seem to think."

When she saw the startled look on Alex's face, she wished she could call her words back, but it was too late.

"You can't be a—"

"No!" Face crimson, she stumbled on. "Not a virgin. Just not . . ." She ran into the kitchen to fumble at the table for her purse and the boxes containing the gun and ammunition.

Alex caught up with her at the door. "Maybe I owe you an apology," he said softly, his hands on her shoulders. She could feel his warm breath on her nape. "We've met under extraordinary circumstances, Kendra. I haven't figured you out. Yet."

"Stop trying so hard. What you see is what you get."

She was shaking again.

"I think I'd better leave now, Alex. I'm not handling this very well."

Alex watched her stumble blindly down the stairs, and wondered if he'd just made the biggest mistake of his life.

Chapter 5

The next four days passed quietly. Kendra saw no one, talked to no one and finally began to enjoy her solitude.

On Tuesday morning, after two productive hours in front of the word processor, she decided she'd earned a break and, stretching languidly, walked out the back door and down to the small dock on the shore of Square Lake.

Promising spring would soon be summer, the breeze raising waves on the water's surface was soft and almost warm. Kendra closed her eyes and breathed it in, relishing the sense of freedom she had here. She was already certain of one thing. She meant to stay on. Except for the periodic intrusion of Alex Moreau's handsome face into her thoughts, she had been able to relax and unwind more quickly than she'd dared dream.

The planks wavered gently as she trod on them, but the dock was solidly built. A few careful steps brought her to the end, where she sat to look out around the point. She could just touch the surface of the lake with the toe of her high-tops. Soon, she promised herself, she would drag Olive's rowboat out of the shed and explore the shore.

Unbidden, a wistful sigh overtook her. Nicer still would be a guided tour, with Alex Moreau as her guide. Irritated with herself for wanting what was not good for her, Kendra kicked at the water. Icy drops spattered back against her cords, soaking through. The air might be warming up, but the water was not.

Suddenly a hot cup of coffee sounded irresistible. Kendra tucked her feet under her and stood, turning, then froze. Someone stood at the other end of the dock, blocking her way to the house.

"You startled me," she said.

He was just a boy. At first, she was not afraid. Then something snapped in place, and she knew with perfect certainty that this was the towheaded boy from the black car. She had not dreamed him after all.

"What do you want?" She took a step closer to him, but he did not move away, and her movements set the dock swaying uncertainly. It felt safer to remain immobile.

"You're not much." His lips twisted into an unpleasant sneer.

"I beg your pardon?"

"You hear me, lady. I said you're not much."

"Okay. I heard you. Would you mind explaining what you meant?" She kept her voice steady, teacher-stern, and tried to appear unmoved by his rudeness. Inside she was quaking.

His eyes ran up and down her body, making her skin crawl. She was uncomfortably aware that her cords were well-worn and snug.

Almost longingly, she thought of the sexless dress-for-success suits she'd left back in Vermont. She credited those clothes with winning at least half the battle of maintaining discipline in her classes. As a new young teacher she'd quickly discovered that wearing the latest styles not only undermined her authority but also got her name plastered on the boys' room walls. The pithy, often physically impossible, suggestions had shocked and mortified her at twenty-two. Now she'd accepted that teenaged boys had rude, crude ways. A few were also dangerous.

Show no fear and don't let them see you smile until Christmas, Kendra reminded herself. The words of wisdom were Henry's and she'd hated their cynicism, but now she put the advice into practice. Glaring at her adversary, she started walking toward him, ready to push him aside and run if he didn't move out of her way.

He waited until the last second to step back. "I got friends," he said softly when she was only inches away. "We'll be back."

The insinuation was there, the sexual innuendo, but Kendra chose to ignore it.

"Why?"

Her abrupt challenge seemed to startle him. He'd expected her to panic and run. Now she was facing him down, meeting his eyes until he looked away.

"I asked you a question. First you run me off the road. Now you try to frighten me on my own property."

The threatening facade cracked slightly. She caught the worried look in his narrowed eyes. Though he didn't say anything to give himself away, she was sure she was right. An urgent need for the truth vanquished what little fear was left. He was just a troubled boy, full of bravado and empty threats. She could deal with him.

With pointed deliberation she looked at her watch. "I expect Deputy Moreau any minute now. Perhaps you'd rather explain yourself to him."

A grin flashed white across the boy's face. "Wrong thing to say, lady. He's in court. Will be all day. And the county courthouse is nearly two hours of hard driving away from here."

"You seem awfully sure of that. Why should I believe you?"

"Because Alex Moreau is my father."

The silence was not absolute. Water lapped against the dock and the shore. A woodpecker was hard at work on a nearby tree. In the distance the loon cried out for its mate. Kendra could even hear her own labored breathing.

"Didn't expect that, did you, lady?" His voice, meant to be taunting, cracked, and the dull red color of teenage self-consciousness spread up his neck and into his face.

Kendra cleared her throat. "No, I didn't. Aren't you taking a risk that I'll tell him you were with the boys who wrecked my car?"

"Who'd believe you? You take drugs. Just because he took you out to lunch doesn't mean he thinks you're clean. He's probably still investigating you, trying to find something he can arrest you for. You'd better stay away from him."

Kendra studied him thoughtfully. There was more to this young man than first met the eye. It bothered him that she'd had lunch with his father. Thank goodness he didn't know she'd been to Alex's apartment.

"I don't expect to see him again," Kendra said bluntly, "unless I have another crime to report."

He couldn't hide the flash of relief from her. For that instant, he seemed innocent, the child he still was. The impression lasted only a moment before he reverted to his conception of a macho threat. "Go back where you came from!"

She hid the smile the Rambo imitation, belligerent stance and all, provoked, and spoke mildly. "But I like it here. This is my home now."

"Anybody tell you what really killed the old lady?"

"You'll have to do better than that if you're trying to scare me off."

The longer she studied him, the more certain Kendra became that Alex Moreau's son was no real threat to her. Whatever was going on with him, it was essentially nonviolent. Like many boys his age, he was mostly bluff.

"We're watching you. At night. Watching everything you do."

"I have a gun and I know how to use it." She could bluff, too. The gun was under her pillow, but it wasn't loaded.

"That won't do you any more good than the fancy locks on your doors. We can get to you anytime. If I were you, I wouldn't be here tomorrow."

A shiver ran up Kendra's spine as she remembered her ghostly nocturnal visitor. That had not been Alex's son. The prowler had been bigger, more massive.

"It's too chilly to stand out here. I'm going inside and make some coffee." Kendra hoped he'd believe that the goose bumps rising all over her flesh were the result of the gentle breeze. She was not afraid of him, but she feared he was part of something bigger and infinitely more dangerous. He knew too much.

Surely the tranquilizers in her possession hadn't become general knowledge. And her intruder certainly wasn't. Even if Alex was in the habit of confiding in his son, the boy couldn't know about that middle-of-the-night visitor unless he also knew Alex had taught her to shoot. He didn't. She'd bet on it.

Halfway to the safety of her back door, Kendra made an impulsive decision. "If you want a cup you're welcome to come in and introduce yourself properly," she called over her shoulder.

She turned her back on him. She expected him to follow, out of curiosity if nothing else, but when she reached the door and looked toward the dock he had disappeared. She supposed the woods from which he had come had swallowed him up. She suspected she'd scared him at least as much as he'd scared her.

While the coffee perked she cursed herself roughly for mishandling things. She knew no more than she had before. In fact, she had the sense of knowing less. Her fine, logical theories had all been shot down.

So much for figuring everything out, she berated herself. If she hadn't dreamed the boy, then she was back to suspicion number one—the plot against Kendra Jennings. She didn't like that idea any better now than she had a week ago in the clinic. And the prowler she'd tried to convince herself she'd dreamed had been real, too. That meant they could get at her, just as he'd said.

Her first impulse was to drive to the county seat and find Alex. Her second impulse was to do nothing, beyond buying and installing new locks. The boy was probably right. Alex wouldn't believe her. She'd start to resemble the boy who called wolf. Why should she expect him to believe that his own son was involved when he didn't believe there had been a car full of boys in the first place? More troubling still, why was his son involved?

The coffee in her cup grew cold as she sought answers and found none. Staring into the murky depths, Kendra wondered, not for the first time, if there had been a reason the brew at the diner had tasted so bitter. Had someone deliberately drugged the coffee, then hired teenagers to run her off the road and plant pills in her purse? It sounded preposterous, and yet what other answer was there?

She tried to return to work, but her concentration had been shattered. She could no longer visualize cloud castles and carefree children. Sweet young children grew up to be disturbed adolescents.

Doubts crept into her mind. What if Henry had been right all along? What if she was wasting her time?

The memory was as sharp and painful as it had been on the last day of the old year. She'd been sitting under the Christmas tree in Henry's living room, sipping eggnog and talking about a June wedding.

"I don't want to teach next year," she'd blurted.

"You're burned out anyway. We'll start a family."

She'd bristled at his callous words, in spite of knowing he only spoke the truth. She'd told herself it didn't matter. She'd found a new purpose for her life.

"I had something a little different in mind," she'd announced. "I had an idea for a children's picture book. I've already started it."

Not registering the dismay on his face, she'd burrowed in her shoulder bag, pulled out three pages of computer printout and a sketch pad and offered her dreams for inspection.

Henry Damon had read them grudgingly, then had impatiently, disdainfully, discounted their worth. "Cloud castles?" he'd mocked. "If you must waste your time writing for a market that pays nothing, at least produce something worthwhile. Write about computers. Or do a kiddie biography of one of those historical figures you're always reading about."

"Children need fantasy," she'd protested, seizing the carefully nurtured pages away from him.

It was a story about two children who imagined a castle in the clouds on a summer's day and turned it into reality. She'd labored long hours over the simple text. It had needed more revision before she could submit it to a publisher. She had known that. But with a few careless words, Henry had sapped her self-confidence and reduced her efforts to rubble.

"Forget this nonsense. It isn't worth your time."

"You mean it isn't worth *your* time."

"If you're going to be my wife, Kendra—"

"I'm not."

Her words had surprised both of them, but she hadn't taken them back. The sense of relief she'd felt convinced her she'd made the right choice. A week later she'd wondered how she could ever have thought she was in love with him. She hadn't missed his company, and she hadn't missed what had passed for romance.

This is the year when fantasies come true, Kendra reminded herself. She'd finished with Henry right along with the old year, and three days later she'd had the first letter from the lawyer in Maine. The next week she'd started taking chances. A grim smile flickered across her face. A small risk had paid off, and soon she'd cash in on it, but not yet. She had things to do first, and no misguided teenager was going to keep her from finding castles in the clouds.

Resolutely, Kendra put her manuscript away and changed into a less revealing top for the drive into Quaiapen. She doubted she'd run into Alex, but perhaps she could discover why Olive Andrews had left this house to her in the first place. And, somehow, she had to figure out why someone wanted her to leave.

In the deserted corridor of the county courthouse, Alex Moreau gave the soda machine a kick and grunted in satisfaction as it reluctantly yielded up a can of cola. So far he'd been waiting three hours and his case hadn't come up. The whole day would be shot before he got back home.

He ran a finger under the collar of his dress shirt and loosened what had been billed in the ad as a "power tie." If there was one part of his job he hated it was the court appearances, especially those like this one, which would inevitably lead only to a slap on the wrist and a suspended sentence. The criminals were back on the streets before the paperwork was finished.

"Bleeding-heart liberal judges," he muttered under his breath.

"Temper, temper," a cheerful voice chided him. Alex turned to find the court's chief civil deputy sheriff bearing down on him.

"Afternoon, Claude. Works best if you kick it."

They'd known each other for years, first working together at the old rattletrap jail when officers did everything and the number of prisoners on any given night rarely exceeded three or four. With the coming of progress, unions and more prisoners' rights laws, a new jail had replaced the old. It was overcrowded, understaffed and barely up to federal guidelines. Alex was glad he'd gone on the road, trading corrections for patrol five years back.

Claude had taken a different route and now dealt exclusively with court matters. His wife was happier, because the job was not as dangerous as other branches of law enforcement, and Claude was content because he no longer had to meet any weight guidelines. He was short and round and, Alex noticed, starting to go gray. In another year or two he'd be playing Santa Claus at the Elks' Club.

"You talked to anybody on border patrol lately?" Claude popped the top on his soda can and fed money into the candy machine.

"Not for a couple of weeks. Something happening?"

"Just rumors. Some small-denomination Canadian bills turned out to be counterfeit."

"Small bills?"

"Fives. Wouldn't think it'd be worthwhile, would you?" Claude shook his head at the oddities of crime.

"Not as likely to be caught," Alex mused. "Almost anyplace in this part of the state will take Canadian money at a discount and not look twice at it."

Nodding, Claude thoughtfully devoured a chocolate bar. "Probably true along the rest of the border, too. First I heard of it was this past week, but it could have been going on for months."

A sudden, unwarranted connection shot through Alex's mind. Vermont also bordered Canada, and someone he'd recently met had been carrying a large amount of cash. Almost as quickly, he rejected the idea. Kendra Jennings had haunted him ever since he first saw her, and here she was again, invading his head, making him grasp at straws to find some excuse to go and see her. He shouldn't want anything to do with her in light of the newest information he'd gotten on her background, but he did.

"You got an idea?" Claude's eyes had narrowed, watching Alex.

"Wishful thinking." Alex managed a self-deprecating grin and started to turn away, but Claude's joking words pulled him back.

"Trying to find a way to blame it on McKee, huh?" He saw the flash of irritation in Alex's eyes, but had known him too long to let it bother him. "Face it, old buddy, you've tried to pin every scam we've heard about in the last ten years on McKee. He'll always come up smelling like a rose."

"They use manure to fertilize roses, Claude. He'll slip in it one of these days."

"Slip is right, but it'll be out of our clutches. Unless you want to plant illegal substances on him, you haven't got a prayer."

Finishing off the rest of his soda, Alex admitted to himself that Claude was probably right. He needed a solid case, not just his certainty that McKee had more money than an honest real estate broker could possibly amass.

"No matter what he's done to me personally," he told Claude as they headed back toward the courtroom together, "when I arrest Wakefield McKee, it'll be on evidence so sound nobody will be able to shake it."

It would have to be. Everyone knew how far back the animosity between them went.

Alex had been very young when he met Jody. He'd never been out of the state. He'd never been in love before. And then, there she was, beautiful, spoiled, and telling him she loved him, too. Six months later they were married. Another five and they were parents. Six more and she'd left him for Wakefield McKee. If her rich daddy hadn't stepped in and whisked both Jody and Denny away, she'd probably have married McKee as soon as the divorce was final.

With an effort, Alex brought his mind back to the case at hand, just in time to hear the judge postpone the hearing. Disgusted at the waste of his time, Alex left the courtroom in a hurry, before he said something to the judge or district attorney that he'd regret. He was halfway home before he thought about McKee again.

If McKee was involved in something illegal now, Jody was in it with him. Sometimes Alex almost felt sorry for his ex-wife, until he remembered the mess she'd made of raising Denny. After a stint in the Navy, Alex had returned to Quaiapen and started rebuilding his life. He'd wanted to spend time with his son, but Jody and her father had successfully kept them apart. Jody and her dad had had a fine time, traveling the world, spending money, until suddenly Jody's father was dead, and there was no money left.

Jody had turned up in Quaiapen hoping to use Denny as bait. She'd claimed to want Alex back. He'd wanted nothing to do with her, or with Denny. The boy had just turned twelve and was as spoiled as she had been. He'd resented being dragged off to the wilderness, and he'd blamed Alex for ruining his life. Alex had rejected both of them.

Looking back, he knew he'd been wrong. He could have developed a relationship with the boy without seeing much of Jody. Instead, he hadn't even tried to like Denny. He'd taken one look and written the boy off as a loss. Before long Denny had started to live up to the role Alex had cast him in, hanging out with other losers. Jody had resumed her liaison with McKee.

McKee, older and wiser, hadn't proposed marriage the second time around. Without her father's money, Jody had had nothing to offer him but her body. She'd settled for a job in his office and rooms upstairs. Alex wasn't sure which he resented more, McKee's attitude or Jody's. It seemed to him in his blacker moments that the two had decided on their present relationship simply to make living in Quaiapen more difficult for Alex.

He'd arrest his ex-wife without a qualm, but he hoped he'd never have to arrest Kendra Jennings. He had to be a complete idiot, but he still wanted her. The most recent information his investigations had unearthed was unsettling, indicating she might be more unstable than he'd thought. In spite of that he couldn't forget how she'd felt in his arms.

Angry at himself, Alex tore his thoughts away from both women and tried to concentrate on Denny. He'd seen his son twice since finding him at camp. For some reason, Denny had turned friendly. Although he questioned the boy's sincerity, this time Alex had resolved not to rock the boat.

He'd always been careful not to sound critical of Jody in front of her son, but if Denny was disillusioned by something she'd done, this was his chance. If her behavior had created the opportunity to build a relationship with his son, he wanted to take it. This afternoon Denny would be meeting him at the diner after school. An early supper together wasn't much, but it was a start.

Kendra's quest for information had gone smoothly. Tara Loomis in the bookstore had been able to identify the notations on Olive's papers as reference numbers for microfilmed records in the state archives in Augusta.

"You can take a day, drive there and go over the material yourself," she said cheerfully. "Couple of years back, Olive got bitten by the genealogy bug. Lasted about three months. Probably she got bored by the time she hit your branch. Just didn't feel like bothering to write about the information."

"Or didn't have interest enough to follow up on it. Maybe she never actually looked at these records."

"Must have. See this reference? It's to the federal census. She took the rest of the information off it for the part of the chart she completed." Olive's notes, charts and papers were spread all over Tara's counter.

"Then why—"

"If I were you, I'd hightail it over to Augusta and find out." Tara shot her an amused glance. "Not afraid of a few skeletons in the closet, are you?"

"Bank robbers?"

"Or bastards. Could be she didn't put it down because she'd have had to run a broken line from mother to child. Lord knows what the official legal documents say. Can't always believe them, you see."

"I do see. In a way it would be a relief to find something like that. What I'm trying to come up with is the reason Olive left everything to me."

"Probably to keep it out of McKee's clutches." At Kendra's startled look she explained. "He's some relation on her husband's side."

"Why wouldn't she want to leave the house to him?"

Tara snorted. "Because he'd be tearing down the place to build condominiums. Speak of the devil!"

The jangle of a small bell over the door was the only warning as Wakefield McKee strode into the bookstore. Kendra remembered him from her first night in Quaiapen, the man in the three-piece suit at the diner. She hadn't paid much attention to him then, except to note that he was giving Millie a hard time, but up close he was harder to ignore.

Physically, he was impressive. He obviously worked out, for well-developed muscles rippled under the fabric of his shirt. In the day's warmth, he'd removed his jacket and loosened his tie. Above the open collar, an unremarkable jaw and mouth were topped by a regal nose and sharp eyes. The effect was startlingly hawklike, and for a moment Kendra had the sensation of being his prey.

"Ms. Jennings, I presume," he said, extending his hand. The fingers were warm and firm but held hers just a little too long for her liking. "Welcome to our fair city."

"Thank you." She fought the urge to wipe her hand on her skirt when he released his grip.

"Don't let me disturb you, ladies. I just need a get-well card." He maneuvered through closely packed bookshelves toward the rack at the back of the store, but not before his gaze raked over the scattered papers and took in their content.

Unaccountably flustered, Kendra started to gather them up. "Thanks for your advice, Tara. I'll follow up on it."

"Tomorrow's supposed to be another nice day. Take you about two and a half hours to drive to Augusta." She burrowed into a file cabinet behind the counter. "Here you go—hours and services. The pamphlet's a few years old but I doubt they've changed."

"Thanks. And you're right. I may as well follow through tomorrow. I can do some shopping, too. I like Quaiapen, but it does have its limitations."

"If you have a picnic cooler, take it along. Then you can stock up on frozen goods at the grocery store."

Tara continued to offer helpful domestic advice, taking McKee's money and ringing up the sale without pausing for breath. As soon as he was out the door, however, she lowered her voice to a conspiratorial whisper.

"McKee tried to talk Olive into going into a nursing home about a year ago. Lot of nonsense that was. She might never have seen ninety again, but she was spry as could be."

"Did he expect to inherit her land?"

"He was a fool if he did. The McKees are only connected on Olive's husband's side. The land was hers. Olive's granddaddy, Oliver Buttenbeck, used to own most of the land around here. His children, they divided the land, and over the years they've all moved away, or died off. Olive was the last one left. She sold her house in town but not that parcel. Used to be the family hunting camp. She put all her money into fixing it up after she was widowed and that's where she aimed to stay till she died."

"So, she got her wish."

Tara snorted. "Her wish was to see one hundred. I never could figure out how she'd have been so careless as to fall and kill herself. I heard she wasn't even wearing a coat when they found her. I ask you, why would she go outside in the middle of winter without a coat on?"

Kendra was wondering that herself as she sipped a cup of Millie's coffee later that afternoon. The obvious answer was that Olive had been old. She'd simply gotten confused. Or maybe, just that once, she'd been careless. It was foolish even to think of foul play. Alex's son had only hinted at that to frighten her. Well, he'd succeeded.

This time the coffee was not at all bitter. Kendra decided to have another cup. For the moment, she was the only customer in the Quaiapen Diner. In the late afternoon sunshine, the walls looked yellow with age and the cracks in the Formica countertop seemed to have multiplied. Redolent with stale grease, freshly perked coffee and baking apple pie, the air was thick. It should have seemed stifling, but somehow, perhaps because of Millie herself, the place had a hominess about it.

Cozy, Kendra decided. The diner was the kind of place people came back to, and lingered in. It was more than Quaiapen's only restaurant and a convenient meeting place. The diner was simply a part of the life of the town.

Two coffeepots sat on a hot plate next to the pastry case on the counter. Anyone, Kendra realized, could have slipped something into a nearly empty pot and been certain that the customer who got the last cup would drink it. She remembered the silent couple, the lumberjack and Wakefield McKee, but other people had gone in and out. She hadn't noticed all of them.

With a sigh, Kendra picked up the newspaper another customer had left behind. It was published in Bangor, Maine, but there was news of the rest of northern New England. On the third page her eyes were drawn to the solitary story with a Vermont dateline.

"Isn't that something, huh?"

Kendra didn't look up as Millie leaned on her elbows and read upside down. "Something," she agreed.

The Tri-State Megabucks jackpot was still unclaimed. A single winning lottery ticket had been sold in a Burlington convenience store but no one had come forward with it. Authorities speculated that a transient had purchased it and hadn't yet found out it was worth two million dollars. The article concluded with the reminder that if the prize was not claimed within a year, it went back into the fund.

"What would you do if you had the winning ticket, Millie?"

"Quit my job."

Kendra smiled. "I thought you owned this place."

"Nope. It's Wakefield's. So are most of the buildings in town."

"Then I highly recommend telling him to take his job and shove it. It's a glorious feeling."

"You quit yours, eh?"

"Mmm. I should have done it sooner, at the same time I broke my engagement to my boss, but I stupidly thought we could still work together."

Millie made sympathetic clucking noises. Kendra supposed she should not have been so free with her confession. Millie could tell anyone in town what she'd said. Somehow, Kendra didn't care. If she was going to live just outside Quaiapen from now on, people might as well get to know her.

"He was a jerk," she blurted. "If I'd stayed with him any longer I'd have been a basket case."

Her thoughts in the past, Kendra missed Millie's sharp glance, and didn't hear the open door behind her. She was remembering all she'd felt on that Sunday a little more than a week ago.

It had started, she supposed, when she sat bolt upright on her sectional sofa and stared at her small color television set. The local news anchor, unaware that he'd been talking about her, had calmly continued reading his evening report.

Her panic had lasted only a moment, succeeded by a burst of pleasure so intense she could scarcely bear not to share it. Quiet elation had replaced both emotions as she'd hugged the delicious secret to herself.

After a moment she'd resumed her usual position, curled up on the cream-colored sofa that dominated her small living room. A meteorologist with way too many glistening white teeth had babbled on about highs and lows and fronts. She hadn't heard a word of it.

Kendra remembered toying with the fringe on the multicolored afghan draped over the back of the sofa. Its fall tones were picked up in orange throw pillows, deep green rag rugs and her one attempt at painting in oils. She'd glanced at it, knowing the bright abstract splash of red and yellow was garish against her off-white wall. Henry had hated it from the first moment he saw it.

Frowning slightly, she'd gotten up and turned off the television. Unless she came forward voluntarily she knew there was no way for the authorities to find her. She could sit tight and go on with her life as it was. Or, she could disappear, giving herself a chance to think through the consequences of what she'd done.

Restless, Kendra had moved from room to room. The apartment had suited her five years before when she'd moved in. It had suited her the previous January, when she'd signed the lease for another year. The living room and bedroom hadn't seemed small. Suddenly she realized that they were so full of furniture and books that she barely had room to move. The kitchen and bath had always been tiny. Of necessity she kept them neat. Her living room too had been artfully arranged. Perhaps that was why she'd always preferred the cheerful disorder of her bedroom.

It doubled as an office, so that a battered kneehole desk shared the wall with her dressing table. Lesson plans and student papers had spilled over both. Better organized was the four-drawer file cabinet she'd rescued from the dump. Kendra had climbed over her unmade bed to reach the corner where it sat and found the folder she wanted on the second try.

She'd stared at the letters for a long time after she finished rereading them, and then the decision had seemed to make itself. She'd go to the place in Maine, cutting all ties with Vermont. She'd take as much time as she needed to think things through.

Smiling in anticipation, she'd reached for the phone. "Henry," she'd purred when he answered. "I won't be in tomorrow. I won't be in ever again."

Astonishment had sent his normally level voice up an octave. "Kendra? What are you talking about?"

She could picture him, running one long-fingered hand over straight, thinning, corn-colored hair. Once she'd thought the gesture endearing. "I am resigning," she'd told him.

He'd started to sputter. "You must be out of your mind. You have a contract. You can't just quit before the end of the semester. Think of—"

"Henry, I just did." She'd slammed the receiver down as hard as she could, then unplugged the phone.

Less than twenty-four hours later she had driven three hundred miles and was still feeling pleased with herself. All the way east across Vermont and New Hampshire on U.S. Route 2 she'd replayed events in her mind. It was fate, plain and simple, she'd decided, and Henry deserved what he got. If there was real justice in the universe, he wouldn't have been able to find a substitute teacher for her seventh-grade language arts class and would have been forced to teach the 7-C section himself.

The sound of Wakefield McKee's slightly nasal voice behind her brought Kendra back to the present.

"Ms. Jennings," he said, "I have a proposition for you."

Spinning around on the stool, Kendra found herself much too close to him. He was exuding used-car salesman charm at her, together with mint-freshened breath.

"Mr. McKee." She shifted uneasily. The bottom edge of his gray jacket was an inch from her knees and she was afraid to move for fear of brushing intimately against him. He made matters worse by leaning forward and placing one hand on the counter. Although they were not touching, she felt as though she were being made to suffer an unwelcome embrace.

"I've had an offer on your property. A generous one. I'm sure you'll be delighted with it."

She had nowhere to look except into his deep blue eyes. They were icy cold. So was the hand that now came up to take hers. She tried to jerk away, but his grip tightened.

"I am not interested in selling, Mr. McKee. I thought I made that clear to your secretary."

"Assistant."

"Whatever." She remembered what Tara had told her and felt distinctly uncomfortable. The lives of people in this town were interlocked to the point where she knew she'd have to be careful whenever talking to one about the other. The subject of their discussion was more than likely to turn out to be a relative or an ex.

"Why don't you let me buy you dinner and we'll discuss it."

"There is nothing to discuss, Mr. McKee. I plan to live in that house. My property is not for sale."

"Surely you'll reconsider. Why would a beautiful young woman want to live way out there all alone?" The cold eyes narrowed and she had the impression that he was trying to mesmerize her.

"Perhaps I'm using it as a hideout, Mr. McKee."

"A dangerous plan."

This time she succeeded in pulling her hand away. "I like living dangerously." It was becoming difficult to sound flippant. She had the unsettling sensation that more was going on here than she knew.

McKee opened his mouth, but nothing came out. His eyes widened as he was abruptly jerked backward and pointed toward the door. In his place was Alex Moreau.

If Alex had been appealing in uniform, and sexy in jeans, he was devastating in a dark blue suit. The tailored jacket accented his broad shoulders and made McKee look puny. The strength of the purely sexual pull she felt just looking at him left Kendra stunned. The quick, unexpected flash of desire took her breath away.

"Damn you, Moreau," McKee snarled. "I'll have you up on assault charges."

Alex ignored him, but Millie, who had been listening avidly to every word, put a stop to his threat. "No witnesses, Wakefield. No one saw a thing. Right, Ms. Jennings?"

Kendra's eyes were wary and fixed on Alex's face. His expression was as carefully blank as she'd ever seen it and she could not sense his mood. "Right," she agreed softly, and was surprised to find that her voice still worked.

McKee left, slamming the door behind him. Alex, eyes still unreadable, inclined his head toward the window. Together they watched McKee walk rapidly, head down, toward his office.

"McKee never listed Olive's house," Alex said bluntly.

"Oh, I see. Now I suppose you think I'm up to something with Wakefield McKee. Don't you trust anybody?"

"No percentage in it. Expect the worst and you'll never be disappointed."

"If you really believe that, I feel sorry for you."

"Is your attitude any different? Seems to me you're quick to think the worst of anyone under eighteen."

Kendra tried to get up but he caught her arm. "What did McKee want with you?"

"He told me he'd had an offer on the place and I told him I wasn't selling. What is it with you, Alex? Is everything I say automatically a lie or do you quarrel with everyone?"

Chuckling, Millie started toward them, but Alex tightened his grip on Kendra's arm and hauled her to her feet. "This way," he ordered gruffly, pulling her toward the only booth with any hint of privacy. It was in the corner, last of a row of eight that hugged the wall across from the counter.

"I have to get home. It's late." But she slid into the seat opposite him and stayed put even after he let go of her.

"Afraid that black car's lurking out there, waiting for another chance at you?"

Kendra had to bite her lip to keep from blurting out the morning's discovery. Just being near Alex confused her. Her elbow still burned with the imprint of his fingers, but at the same time she was furious with him for his stubborn refusal to believe her. In her whole life, no one had ever doubted her word. They'd only had to look into her eyes to know she was telling the truth. Why couldn't he?

"I did see a car," Kendra insisted, "and those teenagers."

He leaned across the table, until she could see her own reflection doubled in his eyes. "Your blood test came back. I was right on two counts. The concentration of drugs wasn't high enough to charge you, but you did lie to me, Kendra. There were traces—"

"No!"

"The lab has no reason to lie."

"If they found drugs in my blood, then I was drugged without my knowledge. I can even guess how. The coffee—"

"According to my sources, you've been behaving irrationally for months. Seems you're paranoid about teenagers, especially boys. Just last month there were some . . . accusations. Delusions—"

"You're still investigating me?" Her heart began to beat faster. She was not afraid of what he might find out in Vermont, only the interpretation he'd put on it.

The incident he referred to had been blown way out of proportion. She'd reported that one of her seventh-grade students had been drinking before school. She'd even found an empty vodka bottle in the trash. In spite of this proof, Henry had hushed the matter up. The boy in question had the wealthiest parents in the school. He'd accused Kendra of buying the bottle for him and trying to molest him when he was drunk.

"Don't pretend to be so shocked." Alex's voice was cold and harsh. "You must have known I'd find out. Investigating is what I do for a living."

"What you're doing is harassment." She lowered her voice. "Do you do this to every woman who turns you down?"

He simply lifted an eyebrow, as if to say she was being paranoid again. Suddenly furious, Kendra surged out of the booth, planning to stalk out of the diner without a backward glance. She stopped short, face-to-face with Alex's son.

The boy's expression became a mask of affronted innocence as soon as she gasped and backed away from him. She could imagine how that looked to Alex. She was acting as if the mere sight of any blond teenager could send her into a panic.

Alex had to be taking in her irrational fear, and he'd interpret the nervous, jerky motions of her hands and her inability to form the simplest words as proof of the instability he'd just accused her of. She didn't need to ask where he'd gotten his information. Someone had talked to Henry Damon. She wondered what else dear Henry had said. She'd be willing to bet he hadn't admitted to once wanting to marry her.

Alex's voice was lifelessly formal as he introduced the boy. "My son, Denny." Kendra fought to control her emotions, but the battle was lost as soon as Alex continued. "He's blond. Perhaps he's the one you imagined you saw the other night."

"Hey, Dad, I wasn't—"

Alex stopped him with a quick slice of one hand. His eyes never left Kendra's face. Watching her, he grew very still. The muscles in his jaw tightened when she refused to speak. In the end it was Millie who broke the charged silence.

"What'll it be, boys? Special tonight is lasagna."

Without another word, Kendra turned on her heel and hurried toward the door. Unshed tears blurred her vision. Let him believe what he chose. Let him investigate and listen to Henry's lies. Why should she care?

The trouble was, she did care. She wanted Alex Moreau to think well of her. Try as she might to ignore it, to tell herself it was crazy to want a man who didn't even like her, she hadn't been able to stop thinking about him.

Chapter 6

On the long drive to Augusta the next morning, Kendra considered the week just past and decided she was doing extraordinarily well. Her manuscript was nearly complete. In addition to finding answers to her questions about Olive at the state library complex she also hoped to locate a recent copy of a writer's market guide. She was almost ready to submit her brainchild.

As soon as she had mailed it, she would start a second book, just as all those articles full of helpful hints for fledgling writers advised. It might be months before she heard any more about the first one. She'd keep producing. Eventually, something would sell.

The day had dawned crisp and clear and as the morning wore on it only got better. Kendra's impulsive car purchase, painted a fiery red on one side and cobalt blue on the other, had a number of unidentifiable creaks and rattles, a heater that had to be worked with a makeshift lever, and several holes in the upholstery, but in spite of such minor inconveniences and the 155,000 miles showing on the odometer, it ran like a dream.

Kendra turned the radio up and hummed along, taking time to sightsee as she drove. The farther south she went the more green showed. There might still be snow on the mountains, but tulips and daffodils were pushing out of the ground. Gradually, she left the fields behind, then passed farms where the earth had just been tilled and apple orchards were blossoming pink and white. Finally, she came to the city.

The statehouse complex was small by national standards but Kendra was glad the legislature was not in session. She'd never have found a parking space otherwise. As it was, she pulled in just to one side of the building that housed the museum, library and archives and got out of the car to stretch.

It was barely ten in the morning, but she'd been up since six. Kendra finished the coffee in the thermos she'd brought with her, then ventured inside. There was much to do, and only a few hours in which to do it. She wanted to be back to her own house before dark.

The next few hours passed quickly. Armed with Olive's notations, Kendra easily located the microfilmed old census records. The ancestor they'd shared, Oliver Buttenbeck, was listed in the 1900 census, together with his family and servants.

Her second reference was to a reel of microfilm in the Brides Index, a listing of marriages from 1895 to 1953. There she found Oliver's daughters, three wed in their hometown, and one who'd gone all the way to Portland to marry Joseph O'Hara.

Abruptly, pieces of the puzzle began to rearrange themselves for Kendra. She glanced back at the census record. There he was, Joseph O'Hara, servant. He'd been born in 1875 in Ireland. So that was it.

She couldn't fill in the details of the next generations, but her father's mother had been an O'Hara. As a teenager she'd wondered if she was related to Scarlett. She also knew that when the Irish first came to America they'd been regarded as second-class citizens.

It was clear what had happened here. The daughter of the house had eloped with the servant. Old Oliver had no doubt cut her off and never spoken to her again. And Olive? Kendra couldn't prove it, but she suspected Olive had been trying to right an old wrong by leaving what remained of the family property to the sole descendant of that long-ago love match.

What a pity all mysteries aren't as easy to solve, Kendra thought as she loaded up her notebooks and went to the library. "Do you have this year's *Writer's Market*?" she asked at the reference desk.

Twenty minutes later Kendra was pulling out of the parking lot when she caught sight of the dark car behind her. Just imagination, she tried to tell herself, but the car drew closer and closer until Kendra could see the driver in her rearview mirror. His face was covered by a ski mask.

"This can't be happening."

It didn't help to say the words aloud. The car was still there. Kendra tried to keep calm, to notice details. Surely he wasn't going to ram her right in the middle of the city. She'd find a policeman. She wasn't foolish enough to think she could drive like a television P.I. and lose him in traffic.

The car was dark blue, not black. She tried to read the license plate, but it had been covered with a layer of mud. Kendra came up on a light just turning red. For a moment she considered running it, leaving her pursuer behind, but habit stopped her. She'd been law-abiding for too many years not to slow to a stop. Her tormentor had no such qualms.

An impact of great force pushed Kendra's car into the middle of the busy intersection.

An eternity later, at the police station, Kendra looked up and saw Alex. His brown uniform drew her eyes like a beacon in a sea of men and women in dark blue. He was talking to her witness, a man in a florist's van who had seen everything, including the ski mask on the driver of the car that had hit her.

Kendra had been shaken but not hurt. Her car had suffered no more than a bent fender. Unfortunately, it had bent inward, so that she could not drive without ruining her tire. The mechanic who'd towed it away had promised to fix the problem first thing in the morning.

How long ago had that been?

How long since the young, no-nonsense police-woman had urged her into one of the white Volvos Augusta police used as squad cars and driven her to this somber, sour-looking brick monolith on the waterfront?

Inside were the plaster walls, high ceilings, over-sized doors, redundant woodwork and wasted space of turn-of-the-century public buildings everywhere. Once the city hall, it now housed police headquarters. Kendra had been brought in to make a statement.

Abruptly, she stood and walked to one of the high, old-fashioned windows. Straight down was the Kennebec River. The fading sunlight sparkled on its fast-moving surface. How had Alex gotten to Augusta so quickly? Why had he come? She remembered telling the police about her earlier accident, but she had not mentioned his name.

This time, at least, no one thought she was at fault. There was no question that the car and driver had been there. Her witness was willing to swear to what he'd seen, and the driver of a pulp truck had verified that a dark blue sedan had sped away from the scene. Unfortunately, no one agreed on a make or model, and a passerby had insisted that the car was green.

Before she turned around, she knew Alex was standing in the doorway of the detective's office. Her pulse rate doubled at the sound of his footfall. It took all her willpower not to run into his arms.

"I didn't expect you to come."

"Cindy's thorough. She called the sheriff's office to check on the earlier accident. Got me."

Cindy, she thought. The policewoman. Why did she suddenly wish Cindy weren't quite so young and attractive?

"Are you okay?" he asked.

She nodded.

"Want to talk about it?"

"I'm all talked out. Are you on duty?"

"Not anymore." His mobile, sensual mouth curved in a smile, revealing bright, even teeth that made her think of the wolf who pursued Little Red Riding Hood. "Come on," he invited softly. "I'll buy you dinner."

"I'm not very hungry." She could feel her back-bone stiffening and willed herself to relax. What harm could it do to let him fuss over her? They knew where they stood, didn't they? She was a suspicious character. He was a cop.

"So we'll eat Chinese." His grin was infectious, and it took no more than a touch of his hand on hers to remind Kendra of the chemistry between them. Protests died on her dry lips as he pulled her along behind him out of the police station and into his cruiser.

"Why are you being so nice to me?" she asked as he turned into rush-hour traffic and headed through the center of the small city.

"Suspicious?"

"Yes." In truth her mind was whirling with conflicting emotions.

Too aware of him in the confines of the cruiser, she breathed in his clean, spicy male scent and watched the tendons flex under his uniform as he gripped the wheel. The lassitude she'd felt with him once before came back, weakening her resolve and sending a thrill of anticipation through her at the same time.

"I guess I'd better phrase this next part carefully." He glanced at her as he stopped for a light. His right arm stretched along the back of the seat and grazed her shoulder. Kendra closed her eyes, disturbed by the weakness that seemed to engulf her. "You need a motel room for the night if you're going to wait and pick up your car in the morning. I called in a reservation from the police station."

"Thank you," she managed to croak. "The garage promised to fix it first thing. I should be on the road again by nine."

"There's a Chinese place in walking distance if we cut through a mini-mall." His voice stayed soft, lulling her toward trusting him, but her hands plucked nervously at the pendant she wore.

Maybe she was dreaming this, but Kendra knew she didn't want him to leave her. Not quite yet. The thought of even a brief separation gave her an odd, empty feeling. Nerves, she tried to tell herself. Who wouldn't be shook up after two automobile accidents nine days apart?

"I'd like to use your room for a minute," Alex said as he pulled into the parking lot at the motel and angled the cruiser into a spot behind a tree, out of sight of the street. "I've got a change of clothes in the trunk. The uniform's pretty conspicuous in a restaurant."

He went with her to register, seeming oblivious to the curious looks he got from the desk clerk. Kendra felt as self-conscious and guilty as a teenager sneaking in after curfew when she asked for a single room, paid for it with her credit card and accepted the key. She hesitated a moment, then tossed it toward him across the lobby, in full view of several amused guests and the clerk.

"Go ahead and use my room to change. I'll wait here. Officer." It was a test for her as much as for him. Surely she could stand a few minutes alone.

He was back ten minutes later, his damp hair giving evidence that he'd also borrowed her shower. Outside, they climbed over a small retaining wall and slid down the bank into a shopping center. He put his arm easily around her shoulders, guiding her over the rough terrain and warming her as evening drew in. Too warm, she thought. He squeezed them both closer to the stores they were passing to let a woman with a baby carriage go by and then his arm dropped down around her waist as they stepped off the curb to cross the parking lot to the cheerfully lit restaurant. Everywhere his fingers brushed they left a trail of fireworks that didn't stop when his hand came to rest on the gentle curve of her hip.

Only when they were inside the restaurant did he break physical contact with her, pulling out a chair so that she could sit down. Kendra rushed into speech, her voice sounding too high and a little breathless.

"Generic Chinese restaurant decor," she blurted.

The waitress looked affronted, handed each of them a menu and left. Feeling slightly foolish, Kendra met Alex's eyes and was relieved to find no mockery there. "I worked in one of these places when I was in college," she explained. "I think they've all been designed by the same firm, right down to the place mats with the signs of the Chinese zodiac."

She knew without looking that the place mat would tell her to stay away from him. For every one of the twelve animal signs, ideal mates were recommended. Whether it was coincidence or some Oriental ideal for the age differences between spouses, these were always four signs away in either direction. She and Alex didn't fit the pattern. She wondered if his astrological sign would be as incompatible and told herself it hardly mattered. They had no future. He might be behaving nicely now, but it wouldn't last. They'd quarrel soon. Didn't they always?

"Penny for your thoughts," he said softly.

Glancing up from the menu, she met dark eyes alight with mischief. He seemed to enjoy her company. For the moment, at least, the circumstances that had brought them together had been forgotten. Kendra grinned and pointed to the place mat.

"Which do you find harder to imagine, the boar marrying the sheep or the rabbit?"

The image of either coupling made them both laugh and for a time they chatted easily. He told her he'd worked on road construction in the summers when he was in school, and Kendra told him about some of her waitressing experiences.

"I'll bet you're a generous tipper," he guessed when they'd ordered. "Most ex-waitresses are."

"You're right. I overtip, to make up for all those terrible customers I had to put up with. There's just no pleasing some people."

"There can't have been many who didn't appreciate your service. Not once they got a look at your legs." The golden flecks in his dark eyes danced.

Kendra's throat went suddenly dry. Without even touching her he'd managed to rattle her again. She reached for the small pot of tea their waitress had placed between them on the table, but her hand was shaking as she poured, until Alex steadied her grip with his own. His touch set her heart beating faster.

"We used to be able to guess at the tip by what people ordered. Someone who's never eaten Chinese food before isn't usually very generous. I always knew I wouldn't be getting a good tip if a customer ordered blueberry pie."

"Why's that?" Now his finger was circling the soft skin around her thumb, burning it with as much warmth as the barrel of her gun. Vibrations hummed between them, elusive but enticing.

All Kendra's willpower was required to give a comprehensible answer. "No pies on the menu in most

Chinese places." She jerked her hand free. "Alex, you're making me very nervous."

"You had a scare. I'm just trying to take your mind off it for a while."

"Talk about yourself, then." Immediately she wished she'd chosen a safe, casual topic instead, but he allowed her withdrawal, seeming to sense her unspoken fears.

"What do you want to know?"

"Why did you feel you had to change your clothes? I hope you didn't think I'd be uncomfortable having dinner with you just because you were in uniform."

"No, I'd be the uncomfortable one. Even people with nothing to hide start acting guilty around uniformed officers. It's as if we aren't supposed to eat like everyone else. And, they assume we're on duty."

Scowling, he fell silent, and this time Kendra was the one to reach out. For an instant she covered his hand with hers. "What is it?"

Alex caught her fingers before she could withdraw, turning her hand to plant a soft kiss on her palm before he released them. Kendra felt the shimmering heat all through her body. "Tell me what made you frown that way," she said quickly.

"Was I frowning?" He shrugged, attempting to make light of it. "I was just thinking of something that happened yesterday. I had lunch during a break in proceedings at the courthouse. I went to a fast-food place, and I was minding my own business, thinking about the case coming up, and trying to ignore the people at the next table, a woman and a little kid, maybe five or six years old. A real brat. He dumped his fries on the floor. Maybe it was deliberate, maybe not, but obviously his mother thought it was. She grabbed him by the arm and pointed at me and she said, 'You behave yourself or that cop over there will arrest you and lock you up and throw away the key.'"

"So much for teaching little kids that policemen are their friends." Kendra spoke softly, willing him to go on. She sensed there was much more than the surface story eating at him.

After a moment, Alex's words confirmed her guess. "I'm not much better than that woman. My own son grew up hating all kinds of authority."

They ate slowly as he talked, telling her for the first time what she had heard secondhand from Tara. He didn't go into detail, and he thought he was hiding his emotional scars, but the story of his marriage, fatherhood, divorce and separation from his son all tumbled out until Kendra saw the hurt behind his flat words. She thought she might be the first person he had been so open with, and that pleased her.

Restaurant smells, other patrons, the soft but inappropriate music from a golden oldies radio station—all those things faded away as Alex gave Kendra an unintentional glimpse of how empty he had let his life become. He didn't need to say he was wary of permanent relationships. After Jody's betrayal she knew he could not be otherwise. He'd dedicated himself to his work and lost himself in solitude on his days off, shutting out the rest of the world. She was certain there had been women. He was too frankly sensual to have lived the life of a monk, but he hadn't allowed anyone to get close to him.

"And now?" she asked softly. "You must see Denny more often. Quaiapen isn't that big."

"It was a case of instant mistrust the first time we met. I hadn't seen him since he was a baby and suddenly he was twelve and had dyed a purple streak down the center of his hair. I was in uniform, and reacted like a typical small-town bigot.''

"I expect you reacted like a typical parent," Kendra told him soothingly. "Twenty years ago parents told their kids to go get a haircut. Now they say, get rid of the purple streak.''

"That was my father's line to my son. He and my mother reacted badly, too. They're very conservative people. Add an unfriendly reception to all the stories Jody had told him about how insensitive and strict I was and it's no wonder the kid tried to stay out of my way." Alex toasted her with his coffee cup. "Meeting you may have changed my luck with the boy. This past week I've had a couple of normal conversations with him. I've finally managed to stop acting like a cop and start acting like a father.''

"It's difficult to parent teenagers even if you've had them all their lives.''

How was she going to tell Alex about Denny's part in the first accident? Alex hardly believed anything she said anyway. If it involved his son, he would have even less incentive to listen to her. Besides, what she had to say about Denny would hurt him. Her instinct had been that Denny was not beyond redemption, and it seemed he had been trying to reconcile with his father. Kendra was reluctant to shatter the frail bond they had begun to build between them. When she got back to Quaiapan, she decided, she'd talk to the boy herself. There had to be some way to get through to him, to convince him to tell Alex the truth.

"You've gotten very quiet. Does the thought of teenagers always do that to you?"

Something in the timbre of his voice had changed. It was harsher, lower pitched, almost ominous. Kendra stared at him, surprised to find she could no longer read his expression.

"Alex? You do believe me now, don't you?" She pushed her plate aside, unable to manage any more fried rice.

"Getting hit by that car in front of witnesses was pretty convincing proof that something is going on." He reached across the table to take her hands in both of his. "What are you getting at, Kendra?"

"If you believe that same car caused the first accident, you have to believe that I saw its occupants, and that one of them was actually inside my car, putting the pillbox in my purse."

He nodded, wariness narrowing his eyes. "I believe you've always told me the truth as you saw it, but sometimes perceptions can be . . . out of focus." The pressure of his grip tightened around her clasped hands. "We have a lot to sort out yet, Kendra, to make sense out of what's happened to you. You just keep on telling me the truth, no matter how farfetched, and somehow we'll find our way through it."

"Don't patronize me!" Jerking her hands away, she stood, heart aching. He didn't believe her after all. "I've been telling you the exact truth from the beginning. Why do you insist I'm distorting it?"

The waitress hovered, fortune cookies and bill in hand, and Kendra bit back her next words. She couldn't let herself be goaded into telling him his own son was involved. In spite of the way he doubted her, she'd come to care for Alex too much to cause him hurt. She could even understand why he hesitated to trust her unsupported word. In his line of work, he

Cloud Castles

dealt with lies all the time. In his personal life he had been deceived and betrayed.

While he paid for their meal, she gathered the shattered remnants of her composure. He wanted to believe her. She didn't doubt that. Somehow there had to be a way to convince him that she was an honest woman who was telling the truth and who was already half in love with him.

The realization came to her without fanfare and she accepted it. She was falling in love with Alex Moreau. The only way to stop it was to keep him at a distance. Surely it wasn't too late for that?

His big hands were gentle on her shoulders as he steered her outside once more. The May evening was cooling off rapidly but it was his touch that made her shiver. How could she even consider falling in love when there was so much between them that was still unresolved? And how could she want him so much?

"Let's talk about your students," he said abruptly. "They're part of the problem."

For a moment she was shaken out of her emotional quandary. He was making no sense at all. "What are you talking about, Alex?"

"You left your job because of a nervous breakdown. That has to have colored your perspective on—"

"I what?" Skidding to a halt in the mall's half-empty parking lot, she just stared at him. "Where on earth did you get that idea?" She wished she could see his face more clearly, but twilight obscured his features. Darkness pooled around them, broken at intervals by mall floodlights.

"Let's go back to your motel room where we can talk in private."

"No, thank you. We've nothing to discuss. You talked to Henry Damon, didn't you?" She spat out the name and didn't wait for confirmation. "He would lie about me, even to the police, because he's vindictive and small-minded." Furious, she spun away, moving rapidly toward the motel.

Alex wanted to believe her. For a little while, over dinner, he'd begun to relax with her, to dream of more meals together, of a gradually growing trust between them. If only that wary expression hadn't come over her features when he began to talk about Denny. It had reminded him of all his investigations had unearthed. She was right, of course, that his source was Henry Damon. Damon was well respected in Burlington, his opinion valued. Then Alex remembered the negative impression Damon had made on him over the phone and hesitated. Maybe people were too quick to take Damon's word.

Sprinting after her, Alex caught up with Kendra at the side of the motel. "Why did you leave Vermont?"

His voice sounded harsh in the stillness. The hand on her elbow brought her to a stop and tugged her down to sit beside him on a bench installed to overlook the deserted motel pool. She had no choice.

Glaring, she kept her answer short. "To come here."

"Damn it, Kendra, give me a straight answer."

Cupping her face between his palms he held her with firm gentleness at arm's length, refusing to let her turn away. In the illumination of the pool lights he studied her expression and she knew he could read the emotions there—defiance, anger, fear and something more, something she hoped he would not be able to identify because it was the result of his nearness.

"Why did you leave the way you did? If Damon's lying, what happened to make him so vindictive?"

"I left him."

For a moment her simple words seemed another evasion. Of course she had left him. She'd quit her job and run away. Then, with a jolt, Alex realized what she really meant.

He felt a brief but violent surge of jealousy. Its intensity both surprised and angered Alex. What was it to him if she'd had a lover? A dozen lovers? For all he knew she'd loved them and left them all over New England.

Only he didn't believe it. And he wanted to pummel Henry Damon. Damon had hurt Kendra, was still hurting her with his lies.

"Tell me." His voice sounded gritty and he released her so suddenly that she swayed toward him, off balance with surprise.

Only by catching the back of the bench could she hold herself away from him. "We were lovers for almost two years." Her voice was so soft he had to strain, leaning closer, to catch the words. "There was no official engagement, but we were talking about a June wedding. Then...something...happened, at Christmas, that made me see what life with him would be like. I couldn't face it. I told him I wasn't going to marry him, ever. He didn't take it well."

"Something?"

"I don't want to talk about it."

"If he hurt you—"

Touching her fingers to his lips she stopped him. They were only inches apart on the bench, very nearly embracing. "Only my feelings," she whispered. "I don't need pampering, but I'd like the man I marry to be sensitive to my emotional needs."

As if she'd revealed too much of herself, she slid away from him and refused to meet his eyes. Nervous fingers plucked at the soft wool of her pleated skirt, smoothing and unfolding and smoothing again.

"Why didn't you leave your job then?"

"I thought we could still work together. I was wrong."

With each word he felt her withdraw into herself a little further. The change was subtle, but he had the sense that she was finding Henry Damon so difficult to talk about that she needed formality. Perhaps it was to protect herself from shedding tears, but now she almost seemed to be giving a lecture.

"A schoolteacher who gets no support from her principal has twice the problems of one who does. The atmosphere in my classes was already rough. This particular seventh grade was the worst in years." At his raised eyebrow, she tried to explain. "That probably sounds cynical, but sometimes it happens with a whole year's children. One of the older teachers said the seventh graders back in 1975–76 were the same way. There were twice as many boys in the class as girls, and they had a certain wildness about them. They had indulgent parents." She gave him a wry smile. "Mothers and fathers who wouldn't listen to one word against their little darlings. It must be the teacher's fault."

Alex understood better than she realized. Hadn't he dealt with parents, wives, siblings, all insisting that their loved one couldn't have committed any crime? He'd encountered his share of young criminals, too. If

Kendra had been teaching here, she'd have passed on any number of her students to his jail.

"You made it till the beginning of May. Why not stick it out to the end of the year?"

Evasively, Kendra stared into the empty pool. "I just decided I wasn't going to take it anymore."

"You're a lousy liar."

"At least that makes it clear the rest of what I've said is true." Her head snapped up and her eyes flashed.

Abruptly, Alex stood. He needed to put some space between them. Why was he letting her get to him this way? Okay, he believed her. Up to a point. There was little reason for anyone to run her off the road. There was still less for a gang of teenagers to do it.

Knowledge that had been nagging at the back of his mind ever since he left the police station with her surfaced again, as unwelcome as before. A redhead in a dark sedan. George Marks. Denny's friend. A blond boy. Denny? Or had Kendra mistaken Gil Paradis's sand-colored locks for yellow?

There were some hard questions he had to ask those boys tomorrow. He'd hold off approaching Denny for a bit. Hadn't his son said they'd dropped him off at camp? If they'd been drinking and caused Kendra's accident, of course they'd run off. But why follow her to Augusta and try again? They must realize she hadn't been able to identify them. He'd have hauled them in by now if she could.

Cursing silently, Alex realized he was going around in circles again, just as he had been since Kendra Jennings first came into his life. She was staring at him as he paced the length of the pool and back. Finally she stood, fumbling in her purse for her room key. She wanted him to go, and he could hardly blame her. Once again he had felt the rapport building between them and ruthlessly crushed it. Once again he regretted the loss.

"Alex?" She sounded tentative, almost fearful.

Had he done that to her? Hardly the sensitive guy she said she wanted. He strained for calm and civil and caring. He managed a noncommittal grunt.

"What did they tell you at the police station?"

"The Augusta police have no clue as to the other car or its driver." Now he sounded as if he were making a report to a superior officer in the military. What was the matter with him? "This is the second time someone's tried to harm you, Kendra. Thanks to my stupidity they might have succeeded."

Her eyes widened at the bitterness in his tone. For some reason, now that he'd finally decided to believe her, he was taking the blame himself. "You couldn't have known—"

"I could have kept an eye on you." Catching her arm again, he pulled her toward the motel. Unconsciously he lengthened his stride until she was almost running to keep up with him. Only after she stumbled did his pace slow.

"Alex, I wouldn't have believed me if I hadn't been there. Nothing about this makes any sense at all."

"I don't like leaving you here alone." They were at the door to her room. Alex took the key from her hand, opened the door cautiously and checked, as he had that first day at her house, to be sure no one was lying in wait for her.

"I'm in no danger." Amusement warred with irritation. "No one even knows where I am, except you."

"Someone knew you'd be in Augusta."

"Sure. Tara. I don't really think she—"

"I ought to go back and check your house."

She nodded, suddenly thoughtful. "You may be right. I was thinking at the police station that if someone wanted to kill me they'd have been more efficient about it. Do you think they just don't want me at the house? The first accident prevented me from reaching it until the next day. The second made sure I wouldn't come home early tonight."

"Damn, I wish this made some sort of sense. I've been all over Olive's place. There's nothing there anyone would want."

"Well, if they wanted me gone for the day, they succeeded. And I'm sure they've been and gone by now. You needn't rush back hoping to catch anyone." Why had she said that? Kendra toyed nervously with a lock of hair. What if Alex took it as an invitation to stay?

In vain, she tried to block out the erotic thoughts flooding her mind. She told herself she was crazy if she thought a night with Alex Moreau would lead anywhere. She knew she'd just be left alone in the morning, full of regrets.

"Go home, Alex." Her voice was teacher-firm. "I'll be okay. I need a hot shower and some rest, and you have to work in the morning." Holding out her hand for the key, she stood stiffly in the doorway. She would spend the night alone and drive back to Quaiapen tomorrow.

With reluctance so obvious that it warmed her, he folded the key into her outstretched palm and kissed her lightly on the tip of her nose. "Take care of yourself. I go on duty at eight tomorrow morning. I'll check your place first thing, then swing back to talk to you sometime in the early afternoon.''

Kendra nodded. That would give her time enough to get home and time enough to brace herself to see him again without wanting him.

"Go home, Alex," she repeated, her voice still firm. "It'll be midnight before you get back to Quaiapen."

Regrets set in as soon as she heard his footsteps fade away. Idiot, she thought.

As she stripped off her clothes and headed for the bathroom, she wondered what would have happened if she'd taken a chance on Alex Moreau.

He wanted her. He'd said that. His eyes at dinner had confirmed it, though the words had not been spoken aloud. But did she want a brief affair? She'd known him such a short time, but already she sensed that a future with Alex would be more than Henry Damon had ever made her dream of, and her pain all the more devastating if it were denied her.

The fine, hard spray from the shower slowly began to ease the aches and tension of the last hours. Kendra had been standing under it for at least ten minutes when she heard the knocking. She tried to ignore it, but the pounding was persistent, and the water was lukewarm.

As she shut off the spray, her heart began to hammer to the same tune as the door. Still dripping, Kendra wrapped one fluffy white towel around her wet hair and another around her torso.

It had to be Alex. Even the thought heated her blood and set her pulses into overdrive. His reasoning had taken the same path as her own and he had come back.

Kendra was so certain that she didn't stop to consider any other possibility. She flung the door wide, her lips already forming themselves into a smile of pure pleasure.

Chapter 7

Alex!"

His eyes swept down and up again, but the flash of desire was replaced almost at once by anger. "Don't you have more sense than to open the door without finding out who's on the other side first?"

Painfully aware that she was wearing nothing but a towel, Kendra backed away. Closing the door behind him and locking it, Alex followed her into the room, but when he turned to look at her, his face was carefully blank. "Put your clothes back on," he ordered. "We need to talk."

Kendra fled into the bathroom to dress in the only clothes she had, the wool skirt and sweater she'd put on for her day in the city. In her hurry, she ignored the stretched-out panty hose. The room was warm enough for bare feet and legs. It felt too warm, now that Alex had come into it.

With a deep breath to give her strength, she faced him. "Why did you come back?"

"There are too many unanswered questions. As long as they stay that way, you're at risk. Damn it, Kendra, what is it you haven't told me?"

That I love you, she thought. That your son is one of them, whoever they are. Aloud she insisted, "Nothing that has anything to do with this."

"Not good enough."

"It will have to be. That's all I have to give you."

A dangerous light came into his molasses-brown eyes and he took a step closer. "Is it?"

Her heart gave a nervous lurch and her breath stopped. As quickly as it had been issued, the sexual invitation was retracted and controlled. He might be out of uniform, but Alex could wrap his profession around him like a cloak when he chose. He was choosing now, and, infuriated by the barrier he was building between them, Kendra lashed out.

"Stop playing cops and robbers with me! Either you believe me or you don't. Either you want me or you don't. We agreed there's no killer lurking in the shadows, so why did you really come back?"

"I couldn't leave." The words seemed wrenched out of him, but she believed them. She felt the same inevitability about their relationship. It was futile to fight mutual desire this powerful. It was almost criminal even to try.

Kendra's face changed, softening, until he could read all she felt in her eyes. She was glad he'd come. She wanted him to stay.

"I keep giving you a rough time. I'm sorry, Kendra."

"More than you know." She moved closer, the damp tendrils of hair dancing around her exquisite face. Her pupils were enormous, wide and black. "I've thought about you far too much ever since we first...met."

The longing in her voice matched that in his heart. With no more hesitation he moved across the small room and pulled her into his arms. "You've become an obsession with me, Kendra," he murmured into her hair. She smelled of flowery shampoo, and soap. "I didn't even reach the car before I knew I had to stay here tonight."

"What took you so long to come back?"

She felt his smile against her forehead. Then he was planting teasing little kisses around the curve of her jaw, the edge of her ear, the bridge of her nose, moving ever closer to her lips. "Had to get someone to cover for me until noon tomorrow."

"Noon," Kendra repeated, mindlessly echoing the word. Impatient, she reached up, tightened her fingers around his softly curling hair and pulled his mouth toward hers. "No more talk," she whispered in the breathless second before their lips met.

Their kiss had all the power of the one that had come before, but this time there was no pulling back, no uncertainty. Kendra made no protest as Alex lifted her off her feet and shifted both of them onto the bed. It felt too right to be lying side by side.

More kisses rained down on her mouth, her eyelids, her brow. Bemused, she began fumbling with the buttons on his shirt. The material was soft, much-washed cotton, and she felt chills ripple along her spine as it came apart to reveal the heated flesh beneath. His skin was smooth, with no thick mat of hair to keep her from pressing against the flesh. Flat, pebbly nipples drew her fingertips, and a sound of pleasure from deep in his throat.

Nothing mattered to her but this man, this moment, as she tugged at the shirt, finally freeing the tail from his belt. Corduroy whispered against her bare calves as she writhed closer.

Smooth, warm fingers slipped under the heather-colored sweater, easing loose the soft camisole beneath while he planted a series of tiny, teasing kisses along her collarbone. Her skin prickled deliciously and she arched her body toward him. The sweater bunched up between them until, with a muffled curse, he slid both it and the camisole over her head and shoved them off the bed.

Delight etched into his face, he looked down at her. She trembled, pausing in her explorations, as he pulled back to poise above her, balanced on one elbow. Even if she had not been able to see his expression, she would have felt the intensity of his gaze. It raked her for a long tremulous moment before he began to lower searching lips.

"So small and so perfect," he whispered, moving his mouth over one breast toward the hardening nipple. Kendra moaned with the pleasure of it. She never wanted him to stop.

Fingers started at her ankle and moved along the sensitive skin on the back of her calf. The touch was feather light but devastatingly erotic. She answered his quest to learn the secrets of a lover's body by renewing her own.

Moving from its worship of her fully sensitized breasts, his tongue possessed her mouth, thrusting in damp, exciting circles, inviting her response. Unable to think, Kendra could only feel, and, feeling, answer his passion.

His hand slipped beneath the hem of her skirt and touched her bare thigh. Then it was inching upward, scorching a fiery trail from the sensitive area in back of her knee to the still more susceptible skin near the apex of her thighs.

When he moved away from her, Kendra whimpered in protest, afraid he meant to stop. Relief surged through her as she realized he had only paused to finish removing their clothes. Her wool skirt, bulky and interfering, became a discarded mound at their feet, whisked out of the way with deft hands. She heard the rasp of his zipper and the whisper of corduroy, and then his heavy body was pressing against her once more.

Slowly, with infinite care and tenderness, he began to kiss her again, building the heady momentum until she felt she was falling into a whirlpool. The wisp of lace and nylon that still separated them was gently tugged away, eased downward until it was gone. His knee gently parted her inner thighs, as his hands pressed into the small of her back, urging her closer.

Kendra tensed at the first, probing touch, but he stroked her gently, whispering that it would be all right. "I've taken care of everything," he said.

She felt vulnerable and at the same time cherished. He had taken time, even in the midst of their tumultuous passion, to ensure her protection. It was, she thought, as much an act of love as what would follow.

Answering his kisses with her own, she gave herself over to her love for him, guiding his entry as she arched toward him.

This was meant to be, she thought. How else could they fit so perfectly?

Slowly, gently, he began to move within her, until his thrusts were creating sensations she had never dreamed possible. Instinct drove her to answer his passion with her own.

"I've wanted you like this since the first moment we met." His whisper was husky, taut with yearnings as yet unfulfilled.

With a sigh, she closed her eyes, abandoning herself to the building rapture. She became deaf and blind to everything around them, aware of nothing but his sweet assault on her senses that was bringing her to the height of ecstasy.

His woman.

The thought was accompanied by a primitive surge of male pride as he watched her sleep beside him. She was a woman who gave sweetly, loved with passion and had chosen him.

With gentle fingers, careful not to disturb her slumber, he tugged a cinnamon-colored strand of hair away from the corner of her mouth. Her lips looked fuller, still swollen from his kisses, and Alex knew he wanted to make love to her again. He wanted to spend a lifetime making love to her. The realization shocked him, but he had no time to analyze it. Kendra had opened her eyes and was smiling at him.

Still sleepy, languid with memories, she said the first thing she thought. "I like waking up with you, Alex. We should do it more often." At his startled look her heart sank. "I never learn, do I? I shouldn't be allowed to speak at all until after at least one cup of coffee in the morning. I just blurt things out. I'm not trying to catch you or anything, honestly. I just meant I was glad we—"

His lips stopped the torrent of words, replacing them with kisses. When they finally subsided, Kendra was breathless.

"Don't ever stop blurting at me, Kendra. That's part of what I like best about you."

"What's the other part?"

With a wicked chuckle, he reached for her. This time their lovemaking was less frantic, but she responded to him with just as much fervor, again reaching the mindless ecstasy that was over far too soon.

"That could become addictive," Kendra murmured as she watched him dress. Ruthlessly, she pushed visions of a future with Alex out of her thoughts. This was sex, not love. They'd made no commitment. Worse, she knew that if she followed his advice and let herself blurt what was in her mind, she'd regret it. First she'd say she loved him. Then she'd be inviting him to move in with her. No man, no matter how tender a lover, was ready for that much frankness. It was too soon. Last night he'd still believed Henry's lies.

"Come on, lazybones," he teased. "I'll buy you breakfast under the Golden Arches."

"Offers like that inspire me to stay in bed." She was tempted to pull the blanket over her head and catch up on missed sleep, but without Alex beside her the sheets had rapidly lost their warmth.

Before she could change her mind, Kendra flung off the covers and swung long legs toward the floor. Alex had already retrieved her clothes and proceeded to hand them to her, piece by piece, and watch her dress.

"Enjoying the view?"

"Immensely. As much as you did a few minutes ago." He laughed aloud as color bloomed on her cheeks and she fled into the bathroom. "You're beautiful," he called after her.

Kendra sighed unhappily as she struggled into panty hose and tried to get a comb through her tangled hair. Alex was a special man. She grimaced at her reflection. He had to be to call a woman who had slept on wet hair beautiful.

In the cold, clear light of day she knew she'd been kidding herself. She couldn't hope to keep evading Alex's questions. Not after last night. There were a couple of truths she was going to have to share with him before their relationship went much further, and she had the sinking sensation that one of them would bring it to a grinding halt.

Confrontation came even sooner than she'd expected. Over sausage and biscuit sandwiches, he turned back into Deputy Moreau. "I'm going to check on a car when we get back," he told her. "Dark blue. Belongs to a nineteen-year-old redhead named George Marks. Think you can identify him?"

"I don't know. I was dazed. It was foggy."

He nodded, but his eyes were wary. No more evasions, Kendra reminded herself. Just blurt it out.

"The boy who put the pillbox in my purse was your son."

She expected violent denial. Instead Alex closed up, hiding his emotions as completely as he did when he put on his mirrored sunglasses. "You only met Denny once, in the diner. How can you be so sure?"

"That's not the only time I saw him." Haltingly, sensing he was withdrawing further and further away from her with every word, she told him about Denny's visit to the house and his threats. "He's confused," she said at the end. "I could sense it. We can help him, Alex. He's crying out for attention, your attention. We can reach him, talk to him."

"Oh, I'll talk to him all right," he promised, "but I'll do it alone."

Kendra stopped the car in front of her house with a sigh of relief. Alex had insisted on driving behind her all the way home. Instead of reassuring her, the constant presence of his cruiser in her rearview mirror had made her increasingly more tense.

Nothing had been settled between them. She thought he believed her. She knew he was going to talk to Denny. What happened after that was the problem. Even if Denny confessed everything, vindicating Kendra, the fragile bond of a night's lovemaking had been damaged. She knew now she should not have let it happen. There had been too many secrets between them, secrets that now were driving them apart. If Denny denied everything, if he convinced his father he'd never gone to see Kendra, there was little hope of a future with Alex Moreau.

How had he become so important to her so quickly? It hurt to know this morning's separation might be permanent. Could she stay in Quaiapen, only seeing him the way his ex-wife did? The prospect appalled her.

"No sign of any activity," he said, as he joined her at the front door. The new locks were still stiff, and obviously undisturbed, but Alex accompanied her inside anyway, going from room to room as he had be-

fore until he was satisfied that it was safe to leave her
there alone.

Kendra checked her computer and the box of disks.
Like the rest of the house, they were undisturbed. She
turned to the living room next, meaning to open the
windows and air out the stuffiness that came from
being closed up. Flies, brought out by the warmer
weather, buzzed on the screens.

The smell assaulted her as she crossed in front of the
fireplace. She stopped, wondering if she'd imagined it,
and sniffed again. Smoke. She wanted to believe it was
wood smoke, left over from the last fire she'd laid in
the hearth, but there were subtle differences. This was
cigarette smoke. She was particularly sensitive to it
because she habitually avoided places where smokers
congregated.

Sniffing delicately, she tried to trace the odor. It was
only in the living room, and only near the fireplace.
Except for the lingering smell of tobacco there was
nothing to indicate anyone had been in the house, but
she sensed with growing panic that her shiny new locks
had been useless. Someone had gotten in.

"Kendra?"

"Can you smell it? Cigarette smoke."

Avoiding physical contact with her, he crossed the
room and stood near the fireplace. "I don't smell
anything."

"I shouldn't have opened the window." The faint,
elusive scent was rapidly dissipating. "I did smell it,
though. Someone was here while I was gone."

But he shook his head. "You're overwrought.
There's no sign anyone's been here. If they did want
to keep you away, it could be something on the lake
that you weren't supposed to see."

"That doesn't make any sense, either, Alex."

Shrugging, he moved toward the door. He'd stop at his apartment and change into his uniform. Whatever had been going on, he was convinced Kendra was in no danger if she stayed here alone. He was the one in danger if he lingered.

It tore at him to see the longing in her gaze. She didn't want him to go any more than he wanted to leave. Perhaps that was why she was babbling on about cigarette smoke. Any excuse to keep him longer. He ought to be flattered, he thought, but her need for him made him want to run the other way. They could both use some distance between them. And he needed to find out, once and for all, if he could believe her. Denny held the answer there. Alex had been ready to accept everything she said until she'd accused his son.

Gruff-voiced, he said, "I'll be in touch," and left quickly.

With a despairing sigh, Kendra locked the door behind him. For all the good it will do, she thought. Moving listlessly through the rooms he'd already searched, she turned on the generator so she could take a hot bath. An hour later, soaking in the tub, she convinced herself that she could forget Alex Moreau and get on with her life. She still had a manuscript to finish. Maybe she'd start a mystery story next, or a romance.

No one was trying to kill her, of that she was now certain. Someone had merely wanted to make sure she was not in this house at specific times. The first accident had kept her from arriving. She'd been neatly sidelined until the next day. That had given someone time to do whatever it was they had to do before she saw the place. The second accident had guaranteed she'd be away overnight. In her absence someone had come in. She didn't have a clue as to why they had to have an empty house at those particular times, but she was certain that was the solution.

Perhaps something had been left behind the first time. That might explain why they'd tried to sneak in at night. Had she slept through it, she might have avoided a bill for car repairs.

Smiling wryly to herself, she stepped from the tub, toweled dry and slipped into a comfortable jogging suit. Now what? She wondered if they were through disrupting her life. "Why don't they just ask?" she grumbled aloud as she made her way back downstairs. "I'll oblige and stay away."

She used the last of her split wood to make a fire in the fireplace and settled down in one of the overstuffed chairs in front of it to reread her manuscript. It was time for the last rewrite. In the morning she'd drive into Quaiapen and send it off to the first editor on her list of children's book publishers.

Alex's afternoon consisted of one petty complaint after another, taking him all over his half of the county and resulting in more paperwork than he wanted to think about. In addition he looked for George Marks, but George was at none of his usual haunts, and there was no sign either of his car or his constant companion, Gil Paradis.

By the time he got back to his own apartment and fed the cat, Alex wanted nothing more than to sit down in front of the television with a beer and watch the Celtics game. He was tempted to put off talking to Denny until he was more relaxed. There was no point in provoking the boy. That was why he'd waited until he was off duty, wasn't it?

The weekend stretched before him, welcome after seven consecutive days on the road. For a time he'd expected to be sharing it with Kendra. Ruthlessly he pushed her image out of his mind and concentrated on Denny. Would he know if the boy was lying to him? That doubt troubled him more than he wanted to acknowledge.

Knowing he had to talk to his son before he saw Kendra again, Alex pulled a frozen dinner out of his refrigerator and popped it into the microwave. While it hummed along, Alex dialed his ex-wife's number.

Chapter 8

The following morning Kendra unearthed a small hacksaw from her cousin's eclectic tool chest and set out around the house to the woodshed. The last time she'd gone out there she'd discovered a huge old-fashioned padlock holding the door closed, and there was no sign of a key in the house. She was hoping the shed was full of split logs, ready to be carried into the house for use in the fireplace and wood stove. If not, she was going to have to learn a new skill.

To her surprise, when she seized the heavy metal lock, it came open in her hand. For a moment she stared at it, positive that she'd tugged on it the last time and found it holding firm. Kendra shook her head, beginning to feel like the heroine of a Hitchcock film. Was anything ever as she thought?

Inside the shed, to her dismay, there was no stove-length split wood, nor any neat piles of kindling. There was nothing at all but a splitting maul, metal wedges, a mallet and an ax, all neatly lined up along the side wall.

"Phooey," Kendra said aloud. Unconsciously she flexed her shoulders, wondering if she had the strength to split wood. In theory it was easy enough. You put the wood on the chopping block, you hauled off over your head with the maul, and you let the wood have it. It broke in two, then quarters on the next stroke, and even smaller, as long as you kept thwacking it. You kept your feet out of the way, and it probably helped to imagine that the piece of tree you were destroying was someone you disliked.

Wood warms you four times, she'd often heard— when you cut it, when you haul it, when you split it and when you burn it. At least the cords of wood neatly stacked at the side of the house had already been cut and hauled.

Wondering why the shed had been locked when it was empty, Kendra stepped inside, exploring the small area more closely. It even appeared to have been swept clean, for where there should have been a layer of sawdust and chips of wood the floor was bare. The midafternoon sun slanted into the room, picking out the evenly cut planks of wood that made up the walls. The shed sat right next to the chimney, Kendra realized, which meant those planks at the back were against her living room wall.

Scarcely daring to breathe, she moved closer. With very little imagination, she could see a door in that wall, a door that would open into the house itself. Tentatively, Kendra reached out, touching her fingers to the rough surface. It seemed solid enough. Then she saw the small indentation at waist level. It was a primitive pull, and with a tug of her fingers, a four-foot-wide section slid sideways and she was facing the rag rug, overstuffed chair and oak end table in her living room.

Kendra passed through and turned, scarcely able to believe she'd found what she thought she would. Then she laughed at her own foolishness. It wasn't exactly a secret passage. The door was merely a clever way to reach the winter's supply of wood without going outdoors. Somewhere on the living room paneling there was an equally unobtrusive pull to open it from the inside.

And that, she realized, is how the ghost got out. Whoever he had been, her midnight visitor had come in through the woodshed and vanished by sliding the door closed behind him. The intruder with the cigarette had entered her house the same way. No wonder her new locks had been useless.

Experimentally, Kendra pulled the door closed until it clicked into place. The release catch was easy to find now that she knew what she was looking for, and she was able to slide the door silently back and forth in its track.

Frowning thoughtfully, Kendra went inside and made herself a fresh pot of coffee while she considered what to do next. Another dead-bolt lock, for the outside of the shed, must be purchased and installed. She'd just have time to do that, but taking an hour to drive into town would mean she'd have to get along without heat for one night. The weather report had indicated the temperature would stay in the fifties. She'd manage. The real question was why she hadn't already gone to Alex with this newest development.

Just the thought of seeing Alex again was enough to make Kendra nervous. The last thing she wanted was to have him think she was making up reasons to contact him. He had certainly talked to Denny by now. What if he had believed his son? If he took Denny's word against hers, and added the blood test, he'd be convinced she was hallucinating.

Tell him you weren't imagining the cigarette smoke, an inner voice urged.

But Kendra knew she had no proof.

Alex might feel obligated to move in and protect you, the voice persisted. Tell him!

Tell him what? Dumping half the coffee down the sink, she went back outside. She hadn't imagined the door but for all she knew it could be a standard part of local architecture. If she were trained, she might find some sign of a vehicle or footprints, but there was nothing near the shed that looked suspicious to her. Her own movements had likely erased all traces. The ground was dry. It wouldn't hold impressions the way the mud had. Someone could easily have backed a truck up to the shed while she was in Augusta and taken away whatever they had stored there.

If that was the case, Kendra had nothing more to fear. They had what they wanted. There was no reason to report her discovery to the police.

Still curious, she got down on her hands and knees and peered at the ground around, next to and under the shed. The search for clues appeared futile and the only objects she unearthed were two rusty nails, a barely recognizable Canadian five-dollar bill that looked as if it had been caught under the corner of the shed for months, and a spider.

Carefully, she smoothed the five out and rubbed the layer of dirt away. Money was money, after all. Slowly the blue and green images emerged. A belted kingfisher was depicted on one side, and a portrait of one of Canada's former prime ministers graced the other.

Not a total loss, Kendra decided, stuffing the bill into the pocket of her jeans. Maybe someone like Alex could tell more about the scene with his trained eye, but she doubted it. The more she thought about it, the more reluctant she was to contact him. She'd tell him about the door when he contacted her. After all, he had promised he'd be in touch.

By now the clerk in the hardware store knew her name. He kidded her as he sold her the third dead bolt in a week. "You'll have the place as secure as Fort Knox if you keep going. What you got up there? Crown jewels?"

"Buried treasure," Kendra confided, grinning. She'd been about to write him a check but reached into her pocket instead. Together with a couple of American bills, the Canadian five gave her enough cash to pay for her purchase. "Found money," she told the young clerk as she passed it over the counter.

"Have to discount it since it's Canadian," he apologized.

"No problem. I still make a profit."

The exchange lightened her spirits and she decided to stop in at the bookstore while she was in town, but a glance through Tara's storefront window made her change her mind. Wakefield McKee was at the counter, leaning into Tara's space, and the two appeared to be quarreling. Another time, Kendra decided. She liked Tara, but Wakefield McKee was a person she intended to avoid.

Back home she had just finished installing the new lock on the shed door when she heard a car pull into her yard. The freshly waxed sheen of brown paint and a flash of late afternoon sun off a set of blue lights had her heart beating rapidly as she rounded the corner of the house, but the officer who got out of the patrol car was not Alex. He was younger, and thinner, and sported an oversized mustache.

"Evenin' ma'am," he drawled. "Everything okay out here today?"

"Just fine." She hoped she didn't look or sound as disappointed as she felt. "For a minute I thought you were Alex Moreau."

"He's off this weekend, ma'am. Won't be back on duty until Tuesday afternoon. Mentioned you'd had a problem with prowlers, so I thought I'd stop by. Name's Johnson."

"Well, thank you, Deputy Johnson, but everything is fine. Very quiet. I don't think I'll be having any more problems."

She wondered how much Alex had told the younger officer, but didn't like to ask. They made desultory conversation about the weather until, with a tip of his cowboy-style hat, the deputy got back into his cruiser and drove away.

Feeling secure with her new locks, Kendra told herself firmly that it was foolish to sit around and wait for Alex to come back. He'd turn up eventually, or not. And they'd have a future, or not. There was no point in wasting time worrying. She spent the evening writing a cover letter to send in with her manuscript.

On Saturday, Kendra drove into town and mailed the story. By the time she got back to the house she had already gotten an idea for her next project. The plot came to her in bursts of inspiration, frequently when she was in the middle of something else, like chopping wood or cooking or taking a shower or trying to fall asleep. As each day passed, she became more involved. This would be a longer book, for middle-grade readers, a mystery involving a house in the middle of nowhere.

Not a plain house, Kendra decided, but one with a tower. There had been such a house in the town where she grew up, standing deserted at the top of a hill that overlooked the school. They'd called it a castle because it was built of stone and had a crenellated stone tower.

Kendra became so engrossed in the emerging story that she almost forgot about Alex Moreau. Almost. He had an unnerving habit of turning up in her dreams.

"I'll be in touch," Kendra quoted as she stared out her kitchen window at the lake. "Hah!"

Her dreams had been more troubling than usual and she'd awakened with a headache and the knowledge that more than a week had gone by since she'd heard from him. Eight days. It was Friday again already, and she hadn't seen hide nor hair of Alex Moreau since he'd walked out her door the previous Thursday morning.

Unless Alex was through with her, there could be only one reason for his continued absence. He'd talked to his son and Denny had lied, and Alex had believed the lie. That knowledge hurt, yet at the same time Kendra could understand Alex's need to trust his son. She could only hope that in time Denny would confess the truth. Until then she had to think positively and hope Alex was having as much trouble forgetting that night in Augusta as she was.

He was mindful of her safety. Though he had not come back himself, he'd arranged for Deputy Johnson to stop by and check on her. Kendra took solace where she could. At least she had not been forgotten.

A loud shout interrupted these early morning musings. "Yoo-hoo!" came the alto bellow.

Kendra couldn't help but smile. She'd never actually heard anyone yell "yoo-hoo" before. Hurriedly stuffing her notes for the new book into the dish-towel drawer, she reached her front porch just as Tara Loomis extracted herself from a bright orange panel van.

"How'd it go in the ah-chivvies?" Tara's salt-and-pepper hair was uncovered and stuck out in random tufts all over her head. No one could have resisted her broad caricature of a Maine accent and deliberate mispronunciation and Kendra was no exception. She grinned broadly at her visitor, taking in the flowing pink-and-white caftan and the green knee-highs beneath.

"Turns out I'm the result of an elopement," she answered. "Or rather my paternal grandmother was."

"Expected you'd be in to tell me about it before this."

"I would have, Tara, but when I was in town you were . . . busy. I didn't want to interrupt."

Tara's snort told her she knew exactly who'd been with her, and she swept into the house with her head held high. Once inside, however, the disdain faded. She looked around her with avid interest, taking in every detail. "Nice place."

"I'm guessing Olive left me the land to repay an old debt."

"Too bad there wasn't any cash left."

"I'll manage."

"Honey, you can't live without money. What are you going to do for a job till your book sells?"

Kendra just stared at her. She hadn't told anyone about her writing. "How—"

"Shouldn't have used the post office in Quaiapen if you wanted to keep it a secret. So, about the day job you'll need until you find a publisher—how about coming to work for me?" She didn't leave time for an answer, rushing on with all the subtlety of a steam-roller. "Look, you like my place, don't you?"

"Yes, but Tara, I don't have a money problem. Honestly. I...well, I guess you could say there's some money waiting for me when I need it."

"Trust fund? Well, I'll be darned."

Kendra neither agreed with her nor denied her guess. She busied herself perking a fresh pot of coffee. Tara would find out the truth eventually, but there was no reason to tell her yet.

"Here I thought you might let pride stand in the way of earning enough to eat on. I really could use some help, you know. Have to close the place down every time I want to go anywhere. That's why I'm on your doorstep so early."

"I appreciate the job offer. Really." Kendra was oddly touched by the other woman's thoughtfulness toward a virtual stranger.

"Also wanted to bring you this." Reaching into her huge black canvas carryall, Tara pulled out a musty, much-repaired, leather-bound volume. The title was obscured by age and layers of dirt, but Tara had marked one yellowed, crumbling page. "Look here," she ordered, turning the book with a flourish. "Your ancestor."

Gingerly, Kendra took the volume out of her hand and noted that it was the county directory for 1872–73. Tara had opened it to the history section and was jabbing one ragged fingernail at midpage. "Josias Buttenbeck," Kendra read aloud, "came from Connecticut with his cousins Thomas and William Grant in 1795. In 1797 he removed to the Carrabec River and started a gristmill at the falls."

"That's just below here," Tara told her. "Keep the book. It's not in good enough condition to sell."

Holding it carefully, wondering if it could be fumigated, Kendra thanked her and poured the coffee into two brightly painted ceramic mugs.

Chatting idly, seemingly touching random topics, they kept coming back to Wakefield McKee. "Does he own your building, too?" Kendra asked. "He always seems to be in there."

The other woman's face went hard. "Not yet. Hates that, too. You wouldn't think it this time of year, but I do a good business in my place. This is tourist country. Skiing in winter. Camping, boating and canoeing in the summer. Foliage tours in the fall. You're here during our only off season."

"I'm surprised there isn't a spring foliage tour. It becomes more beautiful every day."

"Shh. Give us one time to enjoy the place ourselves! Besides, if there was a spring season, we'd have to come up with a new name for the out-of-staters."

"What do you mean?"

"Well, the ones in the fall are leaf-peepers. After Memorial Day they're summer complaints. And in winter, we have ski bums. We'd have to think of something for this time of year. Hardly worth the effort."

Laughing, Kendra agreed. "We should just enjoy the season ourselves. It's certainly colorful. Every time I turn around, there are more flowers coming up."

Most had been naturalized, so that tulips, grape hyacinths and daffodils bloomed among the tall grasses between the dooryard and the woods. Closer to the house were planted beds, colorful with pale blue forget-me-nots, white candytuft, purple and yellow pansies and pink creeping phlox. Even the two rose-bushes by the porch seemed about ready to burst into color, and lilac and forsythia dotted the long drive-way.

"Wait till the lupines come up. And the iris, and daylilies. Nice thing is, you don't have to give them a bit of care." Tara nodded sagely. "Yeah. Place looks good. First time I've seen it, you know. I was never invited out when she was here. She liked to be on her own. Oh, she came in for Grange suppers and garden club, and she was in Eastern Star and the D.A.R., but she wasn't real sociable. Never hosted meetings here. Did you know you had an asparagus patch over there?"

Pointing a bony finger through the window toward one corner near the trees, Tara followed through by catching Kendra's hand and dragging her outside. The thick green shafts, half hidden by grasses, were al-ready a foot high.

"Snap those suckers off three-quarters of the way down and have them for supper," Tara advised. "If you let them grow much longer, they'll go to seed."

"Seems as though I could live off the land out here if I needed to."

"Probably could. That trust fund of yours gener-ous?"

"I won't have to work unless I want to," Kendra told her evasively.

"What would you think of owning half a bookstore?"

"That would be one way to put an end to McKee's harassment."

"God, woman, but you're sharp. It's this way. With the mill rate forcing taxes up and a balloon payment due on my mortgage at the bank, McKee might be able to stage an unfriendly takeover. Just like the old melodrama villains, McKee's always ready to step in, buy up a mortgage and foreclose. Think about it. Profits aren't great but it's a tidy little investment."

"I'll think about it," Kendra promised.

"Speaking of McKee, how'd you like to see him in action?" The sudden image of Wakefield McKee twirling a black mustache and threatening a little girl and her mother with eviction brought a smile to Kendra's face. As usual, Tara didn't wait for her to answer. "He's got an estate auction tomorrow. Out at the old Benson place. Probably what he'd have done here if you hadn't showed up."

"You mean he's selling off the contents of a house? He wouldn't have done that here. I'd have come in June when school got out, or sooner if the place had been sold. He couldn't have disposed of Olive's things without my approval."

"Some people aren't so careful what they sign. Or so conscientious about checking things themselves. Benson's heirs are all from out of state. Couldn't be bothered to come. They'll take McKee's word on the income from the auction, just like they took his appraisal of the contents when the inventory was done for probate. If he slips out the best items first for himself, no one will ever be able to prove it."

"But that's unethical. And illegal."

Tara's blue eyes snapped. "That's McKee."

Long after Tara had left, promising to meet her the next morning in Quaiapen and drive both of them to the auction, Kendra was still wondering about Wakefield McKee. Was he behind all the odd things that had been happening to her? The conclusion seemed logical, if any interpretation could be considered reasonable in light of the strange events of her first days in Quaiapen. Even odder was that nothing had happened since. In mysteries, it was never the obvious suspect who turned out to be guilty. Usually it was the least likely person. That would be Alex, she decided.

On Saturday morning Tara drove her van south from Quaiapen and out into farming country, until they reached a three-story brick farmhouse. Tents had been set up in the front yard to accommodate bidders.

"No antiques at this one, just good solid furniture and some farm tools. And books. There are at least a dozen box lots, and I've got my eye on one of them for a mint-condition first edition of May Sarton's first book."

"How do you know it's there?"

"Preview yesterday. I came by here after I left your place. Of course, lots of other people saw it, too, but I'm hoping I'm the only one who knows some out-of-stater will pay good money for it. I do a lot of mail-order business to fill in with the walk-in trade."

At the back of Kendra's mind Tara's proposal had taken root and grown. Her rapport with the older woman, like her love for Alex, had blossomed quickly.

She was certain they would become good friends, and positive the bookstore was a good investment. Now if only Alex would come up with a similar proposal about merging their futures, she'd know she'd made the right decision when she came to Quaiapen.

Almost as if she'd conjured him, Alex appeared on the far side of the auction tent. He was not in uniform, and Kendra realized suddenly that he must be back on the night shift again. Hard as she tried, she could not stop a wrenching sort of hurt from ripping through her. Why hadn't he come by? Had their night together in Augusta meant so little to him? Surely he'd talked to Denny. Wasn't he experienced enough at spotting lies to know whether the boy was telling the truth or not?

She wanted to run away, but Tara had brought her. She wasn't even sure she could find her way back to Quaiapen on her own if she had a car. Maybe Alex wouldn't notice her, she thought, and then realized that she wanted him to see her, needed to force him to acknowledge her in some way.

"Woo-wee!" Tara exclaimed. "Get a load of Alex. He's brought Jody and Denny to the auction. If that don't beat all. I wonder if they're getting together again."

How could she have missed seeing it? Kendra blinked and focused. She'd been so intent on looking at Alex that she'd overlooked the fact that Jody was with him. No, not just with him, draped all over him. Denny was a little to one side, looking extraordinarily pleased with himself.

Blinking back tears that angered her as much as Alex did, Kendra turned away from the happy family and followed Tara blindly toward the tent.

"That's Eames Gerow," Tara whispered, oblivious to Kendra's struggle to look calm and collected. "He's the auctioneer." She pointed toward a tall, skinny man with arms like toothpicks. His hair was thinning on top and slicked back on the sides. His personality seemed oily, too, and when they were close enough to hear his voice Kendra decided he sounded the way she felt when she'd put too much suntan lotion on her skin.

Intent on rearranging the items on the platform, he took no notice of Tara or Kendra until the larger woman's caftan swung wide and knocked a small vase off a nightstand. "You broke it, you bought it!" Gerow said. "Twenty dollars."

"Stuff it, Eames. It was worth two, tops." She pulled out two ones from her black bag and Gerow accepted them without another word. "Actually only worth one," Tara whispered to Kendra when his back was turned.

The jumble of junk before them was formidable. There was everything from snowshoes to food processors, soiled table linen to art deco figurines. Furniture predominated, from old trunks and a scratched chest of drawers to a beat-up modern recliner with holes in its seat. It wasn't easy to pick their way through, especially with everyone else doing the same thing, but Tara insisted it was necessary to inspect everything before making a bid.

"I don't plan to bid," Kendra protested.

"So you say. The fever will hit you when you least expect it." She continued to explore everything, double-checking the boxes of books she'd pawed through the day before, and even opening drawers in the bureaus to examine the contents.

Dozens of boxes littered the platform, some filled with books and others with glassware or china, and some simply catchalls for unidentifiable objects. Below, Kendra could see a crowd gathering. Folding chairs had been set up under the tent and many were already staked out by avid bidders who had left coats and boxes full of newspaper to save their places. Near the back, Alex Moreau sat between his ex-wife and his son, but he was watching her.

Turning quickly away, Kendra found Tara again and babbled questions. "How do I bid if I want to? Should I sit on my hands for fear of making some move Gerow will take as a bid? Do they take checks?"

With a laugh, Tara led her to the foot of the platform where a woman with a cash box was guarding a stack of numbered cards. "If you want to bid, you wave this."

Nodding, her mind only half on the instructions, Kendra took the card. Tara found seats for them on the left-hand side, in the twelfth row, but Kendra felt as if Alex's eyes were boring into the back of her head. It took every ounce of willpower she possessed not to turn around and look at him.

Once the auction started, it was not as difficult. Gerow was a showman. Banging a gavel on the speaker's podium, he began with a flourish, gesturing toward an assistant holding a cardboard box full of paperbacks. Kendra had noticed it when she'd explored the platform. Unlike most of the things for sale, the contents of this box looked as if they'd been water damaged.

"What am I bid for this fine collection of literature?" Gerow pulled out one dog-eared, mildewed volume and held it up. "A choice specimen. Very sexy cover art." He leered at the cover in question but did not show it to his audience. "What am I bid? Give me a hundred dollars. Start her off here. Give me a fifty-dollar bill. Who'll give me fifty?"

"One dollar," the man in the front row called and held up his card.

"I hear one. Do I hear two? Two, gimme two, gimme two! Come on, folks! Must be forty books in here. They sell for four, five times that these days. Gimme two."

"One-fifty!" Tara yelled, waving her card with one hand and scribbling in a notebook with the other. "Never can resist a bargain," she mumbled under her breath.

"Got one-fifty, gimme two! Two? Two, anybody? Dollar-fifty once. Dollar-fifty going twice. Any takers? Okay, suckers, you lose. Sold to the lady for a buck-fifty! Now we've got a real find."

As Gerow held up a battered wooden duck decoy, Wakefield McKee slid into the empty seat next to Kendra. She tried to ignore him, but he inched closer, taking her elbow and whispering in her ear as Gerow went on with his spiel.

"Beautiful sculpture of a Maine eider drake decoy," Gerow shouted at the crowd. "Seventeen inches long, with original paint. Found in the attic. Could be the twin of one that sold at an auction a few years back for $725."

"Could be," McKee whispered, "but not likely. May I buy you a hot dog, Ms. Jennings?"

"Thank you, no."

But McKee was insistent. He was disturbing everyone sitting near them. Finally Tara suggested they both go with him to the refreshment stand set up at the back. "We'll ditch him as soon as we eat," she muttered to still Kendra's protests.

When Kendra rose, she noticed that Alex had left Jody and Denny and disappeared. Meanwhile, McKee clung like a leech, touching her hand, her elbow, her back. Her skin crawled even when he kept his distance, and she thought she'd rather be mauled by Eames Gerow.

"Sit on the outside when we go back," Tara suggested. "McKee doesn't want my company." She seemed amused by Kendra's discomfiture, but at least the ploy worked. After several futile efforts to persuade Tara to change seats, McKee wandered off to supervise the next items due up for bids.

"That's the box lot I wanted," Tara declared a few minutes later. "Why don't you go wait at the van while I settle up? We'll head back to the shop and I can show you what a good deal it would be for some well-heeled investor."

Glad to escape, Kendra fled the auction tent and rounded the abandoned house to reach the area where the cars had been parked. She was only halfway there when an arm snaked out and Alex pulled her into the shade of a chestnut tree.

"Having fun with McKee?"

"Don't start, Alex. I've had enough trouble with that slug. I don't need an argument with you."

Side by side, not touching, they continued to walk toward Tara's van. "Sorry."

"How could you think I'd want to sit by him?"

"Women have been known to find him attractive."

"Not one with any taste!" The words were scarcely out before she remembered that Alex's ex-wife had supposedly preferred McKee. She hadn't today, though. Kendra wondered why she'd let Alex wander off. Jody struck her as the possessive type.

"I talked to Denny." Alex's voice gave nothing away.

"And?"

"Looks like a misunderstanding." At her lifted eyebrow he came to a halt in the open. "You just misunderstood. Denny went out to your house to talk to you because he'd seen us together in town. He was afraid you would keep me from getting together with his mother."

Obviously a needless fear, Kendra thought, and wondered if Alex had explained to his son that she was just someone he'd needed to get out of his system. When she said nothing aloud, Alex's voice softened.

"Denny's turned over a new leaf. He's even been studying harder. Jody gives me credit for the change."

"So now Denny can do no wrong?"

"I didn't say that. Look, Kendra, I admit two of his friends might have been involved in your troubles, but I don't think Denny was."

"Did you trace the blue car?"

"George, Gil and the car have disappeared. But the point is, they dropped Denny at camp that Monday, before they headed south. He wasn't with them when they ran you off the road. It must have been Gil you saw, not Denny."

"I can't buy that Alex. Talk to Denny again. Please?" Her hands went to his shoulders, instinctively trying to force a reaction. She searched for some spark of emotion in his hooded eyes, but his expression was carefully blank. Then Kendra's gaze was caught by a flutter of color beyond, near the corner of the brick house.

Jody stood there, watching, and when she realized Kendra had spotted her she boldly met her gaze. In the long, tense moment before Jody moved back out of sight, Kendra recognized the determination on her face. Whatever relationship Jody had with McKee, right now she wanted her ex-husband back. She had no intention of letting Kendra take him away.

"Kendra?"

Jerking her hands away, Kendra hurried toward the orange van. Alex caught up with her as she fumbled at the door handle.

"There's more we have to talk about."

"There's nothing left to say." She scrambled into the seat and slammed the door before he could touch her again. The chemistry was still there, but she could keep the elements from coming in contact with one another. She would prevent the reaction from taking place. She had to.

"I'll talk to him again," Alex said quietly. He looked as miserable as she felt.

"It doesn't matter."

"Of course it matters."

"Not any more."

Tara's arrival produced an uncomfortable silence. Ignoring them both, she loaded her two boxes of books into the back of the van, then climbed into the driver's seat. She started the engine before she looked from Kendra to Alex and back again. "Ready to go?"

Kendra nodded.

"Kendra! This is ridiculous!"

In a burst of irrational anger, she rolled down her window just as Tara started to pull away. "Go back to your wife!" she shouted.

Chapter 9

On Tuesday, off duty for the next three days, Alex drove out to his camp. Early in the afternoon, he launched the canoe. He told himself he hadn't meant to head south along the lakeshore toward Kendra's house. He told himself he was just out getting some exercise, enjoying the first day of warm weather on Square Lake. He told himself he'd go down through the connecting lakes to the river, then back. No sense overtaxing muscles that hadn't been used for paddling in months.

Without conscious intention, he looked toward the shore as he passed and realized what he had probably known but forgotten. The inlet curved in such a way that the dock and house were almost invisible from the water.

The other houses and camps along the chain of lakes that ran north from Quaiapen almost to the Canadian border were built to see and be seen. They stood on top of rocky cliffs, or overlooking small private beaches, or in clusters at the ends of camp roads. Only one, the house Olive had left to Kendra, was concealed. By road or by water, it had protection from prying eyes.

Perhaps it was better he couldn't catch a glimpse of her or the house. What if McKee's car was parked in the dooryard? Alex was still simmering, three days later, at the proprietary way McKee had taken Kendra's arm. Jody claimed they'd been seeing each other. Jody claimed a lot of things. He hadn't really believed her, but he'd been looking for an excuse to avoid Kendra. She made him want too much and it scared the hell out of him.

His thoughts turned to McKee. The man had been careful to keep out of Alex's way, but the grapevine in Quaiapen updated his movements. He'd increased pressure on the main-street merchants. Nothing illegal, but unlike McKee's usual tactics. In the past he'd shown more patience, content to sit back and wait for his prey to grow weak enough for an easy kill. And Jody had distanced herself from him. With self-preservation instincts intact, Alex's ex-wife still worked in McKee's real estate office but had moved to a small house on the outskirts of Quaiapen, renting it from Millie's youngest boy while he and his wife went off to survival school in Wyoming.

Just before he reached the falls, Alex turned the canoe around. The last seven nights had been brutal on the job. There had been domestic complaints, a filling station robbery, an untraceable counterfeit Canadian five surfacing at the convenience store in South New Queepeg. To top things off he'd covered an unattended death and two automobile accidents, one between a moose and a pickup and the other between a fully loaded log truck out of Canada and a telephone pole.

The only bright spot to come out of any of these was a share of the moose steaks in his freezer. Any time the driver didn't want the deer or moose that had demolished his car, the sheriff had it butchered and split among the deputies.

Except for that day at the auction, Alex had avoided his ex-wife. Denny's fixation with reuniting his parents had slowly faded. Alex had been appalled when Denny first explained his reason for threatening Kendra. He thought he'd finally convinced his son that the cause was hopeless, but now Jody seemed to be promoting the idea.

Alex paddled harder. He'd done nothing to encourage her. He'd even avoided her when he knew he ought to question her. He wanted the truth from Jody about McKee and Kendra. It had to have been another of Jody's lies. Kendra was too smart to take up with Wakefield McKee.

"You've got no claim on her, Moreau," Alex muttered, thrusting the paddle into the calm, clear water with too much force. His abrupt, awkward movement nearly upset the canoe and forced him to settle down. Usually the peace and solitude of the chain of lakes worked its magic instantly. Today he felt he'd been caught in a whirlpool.

How many times in the past week had he told himself he couldn't afford strong feelings for Kendra Jennings? He'd forced himself to stay away from her. She was all wrong for him. She was a woman who, though she'd been the victim of a senseless crime, had an overactive imagination. She distrusted all teenagers.

She'd interfere between him and Denny. She had already.

Besides, soon she'd tire of Quaiapen. If he let his feelings for her grow, she'd just be at him to move on, the same way Jody had. She might not want to go back to Burlington, but she'd soon miss the so-called advantages of city life—theaters, restaurants, art galleries. Hell, she'd been born in New York. Of course the country couldn't hold her forever.

It occurred to him she might not want to see him again, that she regretted what had happened between them. She'd turned to him out of fear and yielded to that powerful aphrodisiac, danger survived. When the danger was past, so was the excitement.

Good for your ego to think this way, Moreau, he told himself. He'd had no business going back to her motel room. He deserved to be dumped. As it turned out, he'd just beaten her to the punch.

So he tried to believe, but the logic of this argument did nothing to assuage a cloying loneliness that had crept under his skin and into his thoughts, keeping him awake and robbing him of control. He'd handled himself badly when he talked to Kendra on Saturday. He'd been so rattled by the depth of his own feelings that he'd given her no chance to express hers.

Thinking back to Augusta, he wanted to believe she'd meant what she'd said. Kendra had called him addictive. He'd felt the same way about her. Within hours, put off by the first sign of a break in their harmony, he'd convinced himself addictions were a sign of weakness and suppressed his desire for her ruthlessly, cutting them both off. Ever since, he'd been alternating between pride in his strength of will and fury at his own pigheadedness.

Alex took his time, paddling slowly, delaying the moment when he would once more be abreast of Kendra's house. For a while he let the canoe drift and tried to concentrate on his plans for the summer ahead. Then he'd bring fishing rods and a cooler of beer with him onto the lake and unwind slowly. He'd always liked being alone on the water. It bothered him to find he had changed the word to lonely, and was wondering if Kendra had ever been out in a canoe, or fished for lake trout, or camped out overnight on an island.

Underwater currents turned the canoe toward shore and he didn't correct the course. He'd keep his distance, he promised himself. He'd just stop in for a moment and make sure she was all right.

Gliding silently alongside the dock, the canoe brought him close enough to hear the rhythmic thwack of ax on wood. She'd gotten someone out to cut firewood for her, he thought as he tied the bowline and climbed out of the canoe. Not McKee. McKee avoided anything that made him sweat. Unsure whether he felt relieved or frustrated that he wouldn't have to see her alone, Alex rounded the corner of the house and stopped short. She hadn't hired anyone.

Unaware that she was no longer alone, Kendra's concentration was fixed on a foot-long section of birch. She'd already split three logs, varying in circumference from a foot to fifteen inches. Quartered, they had been tossed in the direction of the open woodshed door.

That shed should've been full of wood, Alex thought as he approached, unnoticed. His canvas shoes made no sound. He hadn't checked when he'd shown her how to use crumpled-up newspaper and small, split pieces of wood for kindling. He'd assumed Olive had stockpiled plenty, just as she'd made sure the oil tank that fueled the generator to provide light and power for the pump was full. He knew well enough that the temperature had dropped to near freezing the night before, in spite of weather in the seventies during the day, but he couldn't imagine how Kendra could have used up an entire winter's supply of wood in two weeks.

Exercise had worked up a sweat, and the shirt Kendra had started out in had quickly been abandoned. Now she wore only jeans and a T-shirt that clung damply to her bosom and back as she worked. Her hair had been scraped together into a ponytail and there were streaks of dirt across her brow where she'd wiped moisture away with gloved hands. Alex watched her raise the splitting maul and bring it down, admiring the sway of her breasts beneath the thin cotton. Then his heart lurched into his throat as the blade caught a knothole.

Abruptly halting her downward sweep, the jarring impact threw Kendra off balance. She tried to compensate, immediately releasing the long wooden handle, but that only sent her tumbling over backward. She landed hard, in a shower of sawdust, and grimaced as the chunk of birch tumbled from the cutting block and struck her ankle.

Before she could catch her breath, Alex was there. His hands caught her from behind, hauling her upright and pulling her tight against him. She was so small, so fragile, he thought. She shouldn't be out here doing this kind of work. His voice, close to her ear, was gruff with worry. "Are you all right?"

Stunned by his sudden appearance, Kendra couldn't find words. Everywhere their bodies touched an electric current ran through her. She tried to struggle free, but he only held her tighter, turning her in his arms until her breasts were crushed against his chest and her head was nestled snugly in the hollow of his throat.

Then he was murmuring into her hair and lifting her face to rain gentle kisses on her closed eyes, her cheeks, her mouth. Powerless to resist, she arched toward him, meeting his mouth with a fervor of her own. For several moments they clung, lips locked, savoring the sensation of holding each other.

"I'm all sticky with sweat," she whispered when he released her mouth and began to nibble at her neck.

"I like you sweaty." His lips moved upward to lick the salty beads that had formed in front of her ear. Fevered fingers slid under the bottom of her T-shirt, easing the damp cloth away from her back. "It reminds me that we once worked up quite a sweat together."

"I remember. I've missed you." She couldn't begin to tell him how much. Instead she let her body speak, running her palms up his strong, sinewy arms as she thrust her hips forward and let her head fall back. Her eyes were already glazing over as she watched him through her lashes. There was passion in his gaze—and devilry.

Before she knew what he intended, he'd pulled the T-shirt over her head, leaving her naked to the waist. He cut off her cry of protest with another kiss before his lips moved lower, trailing a line of fiery kisses along the tops of her bare breasts.

"Alex, stop," she begged, but she made no effort to push him away. It felt too good. "What if someone comes by and sees us?"

His answer was a chuckle as he sank back onto the stump she'd been using as a splitting block and pulled her toward him until she sat astride his lap. "I'm not letting you go," he growled as his hands molded themselves to her buttocks and urged her even closer to the proof of his desire for her. His mouth and tongue continued their worship of her breasts until Kendra no longer cared if anyone saw. Alex had come back to her. He still wanted her. Nothing else mattered.

"The shed," Kendra urged as her own needs welled up inside her and threatened to explode. She wrapped her legs around his waist. He wouldn't have to let go.

Alex stood, still holding her tightly to him, and moved toward the door. If he was surprised to see that it opened into the house beyond he gave no sign but carried her straight through until they could both tumble down onto her overstuffed sofa.

Already working on his buttons, Kendra left him no doubt about her growing enthusiasm. The flannel work shirt slid aside, and her fingers caressed his chest. Her lips found and suckled his nipples before she caught one of the few sparse strands of chest hair between strong white teeth and pulled.

The tiny prick of pain brought Alex momentarily back to his senses. She lay beneath him on the soft cushions, willing and eager, and he had to pull away. Swearing softly, he supported himself on his elbows and tried to shift away from her. He could never quite forget that Denny had been produced out of just this same sort of unbridled passion. Unplanned pregnancy had forced Jody into a reluctant and ill-fated marriage. He'd been ready and willing to marry and start a family. She had resented being trapped and soon had hated him for it.

"Kendra, we've got to stop." His voice sounded strangled, and her first response was to catch his waist, her grip stronger than he'd expected, and pull them back into intimate contact.

At his agonized groan, her luminous blue eyes opened wide. She didn't want to believe what she had heard. "Why?" she whispered. Her pupils were huge and passionate, and her eyes brimmed with tears.

"Damn. Kendra, I'm sorry. I didn't expect to end up like this. I didn't come prepared."

The sudden quivering spreading all through her body startled him, and it took a moment for him to recognize it for what it was. She was laughing. Giggles bubbled up from somewhere deep inside her. Her tears of frustration had been replaced by a shy, radiant smile. "That's been taken care of."

"You're on the pill? For me?"

"Of course for you. You're the only one I want, Alex. I'd have gone crazy if you'd stayed away much longer."

Her words pleased him more than he could admit aloud, but he had the unnerving sensation that this one time she could read everything he felt in his eyes. Her smile deepened slowly, smoldering, as if she knew impossibly ancient truths.

"Come here, Alex."

Enthralled, he bent to kiss her again, deftly undoing and removing what remained of their clothing as he relearned her body and let her rediscover his. "I've missed you, too," he murmured as the last thin barrier slipped away.

Mind floating, Kendra gave herself to the sensations without resistance. In yielding, melting like butter on a hot roll, she knew a growing sense of power. He was as aroused as she, as caught in the whirlpool of emotions their mutual longing had produced.

Both relinquished control, letting delicious, desperate desires take them to new heights of passion. They could no longer tell where one's heartbeat left off and the other's began.

Need burned between them, out of control, bringing pleasure and amazement and something deeper, as yet unnamed. All sense of place and time disappeared as they gave and took, melded and caressed. Urgency grew, throbbing, until release flooded over them, through them, and they gasped each other's names aloud.

Silence settled over the living room. They lay, spent, in each other's arms. He was heavy on top of her, but she loved the weight. When he started to move away, she clasped her hands around his neck and kissed him again.

"I'm crushing you." They rose together to kneel on the sofa, face-to-face.

"You make me feel fragile. I'm not, really." She giggled, a girlish innocence in the sound. "But I really do need a shower."

"Go on, then." With one smooth motion he'd set her on her feet and scrambled up behind her. "I'll get a fire started in the fireplace."

Kendra looked outside, astonished. She had lost all sense of time. The afternoon was rapidly drawing to a close. The living room was chilled. Smiling to herself, she hurried toward the stairs. He was going to stay the night. That was why he'd offered to build the fire.

The face that met her gaze in the oak-framed oval mirror in her bedroom looked radiant. A bride's face, she thought, and felt vague surprise that the fantasy no longer frightened her. When she'd washed her hair and bathed, Kendra slipped into the bright green silk robe she'd bought herself one birthday and never found an occasion to wear. She had one now. Already she could imagine how it would feel when Alex untied the sash and ran his warm, loving hands inside the fabric to find her bare skin.

He was standing at the kitchen counter when she went down. A mug of coffee was in one hand, but his eyes were on the printout in the other. It was the copy of *Cloud Castles* she'd received in the morning mail. Rejected twice now, she thought, once by Henry and now by a publisher. If Alex laughed at her effort it would hurt far more than either.

Apparently unaware of her, Alex continued to read, so absorbed that he'd forgotten to drink the coffee. She stayed frozen in the doorway, wishing she could see his face but afraid to go closer, afraid to breathe.

She wished she'd hidden it somewhere, as she had her notes for the new book when Tara visited. Her computer was unobtrusive on one end of the counter. Only the telltale manuscript and rejection slip had been left as evidence.

Trust Alex to home right in on them the moment her back was turned. Kendra knew she ought to feel angry at him, resent his snooping, but a sense of vulnerability was more powerful than any other reaction.

Willing herself to be brave, to withstand the pain when it came, to sound calm, she whispered, "What do you think?"

"It's good, Kendra," he said without looking at her. "Makes me remember what it was like to be eight years old again."

The disappointment she'd felt that morning, when she'd picked up her mail and found the manuscript, finally abated. The manuscript had been accompanied by a form rejection letter that indicated no one had even glanced at it during its brief sojourn in New York City. Alex was the first person to read her polished, carefully nurtured final draft. Henry had seen it only in an early stage. Alex had read her best effort, and approved.

There were no words to tell him what she felt about his response, just as she'd had no words earlier that afternoon. She simply went to him, circling his waist with her arms, and rested her head against his broad back.

Alex took her hands and kissed each palm, and said words she could scarcely believe. "Beautiful, and talented, and mine." Then he was leading her back through the house until they were in front of the fireplace. Clinging mindlessly, they sank to the floor, wrapped together atop the huge oval rug, and once more the rest of the world faded away.

"I'm hungry," Kendra whispered. The fire was nearly out and it was pitch-dark outside the windows. She hadn't felt like eating lunch, not with that rejection letter burning a hole in her heart, and it was now long past supper hour.

She felt the rich rumble of his chuckle beneath her. "Worked up an appetite, did you?"

"Splitting wood will do that."

Turning his attention to stoking the second dying fire, in the wood stove in the kitchen, he didn't respond to her teasing at once. He waited until she had started bacon frying in the kitchen. "Whatever possessed you to play lumberjack? There should have been plenty of wood already cut."

"There wasn't. I cut what we're using tonight over the past week. Today I didn't need more fuel. I needed to take out my aggressions on something inanimate."

Her eyes strayed to the counter. Following the direction of her glance he picked up the form letter. She knew well enough what it said. It thanked her for her submission and regretted to inform her that the publisher was no longer accepting unsolicited manuscripts. The information in the latest writer's guide had already been out of date. She'd heard that happened, that editors and policies sometimes changed rapidly, but it hadn't lessened the hurt that came from failure her first time out.

"So how do you get solicited?" Alex asked. His arms circled her waist and his lips nuzzled the back of her neck.

"This is a good start," she whispered, leaning back and tilting her head for another kiss.

"Much as I like being distracted," he murmured against her lips, "I do want to know. This is a good story, Kendra. When I was a kid, I would have loved it. You already know I see race cars in the clouds. I should have known the moment I admitted that to you that we had something special between us. I've never told anyone else." He kissed her lightly on the forehead. "You'll find a publisher for your story. I have faith in you."

"Don't worry. I'm not about to give up. The children's book industry is something I've been studying carefully. Patience is an essential prerequisite. Even if these people had wanted to buy my manuscript, a year or more might have passed before it was published. For one thing, the text would have to be matched with an illustrator.''

"But you did sketches. In that little booklike thing."

He left her side to fish it out of the envelope.

Checking first to be sure the bacon would cook safely on its own for a few minutes, Kendra went to stand beside him as he leafed through the thirty-two pages.

"I like the way you draw kids," Alex said, throwing one arm around her shoulders and giving her a squeeze.

"Their heads are too big. They're cartoony. A real artist could make them live."

"No. These are great. You should insist they take the whole package. Why else make up the booklet?"

"Dummy," she corrected. As she felt his arm stiffen, she laughed. "It, not you. The booklet's called a dummy. It's designed to give an editor an idea of what I had in mind." She turned to break four eggs into the cast-iron fry pan on the wood stove. Just knowing he thought her writing was good had restored her optimism. "I just have to keep trying."

"Hell of a way to make a living. It must be hard on the ego."

She shrugged. "There will be more rejections, I expect. But I mean to keep at this. Whacking away at the woodpile was just my way of dealing with a temporary setback."

She slid perfectly fried eggs onto two plates, added the bacon and served on the breakfast bar.

"You're amazing," Alex said sincerely. His left hand crept back across the Formica to catch her fingers as she slid onto the stool opposite him.

"I'll have to keep you around, if only as an antidote for the ego problem." Her words sounded light, but she watched him closely, fearful of what she might see in his expression.

The fingers tightened over hers fractionally, then released. "I should have come sooner," he admitted. "I was on night shift, which throws things out of kilter. I hoped you'd call if you needed me."

"I did almost call once." With an economy of words, she told him about her discovery of the empty woodshed with its hidden entry to the house and its keyless padlock.

"Odd way to build it," Alex said. "I've seen sheds connected to houses before, but none with doors disguised as paneling."

"I have no idea what might have been in there, but if someone wanted to remove it, doesn't that provide motive to keep me in Augusta overnight?"

"Makes sense. Especially since that blue car hasn't turned up. Neither have George or Gil. George's mother hasn't heard from him. She's filed a missing person report."

"Does that mean there's an…A.P.B. out for him?"

Alex chuckled. "No all-points bulletins for missing adults. I haven't even got enough evidence to order one in connection with your hit-and-run."

"So we just have to wait until he comes back to find out why he did it."

"We'll probably never know. Television gives you the impression that crimes are solved every time, but in real life there are hundreds of odd little things happening every day that are never satisfactorily explained."

"Poltergeists?"

"I don't rule anything out," he said with a chuckle, "but I've got the feeling both George and Gil are long gone. Got a flashlight?"

Together they examined the inside of the shed, but Alex saw nothing Kendra had overlooked. He locked it from the outside with her new dead bolt and came back in through the front door just in time to see her sliding the panel closed. She turned, eyes softening as she watched him close the distance between them. Then her gaze shifted invitingly to the sofa, and the still jumbled rug in front of the fireplace. He saw her eyes widen just before she sank to her knees, out of sight behind the couch.

He realized what had startled her as soon as he reached her side. The floor was wooden, made of evenly matched, highly polished oak planks. Beneath the area the rug had covered was a deep, jagged scratch, marring the surface.

"Something heavy," Alex said, kneeling at her side to run a finger over the scarred wood. "Moved in a hurry." They both looked toward the paneled wall.

"I really hate unsolved mysteries," Kendra said softly, rocking back onto her heels.

Alex agreed. Secrets bothered him, too. In a rush some of his earlier doubts about Kendra came back, and though he tried to fight them off, the questions could not all be stilled.

"What is it, Alex? You look worried."

Some answers she'd already given. He couldn't believe she'd ever been involved in anything with McKee, personal or professional. But there was still the matter of the cash. "Tell me about the money, Kendra."

He watched her brow furrow in confusion, then clear. "The Canadian five? I already spent it, for the lock."

Her eyes widened as she took in the shock on his face. She was reaching for him when he caught her hand and kept her at a distance. They were kneeling on the floor. They'd made love only inches away, twice. He knew he should no longer doubt her, but he couldn't help himself. Trust came too hard, even with Kendra.

"Alex, what is it? I just forgot to mention it. I found it in the dirt next to the shed. It looked as if it had been there all winter."

Slowly, inexorably, the pieces began to fall into place. Alex didn't doubt Kendra's story, but he had the sinking sensation that her discovery was just the tip of an iceberg. Releasing her wrist he stood, pacing as he told her, succinctly, about the spate of counterfeit Canadian money that had surfaced in the past weeks. "That scrape on your floor could be made by a printing press."

"Now who's got too much imagination?" Kendra repressed a shudder. She'd been trying to discount the nastiness of her experiences, but Alex's theory hinted at deeper danger.

A rueful smile surfaced and was quickly suppressed. "Unfortunately, my theory makes as much sense as any of our earlier explanations."

"Maybe so, but there's still no proof. Whatever was in there is gone now. And those boys have disappeared. It's over." She refused to mention Denny again. If he'd been involved, at least he hadn't taken off with his friends. He'd stayed in Quaiapen, and he had been trying to mend the rift with his father.

Alex's thoughts also went to his son. Reluctantly he admitted to himself that he'd have to talk to the boy again. Even if Denny had nothing to do with Kendra's troubles, he surely knew more about George and Gil than he'd admitted. "I hope it is over," he said aloud. "I'd rather concentrate on us than on crime."

"I'm willing." Kendra breathed a sigh of relief, but knew there was still something bothering him. Alex stiffened when she touched his arm, and turned slowly to face her.

"When I asked about the money I didn't mean the Canadian five. I meant the eight thousand American you brought with you from Vermont. You've got to admit it was a peculiar thing to do."

"Oh, that."

"Yes." Kendra's cheeks flamed with color and she tried to look away, but he caught her face gently between his palms. "What's the big secret? Tara says you have a trust fund. Is that it? Is that how you mean to support yourself while you write books?"

"Not exactly." Fearfully, she met his probing look but quickly recognized the caring and concern in his eyes. This was the man she loved. Of course she could confide in him. He'd understood about her writing. He would understand this, too.

"Tell me," he said softly. "No more secrets."

"It's going to seem silly when you know."

"I won't laugh."

"I don't know why I made such a big secret of it, except that I wanted to keep something to myself for once. I've misjudged in the past, blurting things out before I thought about other people's reactions to what I said."

"I've told you before I like your tendency to blurt. It's a rare gift to always tell the truth."

"Even when the truth isn't what you want to hear? I was scared, Alex. I felt I needed to think through every single ramification. I suppose I ran away. Sometimes, after I got here, I could even manage to forget about it, even though I knew I'd have to face up to it someday."

"Face up to what?" His mind was racing. Crime? Fraud? An abandoned or lunatic husband somewhere? She was right. He was developing a hell of an imagination.

Kendra took a deep breath. "Two million dollars," she said in a rush. "I'm the ticket-holder they've been looking for all month. The one who won Tri-State Megabucks and hasn't claimed it yet."

Chapter 10

After hesitating as long as she could at the end of the dock, fiddling with the buttons on her shirt and re-tying her shoelaces, Kendra finally realized she had to stop procrastinating and tell Alex the truth. "There's one thing left to confess," she said timidly.

Alex knelt at the side of his canoe, holding it steady. He wasn't unduly concerned. Some ten hours had passed since her midnight confession, hours spent together, in her bed, sometimes sleeping. In the bright morning sun he had no nagging suspicions left.

"I'm not really comfortable about going very far out on the lake. It's deep, isn't it? Over my head?"

"You don't swim?" He sounded incredulous, but at least he didn't laugh.

"Not very well. I never liked to let my head go underwater. Mother insisted on swimming lessons but I refused to jump in or dive. I made it all the way to the float on our local swimming hole once, though. And in theory I know how to tread water."

"I guess I shouldn't have expected a city girl to be comfortable on open water. I'll teach you to swim if you like."

Her head tilted, puzzled. "City girl? Where on earth did you get that idea?"

"You were born in New York, weren't you?"

"Sure. Upstate New York. Looks a lot like this. The town I grew up in wasn't much bigger than Quaiapen. We had trees and everything." There hadn't been miles of rural roads between towns, but neither had it been an urban environment. Kendra had always thought of herself as a small-town girl.

Alex grinned at her and stood, holding out his hand. "Good. Then you have no excuse not to enjoy the great outdoors, do you?" Teasing her, his dark eyes glimmered, and she couldn't help smiling back.

"Promise to fish me out if we tip over?"

"We won't tip over, and you'll be wearing a life jacket anyway." From the interior of the bright green canoe he produced two red nylon vests. Struggling into his own first, he then helped Kendra with hers, zipping up the front and dropping a light kiss on the end of her nose at the same time.

Dismayed, she looked down. "I thought these things were supposed to improve a girl's bust line." Closed, the vest flattened her completely.

Alex chuckled. "I like your figure just the way it is, but you're right. The old-style water wings used to be called Mae Wests. These are better. Come on." Steering her gently with one hand on each shoulder, he forced her across the dock to the canoe.

Tentatively, she planted one jogging shoe on the sloping interior but drew back, startled, as the canoe swayed and sank deeper into the cold, clear water. Alex wouldn't let her back up, but eased her forward, until both feet were in and she was sitting on a very small caned seat and facing the front of the canoe.

It seemed terribly flimsy, as if she were sitting right on the surface of the water. Kendra grasped much-too-low sides tightly and felt her stomach clench as the small craft wobbled again to announce Alex's entry behind her.

"Easy now," he said, his voice low and soothing.

"Are you talking to me or this canoe?"

"You are going to enjoy this, Kendra. Trust me."

Already white-knuckled, her grip tightened as the canoe slid away from the safety of her dock. At least they were only going a short distance, along the shore to Alex's camp. She shivered, although she wore heavy socks and blue jeans and had slipped on the warm quilted flannel shirt over a lightweight, short-sleeved sweatshirt. The water beneath them was nearly freezing. It would be July before it warmed up enough to contemplate swimming.

Grin and bear it, she told herself. After all, this was the first of his personal interests Alex had tried to share with her. If it was important to him, she'd just have to learn to like it.

To Kendra's amazement, soon after they got under way, her nervousness faded, her hold loosened and she began to enjoy the sensation of gliding over the water. The morning sun, bright in a cloudless azure sky, glinted off the dew still dotting green leaves and tufts of wildflowers on the nearby shore. There was no sign of the moose Kendra had seen her first day, but Alex pointed out the loon and held the canoe steady while they watched it dive.

Beneath the crystal-clear water, fish darted fearlessly close to the bottom of the canoe. Kendra trailed one hand and watched the landscape below, wondering how far down the sand and pebbles and boulders were. She could see plants growing, too, waving their long tendrils in the current.

Very quietly, Alex spoke. "Look toward the right, in that stand of birch. A vixen and her cubs are watching us."

Kendra stared back, enchanted, until the mother fox decided discretion was the better part of valor and scurried for cover, driving her rambunctious brood before her.

"Want to try paddling?"

"Aren't you afraid I'll tip us over?" To her own surprise, Kendra realized she'd nearly lost her fear of the water. When Alex was with her, nothing could possibly harm them.

"Next time," he suggested, "you paddle and I'll go along for the ride. I'll bring cushions and recline against them, eating grapes and trailing my hand in the water."

"Next time," she agreed. "I'll provide the grapes."

Unexpectedly, Alex turned the canoe and began to paddle toward the opposite shore. "There's something I want to show you."

Vivid sensual images turned Kendra's face crimson and she was glad she wasn't facing him, but Alex had something entirely different in mind. They came ashore at a tiny beach impossible to see from the center of the lake, and climbed up a bank and into the woods until they reached a small clearing. There, their weatherworn gray surfaces dappled with sun and shadow, stood three massive glacial boulders as high as a man's head.

Without stopping, Alex began to scramble up the rough surface of the largest rock and pulled Kendra after him. Once on top, she saw that the boulder had split and now had a pine tree growing from the center of a crevasse. In its shade, they finally stopped to catch their breath.

"This was my thinking place when I was a kid," Alex told her. "I'd spend hours here. That crack, you know, is really a cave. Indian or pirate, depending on my mood."

"Or bear," Kendra suggested. "This is wonderful. I may steal it for my next book."

"Take it as a gift." He sat, his long, muscular legs dangling into the crevasse, and for a moment seemed lost in thought.

Kendra lowered herself gingerly next to him, aware of the utter contentment she felt in this special spot. Alone, she might have been fearful, for there was no longer any sight or sound of civilization, but with Alex beside her she knew she had nothing to worry about.

When they had been still long enough, small sounds began again. A chipmunk came out of cover and stared up at them. A squirrel chattered in a tree above their heads. A woodpecker commenced his attack on a tree.

"This is the best time of year," Alex said softly, trying to lure the chipmunk closer by offering it a leaf left over from the previous fall. "It's too early for the mosquitoes and blackflies. In a few weeks we won't be able to come here without an inch-thick coating of fly dope."

"I'd like to come back in the fall," Kendra confided. "It must be beautiful here with all the colors."

"Need to be wary of hunters then."

"Do you hunt?" He must, she supposed, with his knowledge of guns, but he surprised her.

"I only shoot animals with a camera."

Why had he told her that? He hadn't thought about photography in years. As they sat together in companionable silence, watching the chipmunk make up its mind about them, he had a sudden vivid picture of himself at Denny's age. He'd been too thin, with gangly arms and legs, glasses, and a camera permanently strapped around his neck.

"Do you develop your own pictures?"

"Not any more. Lately all the photo work I've done has been for the sheriff's office at the county's lab. Nice stuff. Fatal accidents. Suspected arsons. Vandalized churches."

When she made no comment, he felt compelled to go on, to explain why it had been so reasonable for him to give up a dream. "In high school I won the annual photo contest three years running. I was your classic big fish in a little pond. Things changed when I went to college."

"Did you plan to study photography?"

"My dad was county sheriff until he retired. I was expected to get an associate degree in criminal justice and follow in his footsteps, but I did sneak in a couple of photography courses. Then I met Jody. After the divorce, I enlisted in the Navy. Dad thought I ought to become an M.P., but I balked. I put in for naval aviation because that branch included photography."

"Let me guess—they made you a cook on a submarine?"

His laugh was ironic. "Not that bad. I was trained as an aviation electrician's mate. You know how they recruit, with the slogan Join the Navy and See the World? I spent nearly the entire four-year tour of duty in Norfolk, Virginia. By the time I got out and came home, I was convinced someone was trying to tell me something, so I settled down like a dutiful son and went into law enforcement."

"Do you ever regret not taking more courses, setting up your own studio?"

He shrugged to disguise the sudden sadness he felt. "Most studio photographers end up taking senior class pictures to make ends meet. I always preferred wildlife." Right now, though, Alex thought, he'd like nothing more than to capture Kendra on film, here in this rustic setting. He smiled at his own fancy and dropped a light kiss on her forehead. "Let's head for camp. It's nearly time for lunch."

Once back on the lake, Kendra was amazed at how quickly she lost sight of the spot where they had beached the canoe. "You'd never find it if you didn't know where to look."

"Just like your place," he pointed out. "You're tucked away, by land and sea."

Neither of them said it aloud, but they were both thinking the same thing. That might be why someone had chosen Kendra's house for his nefarious doings. Alex paddled in silence until they reached the inlet around which several small camps had been built.

Unpretentious, the log cabin was as comfortable as her own house, and Kendra explored while Alex found fresh clothes. The plan was to spend the day together, which meant that soon they would have to talk about the two subjects they'd both avoided since the night before. Unwilling to let their idyll end, she seized on another topic of conversation as soon as he climbed out of the loft.

"Are these prints yours?" She gestured to four oak-framed black-and-white photographs, each of a different forest creature.

He nodded, looking embarrassed. "My mother insisted on framing them."

"She should have. They're wonderful. It must have taken hours of patient waiting to get these just the way you wanted them."

"More like dozens of bad shots for each good one. And a lot of hours in the darkroom."

"Do you have more?"

Humoring her, he unearthed an old album and left her looking through it while he went to make sandwiches and soup. No more than a few moments had passed, however, before she was at his side, making him want more than he could have again, both professionally and personally.

"These shots of clouds are wonderful, Alex. Maybe you should be the one illustrating my book."

"They were taken a long time ago."

"That doesn't mean you've lost your skill."

Alex pretended to be preoccupied with slicing ham until she gave up.

Another thing they had to avoid talking about, Kendra thought irritably. Not for long, she promised herself, and realized they could not put off the other subjects much longer, either.

His reaction to her news about the lottery had been reassuring. After the first shock, he'd seemed to understand why she was avoiding the publicity that would come as soon as her name was released. He'd even grasped her irresponsible need to see and feel the cash from her bank accounts. No check, certified or traveler's, would have been quite the same.

There was something still bothering him about her having all that money, though, even now that he knew she'd come by it honestly. She didn't think he had any moral objection to gambling, but there was a wariness when he spoke of the two million waiting for her to claim it. Surely he couldn't be insecure enough to think that his woman shouldn't have more money than he did?

The other topic they'd avoided was Denny. She still thought she could reach him, if only Alex would permit it. There had been a boy in one of her classes the first year she'd taught, a small, skinny kid named Ricky. His two older brothers had been hell-raisers and dropped out of school as soon as they could. By the time Ricky reached fourth grade, his teachers had written him off. He was just like his brothers. He was a slow learner. He was uncooperative. He was a troublemaker. When Kendra met him as a seventh grader, he had fulfilled all the expectations, and that had made her angry.

Maybe, she'd thought, if just one teacher had taken the time to know him as an individual, he might have been turned around. She'd come too late. At thirteen, Ricky had alternated between sleeping through classes and disrupting them. He'd told her, though, when he and another boy had successfully collaborated on creating a "radio play" on cassette tape, that she was the first teacher who'd ever made him want to come to school. The play had been titled *The Littlest Outlaws*.

Four years later, after dropping out of school, Ricky had been shot to death while robbing a liquor store.

"Don't furrow your brow like that. You'll end up with wrinkles."

Unable to face talking about Denny just yet, Kendra was tired of avoiding sensitive subjects. Either they could work things out or they couldn't. They might as well find out.

"Why does my win in the lottery bother you, Alex? I know it makes you uneasy. I can feel it."

"Sit down," he said, pointing toward the kitchen table. He brought the plates and soup bowls with him and poured two icy glasses of milk.

"Why don't you like the idea of my having money?"

Nervous fingers created a rat's nest in his freshly combed, mahogany-colored hair. "Damn it, Kendra. Every time I think I have things figured out, you throw me a curve."

"What did you have figured out?" Of its own volition her hand crept across the tabletop and closed over his wrist.

"You. Me. When I saw you doing your mountain woman act at the woodpile I figured I'd been wrong about you. You could belong here, stay here. Stay with me."

Their eyes met, mutually yearning. Staying together appealed to each of them, but the very force of their desire made them both cautious. Slowly, Alex slid his hand out of her grip and began to eat his soup. Kendra bit into her sandwich and found it tasted like cardboard. She swallowed, took a long sip of milk and then a deep breath.

"Why should learning I have money change that? It ought to make life easier."

"What will you do with it?"

It was her turn to shrug. "Live on it, so I can write. They don't give me the whole thing in a lump, you know. It's spread out over twenty years, and when the taxes are taken out—"

"You'll still get around a hundred thousand a year." His short burst of laughter sounded forced. "That has to be more than you made teaching."

"So I'll be able to afford to have power and phone lines run in to the house. Don't look so startled, Alex. I told you I meant to stay."

"What else?"

"Well, when my books start to sell, I guess I'll set up a trust fund of some sort, for my children."

His eyes narrowed, glittering dangerously. "What children?"

"Honestly! You are the most suspicious man! My future children. I'd like to have some, but at the moment I'm old-fashioned enough to think I'd like to acquire a husband first."

Jealous. He was jealous of the idea that she might marry someone else and have children. The realization that he wanted them to be his children shocked him into silence. He lifted the soup bowl and drained it, feeling the need for a shield between them. This was not supposed to happen. He was supposed to need her less as time went on, not more.

An awkward silence continued as they picked at their food. Finally Alex broke it, talking softly, not meeting her eyes. "Jody came from a very wealthy background. We fought about money all the time. It wasn't the only problem we had, but it was a big one."

"It bothered you that she had more money than you did?"

"Yeah. It did. I know, you aren't Jody."

"Not even close. She's a beautiful woman, Alex. It's no wonder you fell in love with her." Kendra sat, not daring to move, across from him at the table. His face was open to her, twisted by memories and regrets.

"Not inside, where it counts. She neglects Denny. I think she may have all his life, in spite of the money she lavished on him when he was younger. If she abused him physically I'd have her in court for a custody hearing in a second, but the only scars are emotional, and I'm responsible for some of those myself."

"Don't, Alex. You aren't to blame." Jody had scarred him, too. Kendra wanted to touch him, but she was afraid he would pull away. Clasping her hands in her lap, she waited. He needed to talk about his son, to purge the guilt, but his thoughts had already returned to his brief marriage.

"We fought almost constantly those few months we lived together. Money. My job. Having a baby. She didn't want him. She wanted to trap me, and as soon as I was neatly caged, she got bored. She whined. It nearly drove me crazy. And when that didn't work, she'd holler. You don't holler, do you, Kendra?"

"Only when we're making love."

Her voice was so quiet that he wondered if he'd heard her right. The soft words brought him back from the past into an immensely better present. Desire shot through him. Whatever problems they might have, enjoyment of each other was not one of them. Slowly, Kendra stood to move behind his chair and massage his shoulders until he tilted his head back for her kiss. "I can't seem to get enough of you," he confessed.

Seconds later he was out of the chair, sweeping her out of the kitchen area and up to the loft. The mattress was down-filled, deep and soft and perfect. For an hour, they forgot everything but each other.

Later, they fixed coffee and sat on the back porch, legs dangling off the edge as they watched birds flying over the lake. "Wouldn't it be nice if we never had to see another soul? We could stay here, or at my place, and live off the land."

He chuckled at her fantasy. "Hard work. In the good old days they died young. You'd soon tire of it. I know I would."

"I wouldn't get tired of you."

"I could make love to you all day long." He came very close to saying more, to uttering words that would mean a lasting commitment, but it was too soon, too fast. He told himself they should take their love day by day, if it was love. Kendra hadn't said she loved him. Perhaps, for her, he was only a casual affair. He had nothing to offer her except his passion.

Deliberately, he broke the spell of lake and solitude. "When are you going to claim the money?"

She felt his withdrawal, and shivered. "I don't know. Sometimes I wish I never had to claim it. If only I could sell three or four books right off I wouldn't need the money. I hate the thought of going back to Burlington and being on television and having my name made public. I'll attract all sorts of shady opportunists."

"They won't find you here."

"No." She hugged her knees to her chin and studied his profile, wishing she had some way to reassure him. The money would make no difference in how she felt about him. She said only, "I'll have to go back to Burlington eventually, I suppose."

"You could put in a claim from here."

"The ticket is in my safe-deposit box in Vermont. It made sense at the time. Just like paying my rent for three months and taking the remaining money in cash did. I wasn't thinking very clearly that day." The same day they'd met, she realized.

"You quit your job as soon as you heard."

Kendra nodded. "That was very clear thinking. It felt good. Sometimes I feel a little guilty, though. I had a responsibility to those kids."

"I thought you hated those kids."

"No. For some of them I have great affection. You see, it only takes one student, upset and seeking me out, to make me feel I'm a success."

"It can't have been such a bad career if you stayed at it eight years."

"Some years were better than others. Last year I had a particularly enthusiastic group."

"Think you can help me out with my kid?"

"I don't know, Alex, but I'd like to try."

"Come on, then, back to my place. After school gets out I'll call him and see if we can meet."

They stopped briefly at Kendra's house so she could put on town clothes. She was halfway back downstairs when Alex stopped her. "Why don't you bring a change of clothing and stay with me tonight?"

"Are you sure? Things may not go that well with Denny."

"I'm sure." His intensity frightened her a little.

"Maybe we should just come back here again."

"T.W. gets upset if I stay away too many nights in a row."

She hesitated, but only for a moment longer. Hoping she wasn't making a mistake, she returned to her room to pack a small overnight bag. She had no illusions. At least at first, Denny might refuse to talk if she was present. Alex might have to leave her at the apartment and go alone to Jody's house. In that case, she decided, she'd better have something to occupy her mind. Detouring to the kitchen, she collected both the returned manuscript and her notes for the new book and stuffed them into her shoulder bag.

Alex wanted her with him, no matter how it went with Denny. The thought lifted her spirits. Now that they had no more secrets, perhaps they could dare think of a future.

Without a qualm, she locked the dead bolts behind her and climbed into the passenger seat of Alex's truck. They were almost back to the highway before an alternative reason for his request dawned on her. "Alex, you don't think my house is safe, do you? You think someone's coming back again."

His jaw clenched, and when he spoke, his voice was carefully neutral. "It's crossed my mind. Call it cop's instinct, but there's still something not quite right about all this."

"You think McKee's behind it, don't you?"

A shrug was his only answer. He kept his eyes on the road to discourage conversation, but Kendra was not so easily put off.

"Maybe we should try harder to find out. He doesn't seem very bright. Maybe we can trick him into a confession."

"That's skirting close to entrapment."

"Not if he's already committed the crime."

"You've watched too many cop shows on television."

"That isn't the point, Alex. You know he made a play for me. Why don't I follow up on that, maybe tell him about the bill I found and see what he does?"

Brakes squealed as Alex brought the pickup to an abrupt halt at the side of the road. His hands gripped the wheel to keep them from grabbing her shoulders and shaking some sense into her. "I don't want you anywhere near McKee."

"He's not exactly Jack the Ripper."

"No. He's small-town slime, but he's slippery, and I don't want you falling in over your head. You can't swim well, remember."

"Fine!" She crossed her arms in front of her chest and waited for him to pull back out onto the road. He was upset because he was worried about her. She knew that. It lessened her own anger, but did not erase it. She was sick and tired of letting circumstances dictate her movements.

After a moment he apologized. "McKee's name sends my blood pressure up. I didn't mean to take it out on you."

In truth he thought the counterfeiting scheme was too sophisticated for a local operator like McKee. That's what worried him. If McKee was involved, he was out of his league, which meant there might be some dangerous types, higher up, who hadn't surfaced yet. He'd feel better knowing Kendra was safe, preferably living with him, until he had some answers. He hoped he could persuade her to stay without frightening her. There were parts of his job he did not want to have to tell her about.

T.W. greeted their arrival with patent disdain. He deigned to eat the food Alex put out for him, but he made it clear there had better be no more lengthy gaps between meals if they wanted him to stay. As he filled the cat's water dish, Alex glanced at the clock. "It'll be another half hour or so before Denny's home from school. You want to use the phone to call the lottery commission?"

"Not funny, Alex. I suppose there is someone I should touch base with, though." At his quick, worried glance she almost laughed. "My mother. She lives in Florida and I try to call her every week. Without a phone at the house it's been difficult."

"Is she ailing?"

Picturing her tiny, energetic mother, Kendra smiled again. "Hardly. She's barely sixty. She goes to aerobics classes every morning, plays in shuffleboard tournaments in the afternoons and alternates between bridge and square dancing at night. I just like to keep in touch."

"What does she think about your winning the lottery?"

"I haven't exactly told her yet." Thinking back on their last conversation, the previous Saturday from a Quaiapen phone booth, Kendra wondered what her mother would think. She hadn't been thrilled to hear her only daughter was living alone in the woods.

"Not all of us enjoy wall-to-wall shopping centers," Kendra had teased. Her mother lived in a condo on the Gulf of Mexico near Tampa and loved it. She was in every club she could find, had hundreds of close friends and never wanted to see another flake of snow again. The last time Kendra had seen her, she'd looked ten years younger than she had when she and Kendra's father had been working twelve-hour days to keep their small grocery business alive.

"Go ahead and call your mother," Alex said. "I'll make myself scarce."

Even after he'd disappeared into the bedroom, Kendra hesitated, remembering what else she'd said the previous Saturday. "Mom, I think I'm in love," she'd blurted, the safety valve of hundreds of miles between them making it easy to confide. They'd found they got along better now, seeing each other once a year, than they had when they'd lived within easy visiting distance.

A pregnant pause had greeted Kendra's announcement, followed by a tolerant sigh. "I'm sure he's an improvement over Henry. He's not a lobsterman, is he?"

So she'd told her mother a little about Alex. And described the house and her growing sense of belonging. "It's like living in a Robert Frost poem," she'd said.

Her mother, ever literal, had only corrected her. "Frost was from New Hampshire, dear. You're in Maine."

Twenty minutes later, Alex came back into the kitchen just as Kendra was saying goodbye. T.W. had climbed onto the shelf behind her head and was nuzzling her free ear, hoping for a refill on the food. "So, did you tell her about your windfall?"

"She thought it was nice. Says she won't worry anymore about leaving anything for me when she goes." Alex's lifted eyebrow didn't surprise her. "You know my tendency to blurt things out? I come by it honestly. Mother always says what she thinks."

"Usually that much money gets more of a reaction than nice. Or is it just a drop in the bucket to her?" He wondered, uneasily, if he was fated to fall in love only with wealthy women. For a moment he stopped listening to Kendra's answer. Was he in love with her?

It was becoming more apparent with every hour they spent together that she was not like Jody. Even two million dollars couldn't change her into that sort of woman.

"Mother's not wealthy, but my father left her comfortably well-off. She takes at least one cruise a year on the theory that the money should be spent before the government gets it. She did say to say hello to you."

"You told her about us?" Another curve, he thought. Did that mean Kendra was serious about their relationship? Or did she tell her mother about all her lovers? The thought twisted inside him like a knife.

"She likes to know what's going on in my life."

"So you give her a rundown on your sex life?"

Startled, Kendra blinked, then decided he was teasing. She hoped. "She doesn't want the graphic details, just the highlights. Deep down, she wants what all mothers want—something to brag about."

"Then she must have been disappointed. Dating a cop hardly compares to a doctor or a lawyer, or even a school principal."

"If you're fishing for a compliment, she never did like Henry." What was the matter with him? Did he want to keep their affair a secret? That hardly made sense when he'd asked her to go with him to talk to his son.

"What does she think of your writing?"

"Likes it better than teaching. You scored points on being good-looking and not being a lobsterman. Mother never has liked seafood."

"Nice to know something is lower than law officer."

"What's wrong with what you do for a living? You haven't heard me complaining, have you?"

He shrugged. "Early days yet."

"Alex. I'm not Jody. We're not talking about getting married or having children. We're just lovers. Lighten up."

"Just lovers?" He turned to look out the window.

Did she really hear huskiness in his voice? Was that what was wrong? He thought she was only interested in casual sex when he wanted more? Say something, Alex, she thought. Blurting out that she loved him too soon could shatter everything they had. And saying nothing could drive him away. Why did emotions have to be so complicated?

Alex's thoughts paralleled hers. He wanted to tell her he loved her. Hell, he wanted to marry her. It was crazy. They were only just getting to know each other, but at the same time he felt as if he'd known her all his life.

When he got control of himself, she was no longer looking at him. She was cradling T.W. in her arms and stroking him gently.

For an instant Alex's mind replaced the cat with a human child, their child. She'd be a good mother, he thought, and he'd like another chance to prove he could be a good father.

Gently he removed the cat and set him, indignant, on the kitchen floor. Gathering Kendra against his chest, he kissed her hair lightly, moving slowly down to her forehead, each cheek, and the corner of her mouth. "I don't think much of the 'just' part, but I'm all for being lovers."

Nuzzling against him, she murmured agreement.

"This has all happened pretty fast. I'm still spinning."

"Me, too," she whispered.

They kissed, not to arouse, but to comfort, like longtime lovers. He swallowed, trying desperately for the courage to speak those three incredibly important words. He couldn't quite get them out. He was too afraid of frightening her off. Instead his lips moved back to her forehead.

She waited, and when he did not speak she murmured against his cheek. "Some of us, though, can tell right away what we like." She planted a loud, smacking kiss at the corner of his mouth, then pushed him away. "Call your son."

But there was no answer at the house Jody had rented. Alex checked the school next, and found out that Denny had been absent all week. His temper was fraying visibly by the time he dialed the third number, McKee's real estate office.

Kendra held her breath. This was not the time for Jody to cause trouble. Surely she could not prevent them from seeing the boy?

She would if she knew Kendra was to be there. There had been no mistaking her hostility at the auction, and of all Denny's claims the only one Kendra believed was that he wanted to reunite his parents. Of course Alex was reluctant to talk about a future for them. He had to settle matters with his son and his ex-wife first. Kendra tried to tell herself to be patient, but it was growing hourly more difficult. All she really wanted to do was ask Alex to run away with her, to start a new life with the lottery money on a desert island somewhere, free of the troubles other people caused.

Tension crackled through the kitchen as Alex finally reached his ex-wife. Even T.W. felt it, and fled for the safety of a hiding place under the couch.

Kendra heard only one side of the conversation, but that was enough to alarm her. She went closer, into the circle of Alex's arm.

Questions flew with rapidly increasing speed, and Alex's temper ignited just as fast. He was gripping Kendra's shoulder so tightly she was certain he'd left a bruise, but she made no protest. The questions were the sort every parent dreads: Where is he? What do you mean, you don't know? How long ago? Why didn't you call me? What kind of mother are you?

He winced and held the phone away from his ear, then redialed. "Don't hang up on me again, Jody, or I swear I'll make you sorry."

Kendra could hear the other woman's shrill whine but not her actual words. Alex's jaw seemed set in granite. He wasn't asking questions now, just listening. The tendons in his neck bulged with the effort at control.

When he hung up she waited, dreading what she would hear. Alex was taut with rage, but underneath it she sensed something deeper, something she suspected was fear. In spite of the lies, in spite of the years of separation, Alex loved his son, and something terrible had happened to him.

"Denny's gone," he whispered. "Disappeared. He's been missing since Monday night, right after he got a phone call from George Marks."

Chapter 11

Jody Moreau's living room was still full of packing boxes, left where they'd been dumped the day she moved. Only her suitcases and Denny's had been taken into bedrooms, and no personal touches had been added to the decor preferred by the house's owners. Crossed snowshoes hung over the mantel, and hunting prints on the walls.

Her face looked haggard in the late-afternoon sunlight, but her makeup, hair and clothes were impeccable, and her eyes were hard as emeralds. If the glare she shot in her ex-husband's direction was unfriendly, that launched at Kendra was positively poisonous. "What's she doing here?"

Not bothering to answer, Alex pushed past her into the small house. His temper was leashed, but just barely. "Why the hell didn't you let me know he'd gone missing?"

"Nobody knew where you were." Jody looked haughtily down her petite nose at Kendra. "I might have guessed, but I thought you had better taste."

"I was married to you, wasn't I?" His hand went to his forehead and Kendra could almost hear him counting to ten. "Let's stop sniping, Jody. Just tell me what happened."

With ill-disguised reluctance she waved them farther into the room, seating herself on the only chair not covered with abandoned newspapers, dirty laundry or the remnants of one of Millie's take-out pizzas. "I already told you everything I know, Alex. Monday night he got a phone call from George Marks."

"What did Marks want?"

"How would I know? I don't eavesdrop."

Didn't care enough to find out what was going on, Kendra thought uncharitably. Jody seemed more upset by Kendra's appearance at Alex's side than she was by her son's disappearance, though now she was beginning to give a good impression of a distraught mother, wiping a tear from the corner of her eye and sniffing audibly.

"Get hold of yourself," Alex told her gruffly as he passed a box of tissues. He was too stirred up to sit, but paced the small room like a caged tiger. "What happened after the call?"

What was Jody playing at? Kendra wondered if she could have sent Denny away herself, in an attempt to get Alex's attention. That seemed too extreme, even for Jody, but Kendra inclined her body forward on the sofa, determined to preserve a healthy degree of skepticism, as Jody answered.

"I went to bed while they were still talking. The next morning I got up early. I have to work for a living, you know. I don't usually see Denny before I leave, so I didn't know he'd already gone. I assumed he was still asleep."

"It didn't occur to you to see that he got a good breakfast, or went to school? No wonder he's truant half the time."

Glaring at him, Jody forgot her model mother role. "He's a big boy. He can take care of himself."

In a dangerously soft voice, Alex continued questioning her. Kendra knew that tone. She almost felt sorry for Jody. "When did you realize he was gone?"

"When I got home Tuesday afternoon, I wondered where he was, but it was time for supper before I checked his room. His bed hadn't been slept in and he'd taken clothes and a backpack. That's when I started trying to find you." Her lower lip crept forward, pouting. "You weren't anywhere to be found, were you Alex?"

"Did you call the sheriff's office? They can track me down, you know that. Did you try coming out to camp?"

Conflict was plain on Jody's face. Did she say she had and risk finding Alex had been there, or did she admit she hadn't been worried enough about her son to bother?

"Never mind," Alex snapped. He was standing perfectly still, directly behind his ex-wife. The tendons in his hands tensed as if he were fighting the urge to wring her neck. "The important thing is to find out where Denny is. Did you look for a note?"

"No note, but I told you—he took his backpack and some clothes. He never bothered to pack before."

The hands twitched ominously. "If you were any kind of mother—"

Whirling around in her chair, Jody clenched her fists. "Don't start on me, Alex Moreau—"

"Both of you stop it!" Like an uncoiling spring, Kendra was on her feet and caught Alex's arm just before his hands reached Jody's throat. "The important thing here is Denny, not this petty bickering."

Alex's nostrils flared angrily, but he took a step away from the chair. Still tense, one arm came around Kendra's waist and tugged her close. He clung to her as if she alone could maintain his slipping self-control. After a few moments, his voice sounded almost normal again.

"Did Denny say anything during the phone call to give you an idea where George was calling from? What he wanted?"

Watching him, Kendra knew the tightly leashed violence was a devil he feared. It went against the code he lived by. And it was only in this situation, she realized, that it had any chance of escaping his guard. To protect those he loved, Alex could be driven to extremes.

"No. I told you." Jody's sulkiness increased at the sight of Alex and Kendra linked together. With malice, she added, "I went to bed. Alone."

That brief yielding to baser instincts had forced Alex to fall back on the safety of his professional training. Jody's taunts lost their effectiveness as his face went hard and expressionless and his voice dripped ice. "Where's your phone?"

"Kitchen," Jody snapped.

"Stay here," Alex ordered and stalked from the room, leaving Kendra behind.

Jody watched him go, then reached for a cigarette. With assumed casualness she blew smoke rings and avoided Kendra's steady gaze. "You'd do well to take a close look at him," she said after a moment. "I left him because of that streak of violence. He may be all smiles and laughter with you now, but when you no longer satisfy him, watch out."

More lies, Kendra thought. Alex was one of the gentlest men she'd ever met, and Jody one of the most provoking women. She was tempted to throttle his ex-wife herself.

Reluctant to leave Jody and Kendra alone together longer than he had to, Alex made three phone calls in rapid succession. The kitchen already bore Jody's imprint. With flagrant disregard for someone else's property she'd scribbled phone numbers on the wall. Millie's son would have fits when he got back. Then Alex looked more closely, and copied the numbers into the notebook he'd brought with him.

"Mrs. Marks has heard nothing from her son," Alex reported when he returned to the living room. Neither woman appeared to have moved, but Jody's face was flushed, and Kendra was smiling enigmatically. He had the feeling words had been exchanged. "Mrs. Paradis hasn't heard from Gil, either. The sheriff's office is arranging for the phone company to check their records and let me know where that call came from. Until then, we'll wait here."

"Nice of you to invite yourselves. Don't expect me to serve tea and crumpets."

"Stuff it, Jody. Your mother love is showing."

He caught Kendra's hand and pulled her down next to him on the sofa. "Where's McKee?" he asked abruptly.

"Why?"

"Give me a break, Jody. Just answer the question."

She studied her long, slender fingers. "I don't know. He's out of town."

"Since Monday?"

Startled, she looked up. "You don't think—"

"I think a lot of things. I don't know anything for sure. Why don't you fill me in while we're waiting for the phone company to come through? What's McKee up to, Jody? Why did you move out of the place he set you up in?"

"He didn't...I..." Jody's eyes suddenly filled with tears Kendra could have sworn were genuine. "I never intended to go back to him, Alex. I came back for you, but you—"

"Had sense enough not to be interested!" His grip on Kendra's hand tightened. He wasn't even aware he was hurting her until she winced in pain. "Sorry," he muttered to the woman at his side, but his eyes never left Jody's face. "Cut the crap, Jody."

"You think I couldn't see what McKee had become? I took what he offered because I didn't have any other choice. I was broke, Alex. As soon as I could swing it, I moved."

His eyebrow lifted, full of skepticism. She'd lived above McKee's office for nearly three years. Still, her usual composure was slipping badly. He wondered what she really knew about McKee.

The next few hours were fraught with tension. Jody fixed herself a drink. Then another. Kendra suggested that she leave and go back to her own house, but Alex would not hear of it. "I need you," was all he said, but it was enough. Kendra stayed. He seemed to want to hold on to her, physically and emotionally, even when she knew his mind was miles away.

By dark, the phone was ringing at frequent intervals. George's call had been traced to a Canadian pay phone. Slowly, wheels ground into motion. This time the missing person was a juvenile. Pressure could be brought to bear on the authorities to search.

Kendra had fallen asleep, her head on Alex's shoulder, when loud knocking at Jody's front door awoke them both. Jody, long since retired to her own bedroom, slept on.

"It's Claude," Alex said after a quick surveillance through the drapes. "Friend of mine." But he sounded worried. Most news had been phoned to them. "Think you can weed through Jody's stuff and find some coffee?"

Nodding, Kendra left the room, but she couldn't shake the sense of impending disaster. Why had he wanted her out of the way? Alex's face had been ashen. As soon as the coffee was perking Kendra started back but stopped, just out of sight of the two men in the living room, as she heard Alex utter one terrible word.

"Murdered?" he croaked.

In the moment she stood frozen, fearing the worst for Denny, Claude spoke. His words sent a wave of relief through Kendra even as they filled her with horror.

"The truck exploded when it went over the cliff. There wasn't much left of George or Gil to identify, but with the information you provided we've confirmed that the two bodies were theirs. They died early Tuesday morning.''

"At least Denny wasn't with them."

"No, but we've found no trace of him."

Kendra heard Alex's fist hit the wall in frustration. His breathing sounded labored. She wanted to run to him, to comfort him, but she also wanted to know what was going on. Alex, she suspected, would try to shield her. He wouldn't want her to hear the gruesome details.

After a moment, Claude resumed his story, sounding almost as shaken as his friend. "They call him the fat man. No name. Just an M.O. Getting into the mill was no sweat. Just like we do with the mills around here, the town cops leave the warehouse district pretty much to the mill security men, and they didn't figure anyone would be after rolls of paper."

"Didn't the warehouse have a watchman?"

"When a voice on the telephone sounds like it has the world's worst cold and tells the switchboard he's not coming in, nobody questions it. If the security guys even heard about it, they didn't worry much. Besides, lots of late night pickups get made, and if the name on the cab of the tractor's right, which it was, who bothers to check?"

"Monday night? George called here first, then?"

"Looks like it. Even with all that planning, the operation took some time. They had to get into what looks like a huge bank vault. Inside, the paper is stacked on pallets in square bundles, rows and rows of them. Real special paper. Raw bank-note stock."

Alex gave a low whistle. "You'd think the Treasury Department would guard it better."

"They figured no one knew it was there. Once in, the fat man had his truck loaded and gone in half an hour. Gate guard said it was just another nondescript green Mack tractor with an unmarked trailer in tow. He remembered wishing them a good night. A couple of hours later they seem to have off-loaded into another semi at a scenic turnout. Somehow, the fat man tricked those two fools into going back inside the empty box trailer. He'd left behind maybe a half dozen jerricans of gas, so when she rolled over the edge of that cliff and hit, she went up like a torch. Might have gone unnoticed except there was a scout troop camped in the woods nearby. They saw the flames."

"I need a drink," Alex said abruptly. "It's in the kitchen."

He rounded the corner before Kendra could retreat, and knew at once that she'd heard. The wall supported her weight and her face had gone ghastly white. "I'm sorry," Alex said, his voice full of pain. "There are parts of my job I hate, parts I never wanted you to have to share. There are some sick, sick people out there."

His arms slid around her shoulders and turned her into his embrace. They clung together for a long moment, but the comfort could not last. "I could use your help, to get Jody out here," he murmured against her ear.

"I'll handle it," Kendra promised, grim faced and grimmer voiced. Jody had better be ready to spill her guts, she thought as she stormed into the bedroom.

Waking Jody was no easy task. Kendra endured a diatribe of personal abuse before the other woman finally struggled into a robe and accompanied her to the kitchen. She was unmoved by the news of two deaths, until Alex added an abbreviated version of what Claude had told him.

"This guy, the fat man, gets his kicks by making sure there are no witnesses to any job he's hired to do. He prefers creative executions, and my guess is that Denny was headed straight toward him when he left here."

Kendra felt ill at the thought. The coffee she'd gulped down in order to force her brain to function churned uncomfortably in her stomach. "This is connected to the money I found at my place, isn't it?"

"It may be. If we're right about the printing press."

"What are you talking about?" Jody demanded irritably. "What press?"

"We think there may have been a printing press hidden at my house. That my convenient... accidents... were arranged to keep me away while George and Gil—"

Alex broke in, his voice harsh. "And Denny—"

"While someone came in and removed the evidence."

Jody's vitriolic words were now aimed solely at Wakefield McKee. When she'd finished cursing him roundly, she started to sob. "Alex, I swear I didn't know anything about this. I knew some of what he was up to. I had to. I kept the books. Both sets. But not this. Honest to God, if I'd known what he was going to do with that press he found I'd—"

"McKee found a press?" Alex's voice was cold enough to freeze water. Jody didn't seem to notice. She was too anxious to save her own skin.

"He found it out at the Narrowbridge house. Remember? The old guy who shot himself? McKee was supposed to go over his place for the estate. Out in the barn he found one of the feed rooms had been turned into a print shop. I didn't pay too much attention. It never occurred to me the old guy was making funny money." Her voice sounded bitter, as if she regretted a missed opportunity. "I should have guessed something was up when McKee told me to go back into the house and start the inventory while he stayed in the barn. He usually stuck someone else with the uncomfortable chores, and this was last fall. It was nippy in that barn."

"Before you say any more," Claude broke in, "maybe you'd better have a lawyer."

"Butt out, Claude," Alex snarled, but his friend reminded him that they were both officers of the law.

"We'd better call in the troops on this one, Alex. State Police, Treasury Department, even the Canadian Mounties."

By midmorning, authorities from both countries had arrived at the county seat, and a full-scale search was under way for both Denny and Wakefield McKee. Exhausted, Alex and Kendra went back to his apartment for a few hours of sleep.

For what seemed like the hundredth time, Kendra repeated, "They'll find him, Alex." She was in his kitchen, scrambling eggs. Almost twenty-four hours had passed since they'd learned Denny was missing.

"I'm glad you're here," Alex told her. "I need you to keep telling me that." He'd barely slept and had been on the phone almost constantly since they got up.

"Do you think McKee knows this fat man?"

Shrugging, Alex toyed with the eggs. "McKee's small potatoes. He found a press and some plates and decided he could make a few bucks. The press was probably part of a bigger operation. Maybe the old guy was double-crossing someone, maybe not, but sometime after McKee got the press, the big boys realized he was cutting into their action. Maybe they contacted him and made a deal. Maybe they just decided to take over. I don't know.''

"They must have. How else would George and Gil have gotten involved in the theft? That paper wasn't stolen to make fives. And don't tell me I've been watching too much television. That's only common sense, Alex."

Giving up on the food, Alex caught her hands. "Promise me you won't go back to your place until this is over."

"Is someone watching it? Do you think the fat man is after the press? That he thinks it's still there?"

"Probably not, but I don't want you taking any risks."

"I'll stay right here, with you," she promised.

The afternoon stretched into evening, endless, broken only by phone calls. Each jangle sent Kendra's heart into her throat, but most of the time the caller was just another concerned friend. All of Quaiapen seemed to know that Denny was missing, that his two friends were dead and that Jody had been questioned with her lawyer present and released. Finally, at 9:00 p.m., the sheriff's office phoned to tell Alex that deputies had located the printing press.

"McKee hid it at the Benson place," Alex said as he hung up, "but the plates weren't there. Now they want me to brief some of the other officers, at the office. Seems they also need my statement, immediately, in triplicate." Bitterness and disappointment showed all too plainly on his haggard face, and Kendra, helpless, watched him buckle on a shoulder holster and load his gun.

"Do you want me to come with you?"

"No. Stay here. Keep T.W. company. Try to get some more sleep." He ruffled her hair affectionately and managed a smile.

"Are you sure?" Silently she wondered what he wasn't telling her.

"They won't let you sit in on any meetings. You're a civilian. Besides, one of us should get a little shut-eye, in case tomorrow is another long day."

Reluctantly, she kissed him goodbye. He was halfway down the narrow stairwell when she whispered, "Alex, I love you." She couldn't be sure if he'd heard. He didn't stop.

T.W. seemed glad of her company. After a shower and a change of clothing, Kendra curled up on Alex's sofa with the cat on her lap.

Alex had been right. There were aspects of his job she didn't like. She had the feeling he'd been growing more and more dissatisfied with those parts of his chosen career himself. She'd heard the disillusionment in his voice. Burnout, she thought. It was something she could understand.

No one had actually said the words "organized crime," but Kendra knew that even rural areas were not immune to it. Back in Vermont she'd heard about the drug pipeline that ran through the northern New England states to Canada. Now there was this counterfeiting. She shuddered, wishing she could block Claude's vivid description from her memory.

What was happening to Alex worried her as much as what might be happening to Denny. He'd blame himself if the boy died. Jody, on the other hand, would survive even that. She'd given up all pretense of loving anyone but herself when she'd been on the phone to her lawyer.

Toward midnight, knowing she'd be better able to help Alex cope if she'd had some sleep, Kendra climbed into the bed they'd shared earlier. Sleep came, but not rest. Horrifying scenes flickered through her dreams. Cars hit trees. Trucks bore down on intersections. Cars burned. Semis burned. Houses burned. When the extension shrilled loudly next to her ear she almost screamed.

"Yes!" she gasped, hoping it was Alex, praying for good news.

Strained silence greeted her. There was someone on the other end of the line. She could hear soft breathing, but no sound of speech.

"Denny? Talk to me if it's you. This is Kendra Jennings. Your father is frantic with worry."

Again the silence stretched interminably, but just as she was about to renew her plea, Denny's voice, shaky and very low, reached her. "I need someone to come get me," he said.

Without hesitating, Kendra responded to the need in his words and his tone. "Where are you, Denny? I'll come."

Alex leaned against the door frame of his ex-wife's bedroom, tired, frustrated and angry. She lay sprawled facedown on the bed, a rumpled sheet only half hiding her nakedness. He felt not even a flicker of desire. Once he had loved her to distraction. Now there was only one woman he wanted to make love to, wake up next to, live with the rest of his life. It was not Jody.

Taking a step closer he understood why she had not heard him pounding on her door. She was drunk. Again. He'd picked her flimsy lock and let himself into the house. This time there would be no lawyer to protect her.

"Jody," he said harshly, shaking her shoulder.

She groaned and rolled over, opening bleary eyes and baring flabby breasts. She looked every second of her thirty-five years. "Alex," she said with an alcohol-induced slurring of her words. "I knew you'd get tired of that pasty-faced little bitch and come back to me."

It took every ounce of willpower he possessed not to slap her across the mouth. Only the thought of Kendra held him in check. It wouldn't be much of a future for them if he ended up in jail on assault charges. Gritting his teeth, he disentangled himself from her pawing hands, avoiding the amorous attention he'd inadvertently aroused.

It took an arm lock to convince her he wasn't interested in anything but the answers to a few questions. "This slime who killed George and Gil also trashed Kendra's place. He's probably looking for the plates McKee used to make those phony fives. You want him to come here next?"

Alex was still sickened by the thought of what the fat man had done to Kendra's possessions. He hadn't seen the destruction himself, but Johnson's description over the phone had been enough to convince Alex that she mustn't go near the place until it had been thoroughly cleaned. Thank God she was safe at his apartment. He didn't want to think what might have happened if she'd been alone in her house in the woods with that savage. By the time Johnson had checked the place on his regular patrol, the fat man had been long gone.

"I want my lawyer," Jody whined. Her eyes were puffy, and her breath reeked of whiskey.

"No lawyer," Alex growled, giving one last twist on her arm before he released her. "I'm not on duty now, Jody. This is just between you and me."

"What do you want to know?" She rubbed her arm, heedless of her bared bosom and the fact that they were still sitting on her bed.

"The phone number on your wall. It reaches an answering machine. McKee's voice answers with the number. Can he pick up messages from a third phone?"

Pouting, making patently superficial concessions to modesty by tugging the sheet up and draping it around her, she waited as long as she thought she could get away with it before telling him what he wanted to know. "He can if he wants to."

"Okay. Now, let's assume the fat man is looking for the plates. Where did McKee hide them?"

"I don't know anything about—"

He caught her hair at her nape and jerked her head back onto the pillow. Her eyes bulged. "You and me, Jody. Where?"

"He's got a safe in the office. A wall safe."

"You've got the combination, right?"

When he released her, she nodded, but she was fully sober now and glaring at him. She wasted several more minutes with whining and complaining before Alex convinced her to give it to him. "Now the key to McKee's real estate office."

"Why don't you just break in? You're good at that."

"I could get a search warrant," he reminded her, "but I'm interested in finding Denny. You want it on your conscience that the time you could have saved me cost him his life?"

"A little melodramatic, aren't you?"

"You just don't get it, do you Jody? This isn't penny ante anymore. There's a guy out there who kills people for a living and enjoys his work. Chances are Denny's with your boyfriend, and this guy wants McKee, and those plates, real bad."

Jody pulled her purse from under the bed, tossed a key chain at him and then settled herself comfortably against the pillows, lay back and lit a cigarette. "If there's nothing else you want, Alex, get the hell out of my bedroom."

"Gladly."

He lost no time driving to McKee's office. With a sense of relief he found both the outer door and the safe undisturbed. He was ahead of the fat man. A quick survey of the contents of the safe told him he'd beaten McKee, too. The plates were still there, together with a wad of bills too substantial for McKee to want to leave behind if he had any choice.

A glance at his watch told Alex there were only a few hours until dawn. He wanted nothing more than to go back to his apartment and crawl into bed with Kendra, but even though the odds weren't good someone else would show up at McKee's office under cover of darkness, he knew it was worth his time to wait and be sure.

When he'd returned the money and the plates to the safe and relocked it, Alex turned the lights off and took a seat in a straight chair hidden in the shadows by the file cabinet. The comforting bulk of his service revolver rested beneath his jacket in a shoulder holster.

He was fed up with the slowness of going through channels. If it proved fruitless to stay, at least he was doing something. After the wasted hours at the sheriff's office, talking to one lamebrained state or federal official after another, he wondered why he'd ever thought law enforcement was efficient. They couldn't even agree on who had jurisdiction in the case, let alone how to handle it.

Time to think about a new career, he mused as the minutes slowly ticked by. Once he'd considered running for sheriff himself, but that was administration, not enforcement. Worse, it was politics.

"Tradition," he muttered under his breath. Maybe it was time to break tradition and do something he wanted to do for a change.

No quantum leap was needed to shift his mind from that idea to daydreams of Kendra. He imagined her, asleep in his bed, T.W. standing guard. Another couple of hours and he'd be home. He'd wake her slowly and take her while she was still half asleep. He was aroused just thinking about her.

Bad as a horny teenager, he rebuked himself, but he smiled as he thought it. There was a great deal to be said for finding love at this point in his life. He could still appreciate the physical fulfillment with all the enthusiasm of a young man, and yet he was mature enough to know that what they shared in other ways was just as important. They were two halves of a whole. Until he found Kendra, he'd thought that saying only a piece of sentimental tripe, but now he knew it was the simple truth.

He wished he'd turned on the stairs at her soft whisper and told her he loved her, too. He'd been afraid he couldn't stop with just words, that he'd be going back up those few steps and taking her to bed. He'd thought it was more important to obey orders and report in. He'd been wrong.

The luminous dial of his watch showed him that less than an hour had passed. It did no good to wonder where Denny was or what was happening to him. He decided to plan how he would propose marriage to Kendra instead. He no longer doubted that he would ask her. He was almost certain she would accept.

Locations varying from the top of Mount Washington to the deck of the Blue Line Ferry gave way to his thinking place, or out in the canoe, while eating grapes. Just as he'd begun to fantasize a proposal in his bed, later this morning, immediately following a long, languid session of lovemaking, he heard a sound in the outer office.

The vision fragmented as Alex leaned forward, ears straining for any hint of movement. Slowly, silently, he reached under his jacket and withdrew the gun, gripping the butt firmly as he peered around the edge of the cabinet toward the door.

With infinite slowness, soundless in the dark, the door began to inch open. Someone was coming in.

Chapter 12

I'm on the run," Denny had said.

Kendra wiggled her shoulders to relieve the ache in her back and increased her pressure on the accelerator. Peering ahead into the darkness, she hoped she'd be able to follow the terse directions Alex's son had given over the phone.

The boy must be terrified. There had been no time to do more than leave a note for Alex and then head north in his trusty pickup truck toward the Canadian border. She'd make one fast stop en route, Kendra decided, at her own house—for the gun.

Cautiously, she pulled into the dooryard. It was three o'clock in the morning. Everything looked just as she'd left it. Her car was still parked at the side of the house. No lights showed inside. It wasn't until Kendra stepped onto the porch that she realized the aura of peacefulness was deceptive. The merciless beam of Alex's high-powered flashlight revealed the brand-new, secure, dead-bolt lock hanging limp and ruined in the remains of her door. It looked as if someone had taken an ax to the wood.

If there had been utter silence, she'd have fled, but Kendra reminded herself of something Alex had said, that animals made no noise when there were humans lurking in the woods. Behind her crickets chirped, squirrels and chipmunks skittered on their way and a distant owl sent its greeting to the moon. Surely she was the only human here now.

Still, she hesitated. Would the animals know if someone were in the house? He must be gone, she told herself. She just hoped her burglar hadn't stolen the gun. Taking a deep breath, she turned on the generator, then threw the light switches for the hall, living room and dining room.

Every item that could be smashed lay underfoot, not only splintered, but ground into the floor by angry heels. The furniture had been slashed. In the dining room not a single one of Olive's bisque figurines had been left whole.

The kitchen looked as if a cyclone had been through it. Even her canisters of sugar and flour had been dumped upside down. The stovepipe had been wrenched loose and ashes scattered on top of the broken dishes and twisted silverware.

Kendra gasped at the sight of her computer. The screen had been smashed, the electronics ripped out. She found her computer disks on the floor, the imprint of a man's boot clear on their surfaces.

What kind of beast would do this to her home? Logic told her that he'd been searching, and that if he'd done all this because he couldn't find what he was looking for, then Denny was in terrible peril. "He's after me," Denny had said.

Get the gun, she told herself, forcing reluctant feet to mount the stairs. The second floor was far worse than the first. Her bedroom had been torn apart and defiled with even more viciousness than the rooms below. In addition, the intruder had taken a knife to the clothing in her closet, scattered the contents of the drawers and emptied every bottle from her dresser onto the floor.

Fighting waves of nausea, Kendra searched, knowing she would never be able to wear any of those clothes again, never be able to sleep again in this room. Absurdly, she found the small handgun undamaged in the midst of the destruction, half hidden by a lacy slip.

Kendra retrieved it and was relieved from picking through the debris for the box of ammunition when she spotted it in a corner. It had been flung against the wall and had emptied into a single pile of bullets.

Trembling uncontrollably, tears running unheeded down her cheeks, Kendra stumbled back toward the stairs. Somehow, once she'd reached the dooryard, she managed to load the gun and tuck it into the pocket of her windbreaker. Then she climbed back into Alex's truck. Much as she wanted to run back to the safety of his apartment, Kendra knew there was no time to lose. Everything in this house could be replaced, but Denny had only one life.

In McKee's office, Alex waited, tense and ready. A flashlight was directed at the wall safe. Fingers worked the combination with the ease of long practice and Alex smiled. McKee had come back, like a thief in the night, to get the money and the set of plates he'd been using to print Canadian fives.

"Hold it right there, McKee," Alex said softly as he switched on the desk lamp. He had the gun aimed and ready, but, as in his meeting with Jody, this was between the two of them. He was a father, not a cop.

"Let me go and I'll tell you where Denny is," McKee begged. His color drained away until his face was pasty white and his Adam's apple bobbed as he swallowed nervously. "There's still time to save his life."

Alex's stomach muscles clenched. McKee's words confirmed his worst fears. There was a possibility that he'd never see his son alive again. His voice was disarmingly calm and reasonable. "Tell me and we'll talk about it."

Obviously relieved, McKee slumped into his desk chair. He gave Alex's gun a wary glance as he attempted to regain his composure but achieved only petulance. "Must you point that thing at me?"

The gun did not waver. "Spill it."

"You do want the boy back, don't you, Moreau?"

With a shrug, Alex replaced the gun in its holster. "I don't need a weapon to make you talk." He leaned across the desk until brown eyes locked on blue. McKee was the first to shift his glance away.

He cleared his throat, swiveling in the chair so that he stared at the real estate photos on his bulletin board. His usual oily charm was only partially intact. "For some reason a certain party thinks the boy is my son. He left a message a short while ago, at a phone number I keep for emergencies. He wants me to meet him." As Alex circled the desk, McKee essayed an unconvincing laugh. "The man must think I'm a fool."

"Tell me exactly what he said, McKee. Word for word."

Reluctantly, eyeing the bulge of the gun under Alex's jacket, McKee cooperated. "He said he'd keep Denny in one piece if I brought the plates."

"Where?"

"Now, Alex. Surely you don't think you can get that information for nothing. After all, if you kill me, you still won't know. Let's talk about you forgetting you ever saw me tonight, and then we'll discuss Denny's whereabouts."

Leaning against the wall, Alex bared his teeth in a mockery of a smile. "If this 'certain party' of yours killed George Marks and Gil Paradis, you're an accessory to murder, McKee."

The realtor's eyes widened. "What are you talking about, Moreau?"

"They're dead. Murdered by whoever instigated the theft of some very special paper."

Genuinely shocked, McKee seemed to shrink into his swivel chair. "I didn't know." The nasal whisper was barely audible. "I swear I didn't know. How could I have known?"

"Same way you knew to stay out of Quaiapen until now. You're right, McKee. I'm not likely to kill you. But I'd really enjoy damaging you."

Fists curled, lips curved into a snarl, Alex glowered down at him. They'd appear evenly matched to a casual observer, but McKee's muscles were all for show. He was a devout coward.

"Okay, okay. I'll tell you what I know. Denny went north to meet George and Gil. They were to call me at an answering machine when they were ready to be picked up, but no one called, not until about an hour ago.''

McKee was plotting as he talked, searching for a loophole. Alex could almost hear the gears clicking. He tensed, ready for anything. McKee was giving him only part of the truth, but it didn't matter, not if McKee knew where Denny was. ''Then what?''

''Just a voice, saying he's got my son and he wants the plates in exchange. That's when I decided to take the money and run.''

''And leave my son!'' Alex had closed the distance between them before McKee could move out of the chair. Seizing him by the collar, Alex jerked him to his feet. The first punch struck a weak chin and chipped a tooth. The second broke McKee's nose. ''Where's Denny? Where were you supposed to meet this piece of slime?''

''The campground,'' McKee gasped. He made no attempt to fight back, but collapsed in a heap on the floor of his office, blood flowing freely from what remained of his once regal nose. ''My campground near the border.''

Abruptly Alex hauled him back to his feet and jerked one arm behind his back to march him toward the door. ''Let's go.''

''Denny?'' Kendra whispered.

Following his directions she'd arrived at a rustic campground, McKee's Lakeside Sites, located within a mile of the Canadian border. She'd opened the unlocked gate and driven in, past the small closed office, across a rough bridge that spanned two small lakes in the same chain that passed her house and on up a hill to the area's only amenity, a log-cabin-style comfort station.

Everything was silent when she shut off the engine and got out of the truck. It was still preseason, since even the bravest campers waited for Memorial Day weekend to come this far north. There had been no campers or tents in any of the sites she'd passed and on the beach had been only a solitary motor launch, half hidden by the trees that grew close to the shore. She hadn't gotten close enough to tell if it was old and abandoned or the means by which Denny had gotten this far.

No light showed inside the square, sturdy-looking building, but the predawn sky and the flashlight she'd taken from the glove compartment showed her latticed walkways leading to doors on either side. Kendra hesitated. Where were those comforting animal and bird sounds?

He'd said he'd be hiding where he could watch the comfort station. That was the reason for the silence. Denny was near, keeping an eye out for her. He was just being cautious, making sure she hadn't been followed before he showed himself. Kendra felt for the gun in her jacket pocket and tried to stay calm. Of course that was it. He was making sure she hadn't brought the police.

The building was circled by a dirt road, with a simple playground nearby. On the outer side of the circle were individual campsites, just as there were around the two lakes below. Denny could be anywhere, Kendra thought.

Squinting into the shadows was making her increasingly nervous. "Denny, it's okay," she called out. "I'm alone. Let's get out of here!"

No one answered her. What if he was hurt? Would he have crawled inside the building? Reluctant to move that far from the safety of the truck, she was still more unwilling to give up now that she had come all this way. Wiping clammy palms on her jeans, she began to make her way cautiously over the flagstone path toward the men's side of the oversized outhouse.

Her breath caught at the sight of locks, broken. The door looked just like the one at her house. Before she could turn and run she was roughly seized from behind.

The flashlight flew out of her hand and crashed to the stones at her feet. Its comforting beam was immediately extinguished from the impact. Rough hands pushed Kendra against the side of the building and began to search her, thoroughly and professionally, for weapons. Short, stubby fingers probed up her legs, down her arms, over her breasts, but the chortle of pleasure came only when they located the gun.

She had the sense of a big man, fully twice her size, as he removed the gun, then shoved her forward, into the building. The fat man. Fear coiled through her, robbing her of all coherent thought.

An instant later Kendra landed painfully, full length, on a hard concrete floor. The shock jolted through her as she struck knees, breasts, palms and one cheek. For a moment she lay still, stunned. Then, before she could right herself, the door slammed loudly shut behind her. She heard the sound of a bar sliding into place to hold it closed. Even broken, she knew that door was strong enough to keep her in. She was a prisoner of the fat man.

Slowly, Kendra rolled over into a crouch. She hurt everywhere, but she forced herself to disregard the pain. She had to get out. Her life depended upon it. That was the fat man out there—the man who killed for fun.

In the pitch darkness of her prison, she dared not move far. The wait, while her eyes adjusted to the blackness, seemed endless. Her breathing came in rasping gulps, and her heart was thudding out of control. She knew she was in deadly peril and took little comfort from hearing the engine of Alex's truck come to life and the receding hum as it was driven away.

"Oh, God," she sobbed aloud. "Alex."

"I'm sorry," a low voice said.

Kendra turned toward the sound. "Denny?" The dark seemed slightly less impenetrable. Faint shapes and shadows had begun to emerge, but she could not find one that looked like Alex's son.

"Yeah," the voice agreed. "It's me. I'm sorry I got you into this. I figured it would be my father who answered the phone."

Kendra drew a deep steadying breath and started to crawl toward the sound of his voice. "I left a note for Alex. He'll be coming soon." Her voice was shaky, but she was regaining control. She had to, for Denny's sake. She only hoped what she'd just said was true. Alex might as easily still be at the sheriff's office, unaware they needed help.

After a moment she realized that Denny had made no move nearer, and had fallen silent. Was he hurt? She stopped her unsteady progress across the floor. "Where are you?"

"Tied to the plumbing. Nice touch, huh?" His voice went up in spite of an effort to sound nonchalant.

"Keep talking so I can find you. Maybe I can get you loose." Concentrate on Denny, she told herself.

Get him free. Together they might find a way to escape from the fat man.

The ropes were clothesline, tightly knotted. Kendra broke three fingernails but finally succeeded in freeing Denny's wrists. Trembling, sweat running freely down her face, she leaned against the rough log wall while he flexed his hands and worked on the ropes holding his feet.

"So," she said blithely. "Feel like explaining how you ended up like this?"

"Stupidity."

"Besides that." Keep it light, she thought. Don't panic.

"Long story."

"Looks like we have time." I hope, she added silently. She reasoned it would be a good idea to find out what Denny knew before they started planning an escape.

Kendra thought she heard a chuckle in the dimness. "You're something else, lady. You sure gave McKee a start when you turned up at Millie's that first night."

Was that grudging admiration in his tone? If it was, she couldn't tell if it was for McKee or for herself. "Why's that, Denny?"

"He planned to use your house until June, and all of a sudden he had about an hour left instead of a month. Had to think fast."

"So he sent the three of you to wait for me, to make sure I had an accident, and to plant the pills."

"Yeah. McKee takes pills like there's no tomorrow. Uppers. Downers. You name it. Thinks nobody knows, but the guys did, and me and Mom. Anyway, he had the stuff on him, so he drugged your second cup of coffee at Millie's. He figured you wouldn't make it very far.''

"Don't you think the pillbox was overkill?''

"Not the way Doc Gray feels about drug and alcohol abuse. McKee wanted to be sure she found it. Figured you'd be so put off by the unfriendly welcome that you'd just go home. Anyway, he couldn't have you seeing Olive's living room the way it was. The press was right out in the open and there were boxes of fives everywhere.''

Poor Alex, Kendra thought. If we get out of this alive, he'll have to arrest his own son for counterfeiting. Then she remembered something else. "Denny? You were just trying to scare me when you hinted Olive's death wasn't an accident, weren't you?''

"Oh, yeah. Hey, that whole scene was McKee's idea. We got the money out after I put the pillbox in your purse, but we didn't have a truck for the press so we just hid that. We knew we'd have to come back if we couldn't drive you away. I was supposed to stick around, at camp, but my dad turned up and spoiled that plan. Then George tried to spook you, one night, but that didn't work, so I took a shot. Then McKee got lucky. He overheard you telling Tara Loomis you were going to Augusta the next day.''

"And George tried to kill me there.''

"Hey, honest, no one tried to kill anybody.''

Kendra wished she could see Denny's face. Did he really believe that? And did he know what had happened to his friends? "How did McKee get you into this?'' she asked abruptly.

She could almost see Denny shrug. "He paid me for all kinds of odd jobs. A little of this. A little of that. Nothing heavy.''

"Till now."

"Yeah, well, he saw a chance for some real money. Figured he'd double-cross the Canadians for a quick profit. Something went wrong, I guess."

She felt him shudder, and his voice didn't sound as cocky anymore. "George called me to tell me where to meet them after the heist. I slipped out of the house that same night and stayed with McKee at the Benson place. Then I went up by water, Tuesday night, in McKee's powerboat. But instead of the guys and a load of paper, there was a fat man with a gun. He was expecting McKee."

"What happened when he saw you instead?"

"He roughed me up a little. Asked questions. Hey, I'm no fool. I told him everything he wanted to know, except where McKee was. I didn't know that."

If the fat man had done no more to Denny than rough him up, the boy could count himself lucky, Kendra realized. She knew the kind of monster Denny had faced. She was glad he'd opted to save himself.

"He kept me locked up, like he was waiting for orders. Then, last night, we came south, in McKee's boat. I was tied up but I knew we were at your place. He was some mad when he came back out. Then we came all the way back north again, to the place I was to have met George and Gil. He had a second boat nearby, with a CB radio. While he was checking in, with his boss, I guess, I got away from him."

Kendra said nothing. If Denny had gotten away, it was because the fat man had wanted him to.

"We had a pretty good chase down through the lakes, until he shot a couple of holes in McKee's boat. She sank. I swam for it. Thought I'd lost him. There's a phone in the campground office. That's where I called you from. I was feeling pretty fine when I hung up, until I turned around and saw him leering at me, gun in hand.''

Denny's sudden silence worried her. She didn't like to imagine what the fat man might have done next. With relief, she heard his account continue.

''Funny thing, but that fat guy thinks McKee is my dad. Made me call him. There's this number with an answering machine we use for emergencies. The fat man left a message. McKee's supposed to trade the plates for me.''

''Don't count on it.''

''Yeah.'' Suddenly tentative, he asked what must have been preying on his mind since his capture. ''What happened to George and Gil?''

There was no point in hedging. ''Your friend out there killed them.''

A sharp intake of breath was the only sound for a long moment. Then she thought Denny might be softly crying, but she wasn't sure. She left him to his grief and tried to think of some way to get them out of here. She didn't believe for a second that the monster who had locked them in simply meant to go away and leave them. She remembered what Claude had said about him. He liked to kill. He liked to kill in a big, flashy way. He was only keeping them alive until he could come up with something that turned him on enough to make their deaths worthwhile.

''Denny, when you called me, did you call your mother, too?''

A short, ironic laugh was followed by a brief silence. ''What for? She doesn't care what I do. She never even wanted to have me. She's told me that often enough.''

Kendra fought the urge to hug him and murmur comforting words. At fifteen he was too big for that, but her heart went out to him all the same. "Did she know what you were up to?"

"Some of it, I guess. The small stuff. McKee didn't mean to take her along when he left. Neither did I."

"Why does the fat man think you're McKee's son?"

"It was a joke. George used to call me the boss's kid. Hell, why not? My own father didn't want anything to do with us when we came back because we didn't have any money anymore."

"Denny, that's not—"

"He wouldn't let us stay with him, or at camp. My grandparents had a great big house and they were heading for Arizona to retire, but they wouldn't let us use it. They sold it instead. Mom had to take up with McKee or starve. So I figured, who cared if I broke a few dumb laws. All I wanted was to make enough money and get us out of Quaiapen again."

When Kendra reached for his hand in the darkness he didn't pull away. "I've been squirreling every cent away for almost three years, and if this deal had gone through, I would have had enough. Funny thing, though. At first I was doing it for Mom and me. Lately I've been doing it just for myself. And then, because I had to hang out with my father, to string him along and convince him you were the one who was lying, I actually started to like the guy."

After a quick, hard hug, Kendra released him. "He's started to like you, too. And tonight you tried to call him." It was the most positive sign she'd seen yet. "Keep giving him that chance, Denny."

"A chance to what? Arrest me? Maybe that nut case out there will be doing me a favor if he kills me."

"Don't say that! Don't even think it. No matter what happens, you and Alex need to talk, really talk, to each other."

"Yeah, sure. Think he'll visit me in the Maine Youth Center?"

It would do no good to blurt out encouraging platitudes, Kendra realized. She didn't even know how Maine law treated juveniles. What she did know was that Denny was a very confused young man who felt rejected by both parents and was now caught in a situation where his life seemed of little value. He was capable of reckless, suicidal behavior. She had to think of something noninflammatory to say.

Before she could, Denny himself changed the subject. "You sleeping with my old man?"

"Yes. I love him," she said simply. "Does that bother you?"

Again she sensed the shrug. "I guess not. Better you than my mother. I was just pretending I wanted to get them back together again, you know."

"Ever consider acting as a career? Your father bought it."

"I was aiming for a career as a con artist," he said with a flicker of the old cockiness. "It's steadier work than acting."

"You inherited your father's sense of humor," she told him. "Listen, Denny, I'd like to get out of here. For one thing, I'd like to see your father again. I've got a few choice words for him on the subject of raising children. Do you have any ideas?"

The high, dirt-streaked windows were too small to squeeze through, even if they could get them open. The door was barred. "It ought to be a flimsy building," Denny said thoughtfully. "McKee built it."

"Good. Maybe we can find a loose plank or some-thing." They separated, crawling on hands and knees in opposite directions around the room. "Is the water hooked up?"

"Yeah. Runs off a propane-fired generator. You gotta go to the can?"

"No. I wondered if flooding the place would help."

"Only if you want to drown us."

Silence descended again, broken only by a muted thud and muffled curse as Denny found the underside of the sink. Finally they met again by the door. It was every bit as firmly secured by the bar as it had been before.

"We could jump him when he comes back."

"Did you get a good look at this guy, Kendra? He makes sumo wrestlers look puny."

Very faintly, the hum of a car engine sounded in the distance. It seemed to stop in the campground below.

"McKee," Denny whispered. "He came through after all."

"Or your father. Either way, the fat man has to come here for you. Let's try to pull him inside when he opens the door, then make a run for that car."

"Why not?"

A few minutes later, just as the heavy tread of soli-tary footsteps sounded outside the door and the bar began to slide aside, indoor lights flickered on. Six propane-fired lanterns, set along the walls, were blinding in the sudden brilliance. Poised on one side, her arms lifted with the fists locked together, Kendra froze, blinking. Denny was on the opposite side. He'd planned to push their captor to his knees as soon as she'd distracted him with a blow. The shadowy figure of the fat man laughed. Safely outside, he loomed large, another light fixture illuminating one beefy hand and the huge gun aimed at Kendra's head.

"You," he growled at Denny. "Outside."

As soon as Denny obeyed, the fat man's powerful backhand swung toward Kendra's face. She jerked away, taking the blow on her shoulder, but it still sent her reeling backward with a cry of pain. As she fell she heard the door slam shut and the bar slide into place once more.

"Not a word, McKee," Alex reminded him as he moved forward to make the exchange. "Once Denny's free, we'll get you out, but if anything happens to him because of you, I'll kill you myself."

There was backup moving into place all around them, under cover of the tree-shaded campsites. No one had approved Alex's plan. He'd simply put it into motion before they could stop him. He'd probably be looking for a new job by daybreak, but the only thing that mattered to him now was getting Denny out safely. He didn't care if McKee survived.

Sparing one brief thought for Kendra, he was glad she was safe, back in his apartment. He hoped she was asleep. There'd been no lights showing when they drove past on their way north. When this is over, Alex promised himself, it is going to be marriage, family and no more worrying about that nest egg. She could use the two million any way she liked. He already had an idea for a new line of work that could support them both.

Dreams dissolved as the dangerous form of the fat man moved down the hill from the comfort station. Alex had already spotted his getaway vehicle, a small motor launch. With luck the backup had, too, and had disabled it. Alex's thoughts focused on Denny, held in front of the fat man like a shield.

"Moreau, you can't do this," McKee whined. "He'll kill me."

"I'll kill you if you make another sound. He wants you alive, McKee, to take him to the plates." Pushing the terrified man ahead of him, Alex advanced until the four of them were only a few yards apart.

Denny stumbled forward, eyes wide with fear. McKee was thrust into the fat man's clutches. Then father and son were running, sprinting toward the shelter of Alex's cruiser. Denny started to speak but the first gunshots covered his words. In the misty dawn light, it was difficult for the fat man to aim, and he had his hands full with McKee, who was fighting for his life. Roughly, Alex shoved Denny into the back of the cruiser and locked him in.

Scrunched low behind the wheel, he started the engine, then backed up, full speed, skidding into a beachfront campsite to turn. He was dimly aware of Denny's frantic pounding at the heavy plastic spitshield between the back and front seats. His son could not get out. The door handles had been removed.

The gate at the entrance to the campground was in sight before he slowed. More shots sounded behind them, and another police vehicle screamed through the gate, speeding by as Alex abruptly braked his cruiser and turned around to look at his son. Denny's words had penetrated at last.

"You've got to get her out!" Denny was sobbing, almost incoherent as tears of frustration streamed down his face. "He broke the valve off one of the propane tanks. If she doesn't suffocate, it'll blow!"

"Who? Who are you talking about?"

Alex's heart nearly stopped as Kendra's name passed Denny's lips. He tried to deny it was possible for her to be here, in the middle of this nightmare, but with cold certainty he knew Denny wouldn't lie, not this time. Without another word he turned the car and started back.

Dizzy, Kendra struggled to stand up. There was an odd smell in the room now that the lights had gone out again. She felt nausea overtake her and stumbled toward the toilets. The generator was running. That meant she could flush after she threw up. The thought was oddly comforting until she realized with sudden, terrifying insight that it also meant that what she smelled was propane gas. There was a good chance the entire building was about to explode, with her in it.

Fire, she thought, too frightened to move.

Water, she thought. Dropping to her knees, she crawled blindly toward the shower stalls as gunshots rang out down the hill.

Someone was running exploratory hands over her rib cage. At first she thought she was dreaming. "Déjà vu," she whispered, and wondered why her throat was sore.

"Thank God." Alex's voice was close to her ear.

"What happened?" But she was already remembering. "I got in the shower and turned on the water," she murmured. "Did the building blow up? I thought maybe if I got wet enough I could jump through the fire."

Alex seemed to be laughing and crying at the same time. He was definitely hugging her tight. Apparently no bones were broken, but she was soaked to the skin.

"No explosion," he said. "But there was a gas leak."

She remembered that, but knew there was something else, something she'd forgotten, something important.

"I thought I'd lost you," Alex whispered. Then he gathered her up as though she weighed nothing and carried her toward an arriving ambulance. A white-coated paramedic was in the back, armed with oxygen.

"I never seem to look my best when you're around," Kendra murmured. Her voice was slurred. She was going to pass out again, soon, but she wanted to remember what was so important first.

"I love you any way," Alex said. "Sweaty, wet, grimy. Any way at all. Every way."

"You love me?"

"I love you." Alex thought he'd never seen anything more beautiful than her smile. Reluctantly, he eased her into the ambulance and gave place to the paramedic, but he kept hold of her hand.

Suddenly she began to struggle again, tearing at the oxygen mask. "I remember!" She looked panic-stricken. "Denny? Is Denny okay?"

"Denny wasn't hurt," Alex reassured her. "He helped me get you out."

"Thank God. He's a good kid, Alex."

"You riding in with her?" the paramedic asked.

Alex nodded. He couldn't leave her now, not even for Denny. The ambulance doors had closed behind them before he looked toward his son.

In the broader sense, he had lied to Kendra. Denny had been hurt. Alex was hurting him even now, by leaving him in Claude's custody. Surprisingly, though,

Denny had seemed just as concerned about her. "Don't let her get away," he'd told his father. "She's prime stepmother material."

Denny was watching the ambulance as it started to move away. His eyes sought and found Alex's and in that last second before they lost sight of each other, Denny raised both hands, thumbs up. Everything was going to be okay, he seemed to signal. Alex hoped he was right.

She was lying on her back on a hard mattress, wearing a short hospital gown and covered by a light blanket. Kendra winced as a smile started to form. This time she had no lapse in memory. And this time, she was not alone. Alex was in the room with her. She could hear him pacing, and smell his after-shave.

"Honest, officer, it wasn't my fault," she said.

A heartbeat later he was at her side, his hand gentle on her bruised face. "Damn it, Kendra, you scared me to death. You've been out like a light for the better part of eight hours."

"You're just mad because there's only room on this bed for one," she teased. "Come here."

The kiss was slow and deep, and so arousing that she forgot the aches and bruises. His hand was inching toward her breast when Colleen Gray loudly cleared her throat.

"Looks like you can be discharged anytime," she said, hard put to disguise a smile of her own. "Just take it easy for a while."

"How easy?" Alex looked worried.

The doctor's laugh was frankly ribald. "Put her to bed and keep her there," she advised. "Now get out of my clinic. I might need this room for sick people."

Even when they were alone again, Alex kept a little distance between them. He got the clothes he'd brought from the apartment for her and helped her hop down off the hospital bed. Kendra started to feel as uneasy as she had the last time they were in this situation.

Seizing the clothes, she fled into the bathroom. Something was wrong. She struggled into jeans and a knit top. He'd said he loved her, back there in the campground. Maybe he regretted the hasty words. Maybe she was only a casual affair to him after all.

Her hair was hopeless, again. She ran her fingers through it once and gave up. If it was over with Alex, what did it matter how she looked? The bruises on her face were enough to dampen anyone's ardor. Closing her eyes against the hideous sight in the mirror, Kendra took a deep breath, turned and opened the door.

"Ready," she said lightly.

"I, ah, hope it's okay if we go to my place instead of yours?"

"You don't have to protect me, Alex. I've already seen what that animal did."

Dismay flooded his features, rapidly followed by relief. So that's it, Kendra thought. He was afraid of how I'd react to the news. "No more secrets, Alex," she reminded him. "Not even to protect me."

Nodding, he took her arm. "The fat man is dead."

"I remember hearing gunshots."

"Police sharpshooters. They picked him off as he tried to get McKee into his boat. McKee's confessed. Both he and Jody will be spending time in prison." They'd left the clinic before Alex spoke again. "I'll arrange to have your house cleaned."

"I'm not going back there. Alex, I—"

"If you think I'm going to let you get away now—"

"Alex, I—"

"I'm under orders, Kendra. My son says I'm to 'go for it.' Marriage and everything."

They were standing next to the white pickup, in broad daylight. Millie's nose was pressed to the diner window. Tara watched them from the bookstore. Even Doc Gray had paused on her way to her own car and was waiting to see what would happen next.

"Alex, if that's the only reason, then—"

"It isn't. Damn it, Kendra. I had all these romantic plans made. I wanted to do this right, but I don't dare take the chance of letting you out of my sight again. Will you marry me?"

A slow, painful smile crept across her face. "If I promise not to say no, can I take a rain check on the romantic setting? I'd like to be proposed to when I look a little less like a refugee from an insane asylum."

Heedless of the watching eyes, Alex took her in his arms. Setting, dress, hair, bruises and sprains were all forgotten. "You've got it, lady," he promised.

"Let's go home," she whispered. "I should be in bed." Her face flamed with color, but she'd never been happier, or more anxious to show him how she felt about him.

"Yeah," Alex agreed, his eyes alight with mischief. "The cat hasn't been fed for hours." He opened the door for her and helped her into the cab.

"By all means, let's go feed the cat." She slid across the seat and met him as he climbed in on the other side. "And, Alex, about the note I left for you in the kitchen—I really meant the last part, where I said I loved you."

Six months later, Kendra Moreau glanced out of the window of her tower office at the icy lake below. The angle of sun on snow told her it was nearly noon. Time for a break.

She walked through the new house, still amazed at how perfect it was. The contractor had been willing to construct it exactly as she and Alex wanted it. Why not? He was getting plenty of free publicity from the fact that a lottery winner had hired him to tear down Olive's house and build this one.

On her way to Alex's photo lab, Kendra paused at the door to Denny's bedroom. T.W. was the only one there, curled up asleep on the bed. Denny was in school, and his grades had been improving steadily. His walls were decorated with black-and-white prints he had done with his father's guidance. It looked as if Denny had inherited Alex's skill with a camera.

They'd been lucky, she knew, that Denny had gotten off lightly. Because he was under eighteen he'd undergone what was called an informal adjustment. A juvenile caseworker, not a judge, had determined that he should be put in his father's care and do two hundred hours of public service work to make up for the trouble he'd caused. It seemed that not reporting a crime wasn't a crime in itself, and that in spite of his involvement with the others, Denny had actually done nothing more criminal than moving boxes of money from place to place and making some veiled threats.

Best of all the changes in the last months was the fact that both Kendra and Alex now worked out of their home. Alex had resigned from the sheriff's office before they could fire him for mishandling McKee, and within a month had obtained a private investigator's license. The publicity from the counterfeiting case had gotten his business off to a flying start, but he'd been even more excited when he'd made his first photo sale.

She tapped lightly on the darkroom door. "Hungry, Alex?"

"Come in. I've just finished printing."

Kendra squeezed in next to him, though the darkroom was spacious. Even after months of marriage, the passionate attraction that had brought them together had not dimmed.

"You know," she told him, "we've never christened this room properly."

Alex dropped a kiss on her nose as he agitated the water with a pair of plastic tongs. "Just a minute more, love." Then he realized what she meant.

"Nice soft carpet in here, too."

"Ah, Mrs. Moreau, I do love it when you get . . . hungry."

Abandoning the tanks and trays, Alex turned all his attention to kissing his wife. It was a quiet loving, but when it was over they were both as utterly content as more frantic couplings left them. There was, they had long since agreed, infinite variety in pleasing each other, enough to fill all the years ahead.

"Nice," Kendra murmured, snuggling against his chest.

"Nice. Is that all? Maybe I'd better try for a higher rating." He moved to nip at her breast, but she rolled away and snatched up her clothes.

"Later. First show me what you've been working on all morning while I've been slaving over a hot computer.'' She'd yet to sell *Cloud Castles*, but two children's magazines had bought short stories.

He helped her dress and she played valet to him. It was sometime later before they turned back to the tray and the single photo floating upside down in the water.

Above the long counter, Alex had pinned some of his favorite prints. Kendra's eyes went directly to one, the last shot in a whole series of candids Alex had taken of her on the day he officially proposed. It showed her sitting on one of the rocks at his thinking place, wearing a diamond ring and a sated smile.

Most of the other photographs fastened there were animal portraits, which were Alex's specialty. Kendra looked from the squirrel and his nut, the family of deer, and an action shot of T.W., chasing his stubby tail, to the tray. She expected to see something similar emerge.

''Got it,'' Alex whispered, holding the wet photograph so that he could see it and she could not.

''Better than nice?'' she teased.

''Perfect,'' he assured her. ''My early Christmas present for you. I'll get it framed and wrap it up and put it under the tree, but since you've been so... nice... you get to see it ahead of time.''

It was not an animal portrait.

The photograph showed a single cloud, puffy and white against a darker sky. The shape was unmistakable. For Kendra, Alex had used his camera to capture a cloud castle.

*   *   *   *   *

Silhouette Intimate Moments®

COMING NEXT MONTH

#309 THE ICE CREAM MAN—Kathleen Korbel

Could the handsome new ice cream man in Jenny Lake's neighborhood be selling more than chocolate and vanilla? She didn't want to believe the rumors that he could be a drug dealer, but there was something strange about an ice cream man who clearly disliked children. For undercover detective Nick Barnett, this assignment was unrelieved misery—except for Jenny, who was charmingly capable of making his life sweeter than it had ever been.

#310 SOMEBODY'S BABY—Marilyn Pappano

Giving up custody of her infant daughter to care for her critically ill son had been Sarah Lawson's only choice. Now, a year later, she was back to claim Katie from her father, Daniel Ryan, as per their custody arrangement. But Daniel had no intention of giving up his adorable daughter, agreement or not! Then, through their mutual love for Katie, they began to learn that the only arrangement that really worked was to become a family—forever.

#311 MAGIC IN THE AIR—Marilyn Tracy

Bound by events in the past, Jeannie Donnelly tried to avenge an ancient wrong and become the rightful leader of the Natuwa tribe. But she found her plans blocked by Michael O'Shea, surrogate son of the man she had to depose. The pain of yesterday could only be put to rest when they learned that trust and compromise—and love—were the only keys to the future.

#312 MISTRESS OF FOXGROVE—Lee Magner

The hired help didn't mix with the upper class—at least that was what stable manager Beau Lamond believed before he fell for heiress Elaine Faust. Surrounded by malicious gossip and still hurting from a shattered marriage, Elaine turned to Beau for the friendship and love she so desperately needed. But Beau was not what he seemed, and the secret he was keeping might destroy their burgeoning love.

AVAILABLE THIS MONTH:

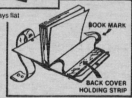

INDULGE A LITTLE SWEEPSTAKES
OFFICIAL RULES

SWEEPSTAKES RULES AND REGULATIONS. NO PURCHASE NECESSARY.

1. NO PURCHASE NECESSARY. To enter complete the official entry form and return with the invoice in the envelope provided. Or you may enter by printing your name, complete address and your daytime phone number on a 3 x 5 piece of paper. Include with your entry the hand printed words "Indulge A Little Sweepstakes." Mail your entry to: Indulge A Little Sweepstakes, P.O. Box 1397, Buffalo, NY 14269-1397. No mechanically reproduced entries accepted. Not responsible for late, lost, misdirected mail, or printing errors.

2. Three winners, one per month (Sept. 30, 1989, October 31, 1989 and November 30, 1989), will be selected in random drawings. All entries received prior to the drawing date will be eligible for that month's prize. This sweepstakes is under the supervision of MARDEN-KANE, INC. an independent judging organization whose decisions are final and binding. Winners will be notified by telephone and may be required to execute an affidavit of eligibility and release which must be returned within 14 days, or an alternate winner will be selected.

3. Prizes: 1st Grand Prize (1) a trip for two to Disneyworld in Orlando, Florida. Trip includes round trip air transportation, hotel accommodations for seven days and six nights, plus up to $700 expense money (ARV $3,500). 2nd Grand Prize (1) a seven-night Chandris Caribbean Cruise for two includes transportation from nearest major airport, accommodations, meals plus up to $1,000 in expense money (ARV $4,300). 3rd Grand Prize (1) a ten-day Hawaiian holiday for two includes round trip air transportation for two, hotel accommodations, sightseeing, plus up to $1,200 in spending money (ARV $7,700). All trips subject to availability and must be taken as outlined on the entry form.

4. Sweepstakes open to residents of the U.S. and Canada 18 years or older except employees and the families of Torstar Corp., its affiliates, subsidiaries and Marden-Kane, Inc. and all other agencies and persons connected with conducting this sweepstakes. All Federal, State and local laws and regulations apply. Void wherever prohibited or restricted by law. Taxes, if any are the sole responsibility of the prize winners. Canadian winners will be required to answer a skill testing question. Winners consent to the use of their name, photograph and/or likeness for publicity purposes without additional compensation.

5. For a list of prize winners, send a stamped, self-addressed envelope to Indulge A Little Sweepstakes Winners, P.O. Box 701, Sayreville, NJ 08871.

© 1989 HARLEQUIN ENTERPRISES LTD.

DL-SWPS

INDULGE A LITTLE SWEEPSTAKES
OFFICIAL RULES

SWEEPSTAKES RULES AND REGULATIONS. NO PURCHASE NECESSARY.

1. NO PURCHASE NECESSARY. To enter complete the official entry form and return with the invoice in the envelope provided. Or you may enter by printing your name, complete address and your daytime phone number on a 3 x 5 piece of paper. Include with your entry the hand printed words "Indulge A Little Sweepstakes." Mail your entry to: Indulge A Little Sweepstakes, P.O. Box 1397, Buffalo, NY 14269-1397. No mechanically reproduced entries accepted. Not responsible for late, lost, misdirected mail, or printing errors.

2. Three winners, one per month (Sept. 30, 1989, October 31, 1989 and November 30, 1989), will be selected in random drawings. All entries received prior to the drawing date will be eligible for that month's prize. This sweepstakes is under the supervision of MARDEN-KANE, INC. an independent judging organization whose decisions are final and binding. Winners will be notified by telephone and may be required to execute an affidavit of eligibility and release which must be returned within 14 days, or an alternate winner will be selected.

3. Prizes: 1st Grand Prize (1) a trip for two to Disneyworld in Orlando, Florida. Trip includes round trip air transportation, hotel accommodations for seven days and six nights, plus up to $700 expense money (ARV $3,500). 2nd Grand Prize (1) a seven-night Chandris Caribbean Cruise for two includes transportation from nearest major airport, accommodations, meals plus up to $1,000 in expense money (ARV $4,300). 3rd Grand Prize (1) a ten-day Hawaiian holiday for two includes round trip air transportation for two, hotel accommodations, sightseeing, plus up to $1,200 in spending money (ARV $7,700). All trips subject to availability and must be taken as outlined on the entry form.

4. Sweepstakes open to residents of the U.S. and Canada 18 years or older except employees and the families of Torstar Corp., its affiliates, subsidiaries and Marden-Kane, Inc. and all other agencies and persons connected with conducting this sweepstakes. All Federal, State and local laws and regulations apply. Void wherever prohibited or restricted by law. Taxes, if any are the sole responsibility of the prize winners. Canadian winners will be required to answer a skill testing question. Winners consent to the use of their name, photograph and/or likeness for publicity purposes without additional compensation.

5. For a list of prize winners, send a stamped, self-addressed envelope to Indulge A Little Sweepstakes Winners, P.O. Box 701, Sayreville, NJ 08871.

© 1989 HARLEQUIN ENTERPRISES LTD.

DL-SWPS

INDULGE A LITTLE—WIN A LOT!

Summer of '89 Subscribers-Only Sweepstakes

OFFICIAL ENTRY FORM

This entry must be received by: Sept. 30, 1989
This month's winner will be notified by: October 7, 1989
Trip must be taken between: Nov. 7, 1989–Nov. 7, 1990

YES, I want to win the Walt Disney World® vacation for two! I understand the prize includes round-trip airfare, first-class hotel, and a daily allowance as revealed on the "Wallet" scratch-off card.

Name_____

Address_____

City_____ State/Prov._____ Zip/Postal Code_____

Daytime phone number _____
                                        Area code

Return entries with invoice in envelope provided. Each book in this shipment has two entry coupons — and the more coupons you enter, the better your chances of winning!

© 1989 HARLEQUIN ENTERPRISES LTD.

DINDL-1

INDULGE A LITTLE—WIN A LOT!

Summer of '89 Subscribers-Only Sweepstakes

OFFICIAL ENTRY FORM

This entry must be received by: Sept. 30, 1989
This month's winner will be notified by: October 7, 1989
Trip must be taken between: Nov. 7, 1989–Nov. 7, 1990

YES, I want to win the Walt Disney World® vacation for two! I understand the prize includes round-trip airfare, first-class hotel, and a daily allowance as revealed on the "Wallet" scratch-off card.

Name_____

Address_____

City_____ State/Prov._____ Zip/Postal Code_____

Daytime phone number _____
                                        Area code

Return entries with invoice in envelope provided. Each book in this shipment has two entry coupons — and the more coupons you enter, the better your chances of winning!

© 1989 HARLEQUIN ENTERPRISES LTD.

DINDL-1